LOSING THE PLOT

When there's no one left to trust,

it's time to change the script

Richard Grainger

No.1 in the Richie Malone series

First published in Great Britain in 2019 by Otterdene Publishing

ISBN pbk: 978-0-9561341-1-0
ISBN ebk: 978-0-9561341-2-7

Typeset by www.shakspeareeditorial.org
Cover illustration by www.creativeparamita.com

FOR
ROSANNA
AND
CAMERON

"I always wanted more

– more of everything."

George Best
The Guardian
21 July 2002

PROLOGUE

NINE MONTHS AGO

I leave the Moët Bar feeling mildly pleased with myself.

And why not?

I have a new nickname – 'Belfast Boy' – which carries a certain gravitas, swinging precariously between intrigue and decadence.

I can't remember exactly who it was who called me this, but I didn't sleep with her, which for me is quite unusual.

I'd been double-parking shitty Spanish beer with equally shitty cheap white wine for several hours and, truth be told, the prospect of sex somehow got shunted down the to-do list.

But I remember she had the deepest green eyes I could swim in without drowning, long, tanned legs that I would gladly die between and an accent that located her somewhere near Belgrade.

I know these things; don't ask me why. There's the intrigue bit coming out.

Anyway, the point is that despite the fact that I would gladly have swum up the Lagan to hand-wash her underwear, there were too many other attractive women in my backfield. To cop off with one would have diluted my chances of nailing the others at a future opportunity.

Tip number one: sometimes, amigo, it's necessary to take a strategic 'did not bat' in the interest of the bigger picture.

Anyway, in addition to being a stunner, she had one of those quirky names that stubbornly wouldn't stick in my mind. I'm pretty good at getting a bird's name, but I'm struggling here.

I'm thinking maybe Agata? The first and last letters were definitely 'A's, so – I'm guessing – Agata would definitely be in the ballpark. Birds love it when you get their name right, when you admire it and show you've remembered, but don't overuse it because that's just tacky, like sending flowers after the first shag. Or even worse, getting flowers delivered to a bar you know she'll be drinking in with her mates. That's stalking, and it's also tacky.

Okay, so this is how things finished up:

I insult the new waitress – who turns out to be the owner's daughter – but repair the situation to the extent that I'm given a drink 'on the house'.

I call a man with a small, bemused-looking dog a drug-dealing homosexual, and he also offers me a drink.

I tell the doorman – who intervened after I had insulted the waitress – that if he continues to look at me in the disdainful manner appropriate for the English tourist, he will have to surgically remove my glass from his anus.

Maybe a little of this is lost in translation, but he also bought me a drink.

And so, all in all, things could have turned out a whole lot worse.

So what is it about me?

You see, I can't go anywhere where I have an audience and behave anything other than badly.

Especially when young, attractive women scaffold my ego. They accelerate this fucked-up mentality that pushes the 'twat' button in my psyche. It's like a drug – I have attention, but I crave more.

***

My name is Richie Malone. Let me tell you a bit about myself; that is, if you don't already know me.

I'm fifty-two years old.

I'm incredibly good-looking – think George Clooney-slash-Keanu Reeves. Despite thirty years of depravity, my physical decline has been slowed by a fixation for running and the gym which almost rivals my obsession with women, so I look much younger than my years.

I'm a writer and a sex addict.

Fuck, that was harder to say than I'd expected – I mean, the writer bit. I'll tell you why in a moment.

I was married for an eternity and then I lived with a woman for almost ten years until last December, when she decided to become a lesbian and moved in with her lover.

So then I moved to Spain; not because I have a love of bullfighting and the peel of church bells, but because even a total, imbecilic fuckwit can pull beautiful women. Which is pretty much all I've been doing since I moved here; I can't beat them off with the proverbial shitty stick.

Until, that is, something went terribly wrong: you'll know what when you've read the next chapter.

But now you know me.

Remember the name: Richie Malone.

Belfast Boy.

ONE

TODAY, 05.45

You've got to understand this. No one is what they appear to be. If they tell you that they are, then they're lying.

And you'll see exactly why I say this when you've read this sorry narrative.

For my money, all women are basically the same. The only ones I tend to remember are the truly dreadful ones. You know, the ones who bite you like some fucking Transylvanian freak or consider it's witty to text that they don't do anal on a first date.

And sometimes I get confused between my ex-wife and my X-any-number-of-women I've slept with because it all breaks down into that dreadful cauldron of white noise that is the catharsis of any relationship; and doubtless they think the same about me, but that's not really the issue right now.

The issue right now is the dead girl lying next to me.

Just the bare facts would do for now, like who is she, how the fuck did she get here and, of course, what is she doing being dead?

TWO

EIGHT YEARS AGO

I found my genre somewhat late in life and quite by accident.

For ten years I'd struggled to write passable fiction; you know, the sort of stuff that guys who don't read would read.

Robert Harris once wrote: 'In the absence of genius, there is always craftsmanship.' Genius certainly hadn't come knocking on my door, so mediocrity would have to do. But please, amigo, by all means feel free to challenge that comment.

I chose for my template the style of James Patterson. If you don't know him: trademark big print – so no more than three hundred words to the page – plenty of dialogue and page breaks, and no chapter ever takes longer to read than the time you'd need to take a crap.

Before I discovered my genre, I'd had three novels published, two of which sold passably well. The third, written under a pseudonym for reasons I'll explain later, staggered into the Amazon bestseller list. But I would freely admit that I popped the champagne cork a little too early when a well-known publishing house took a punt on this work of satirical fiction based on the Irish Troubles that just about returned them their advance. It was no Harry Potter; no release from the doldrums of teaching creative writing to wannabe disillusioned undergrads after eighteen years in the Royal Marines.

It was pure coincidence that I started to write filth.

Filth sold. Filth bought me the Aston Martin, the villa in Marbella with the yacht in Puerto Banús and the chalet in Zermatt. Filth was good to me, and I was good at filth.

It is most unlikely that I would ever have penned the word 'pussy' were it not for Mandy. We met on a residential writers' retreat in the frozen Scottish Highlands one January, twelve years ago.

We were instantly attracted to each other. I'd like to say that it was love at first sight but, in all honesty, it was lust. She'd just left her husband, and my marriage was as dull as the fiction I wrote.

But, truth be told, Mandy is one of only two women I've ever been in love with; and I suppose, if I'm honest, until this all happened, I still was. Truly, madly, deeply.

One afternoon, bored with the pretentiousness of our fellow residents and the drabness of the workshop, we went for a long walk in the snow. Eight hours and as many pints later, we were in bed screwing each other's brains out.

Within a year, she was divorced and I'd left home. The sex was terrific; but more than that, Mandy had liberated me.

For years I had unwittingly carried the burden of a repressed childhood: the awful relationship with a despotic mother; the early years at boarding school, being buggered senseless by Twiss, the near-blind music teacher. My social isolation and the introversion that closed everything away behind the locked door of my subconscious mind were in complete lockdown.

The Corps had been the only release from the emptiness of this emotional void; most of my colleagues were as repressed, as cold and detached as I was. It was what made you an effective killer.

Mandy coaxed it out of me, gradually teasing me with a mixture of bluntness and ridicule that no psychiatrist would have even contemplated, let alone practised. But it worked. It was cathartic, and gradually I began to offload the past as my new life brought new meaning; brought new but welcome chaos out of my old, dull order.

My rehabilitation began with the emails, which were, to say the least, pretty graphic, both of word and image. She lived in Hull and I lived in Cornwall, so time together was a challenge. Despite leaving enough clues, it took almost a year for my wife to hack into my email account, discover the relationship and kick me out.

Mandy's honesty about sex was like a breath of fresh air. She'd had many partners, mostly before she was married, and claimed to be bisexual. Rupert, her husband, had told me he'd considered filing for divorce on the basis that she was a frigid lesbian.

Wrong, Rwoopardo, old boy; wrong on both counts. At least, certainly at that stage.

And anyway, Mandy stitched the fucker up and beat him to it.

***

It began by writing down our fantasies.

She used to subscribe to a swingers' magazine called *Carnal Desire*, and she took a few back issues on our first holiday to Antibes. The periodical ran a competition each month for 'readers' erotic fantasies', with publication and the princely sum of fifty pounds for those considered worthy.

'They're mostly shit,' she'd said disparagingly. 'My grandmother could write better. Most people think that to write erotic fiction you only have to write cunt, jism and spurt enough times on each page, chuck in a bit of woman-on-woman and a splash of anal and, hey presto, you've got something that holds the reader. But that's just bollocks; you have to have a hook, Richie,' she said, hooking the groin of my Speedos with her middle finger.

'Oh, go on, Richie, write up last Saturday night. It'd be a laugh.'

I did, but I'm not going to share this narrative with you, amigo. Sorry.

I won fifty pounds, submitted a few more which swept aside the opposition and was then invited to become a 'contributing editor'.

Within a year I had a five-book deal with Randy House under a pseudonym – a name which you will certainly be familiar with, but again, sorry amigo, that goes to the grave with me – and a six-figure advance on my first novel, *A Pussy Way to Die*.

I had made it in filth, and nobody even knew my name.

And this should have been enough to make me happy, and doubtless it would have been for lesser mortals. But all I'd ever wanted was to publish a novel in my own name; a novel that stood out, so people would actually know who I am?

Pathetic, isn't it … but true.

THREE

TODAY, 05.49

By now, amigo, maybe you're wondering two things?

Maybe even three things, but I'll come to the third one later.

First, what about the dead girl? Who is she?

Come on, Richie, you write an opener like that and then you take us on a sideshow road trip where the view from the window's some boring backstory about your past? Cheap trick – even for a porn writer.

Ouch … that hurt. But sure, you've got a point.

And by the way, did you kill her?

Well, I hate to tell you this, but I don't know the answer to either question … who she is, or did I kill her?

And, of course, you're probably wondering how do I know she's dead?

Let's clear up the last one first. She's dead, all right. You don't have to have seen eighteen years' active service – mostly covert shit in Northern Ireland, Iraq and Afghanistan – to recognise a dead person when you see one. Trouble is, right now I seem to have some sort of short-term memory loss.

Try as I might, I cannot remember where I was or what I did last night. So until I can figure that out, I can't figure out what to do about the girl I woke up next to.

And the only way I can figure this out is through the shit that I *can* remember. It's an old trick I picked up in the Corps; useful after you've just witnessed your corporal get his legs turned into toothpicks by an IED and you don't recall shit about what led up to it.

Trouble is … clock's ticking.

FOUR

NINE MONTHS AGO

So what happened to me and Mandy?

Nearly twelve years together, then you split up?

Truth be told, she was one of only two women I ever really loved, but maybe I loved her so much because I loved my wife so little.

Your wife?

Okay, my wife? Let's get that one out of the way first. I met Susie while I was an officer cadet at Sandhurst Military Academy, the toughest forty-four weeks of my life. Occasionally we were granted an exeat, and so one night I'm enjoying a drink with a few mates in the Bird in Hand when I clock her behind the bar. Slender, shoulder-length black hair, intelligent green eyes … an arse to die for – she could easily have passed for Italian, had she wanted to. She was one of those women who you could justifiably describe as 'petite'. We got chatting.

At Sandhurst, women and alcohol are pretty much off the radar if you want to pass out with a decent commendation, and my goal was the Sword of Honour: top dog.

So, if you ever get the chance to cop off while out with mates who go through hell with you and for you on a daily basis, you have to be pretty certain that it's going to be worth it.

It was.

Long story short, I passed out as Second Lieutenant, winning the Queen's Medal: second top dog. Of course, I was gutted it wasn't the Sword.

Susie completed her law degree at LSE and we got married the following year. Between '85 and 2000 I did four tours of undercover shit in Northern Ireland, where I blended in working for the Special Resistance Unit – a unit so secret even the Home Secretary didn't know it existed.

Then I had a walk-on part in Desert Storm followed by three tours as part of the so-called peacekeeping mission in Iraq, whose role it was to perpetrate and shoot the fuck out of insurgents, or anyone who looked as if they may become an insurgent.

After that, I'd had enough.

But for Susie and me, all this time apart meant that our time together was, shall we say, difficult?

By the mid '90s she'd become a senior barrister for a firm specialising in medical negligence litigation. No problem with that. But we both knew by then that children were off the agenda, thanks to her career and my absenteeism. No problem with that, either.

But when she was recruited by a firm who specialised in delegitimising the Iraq war and chasing the ambulances that lads from my unit were shipped out in, the foundation stone of our precarious relationship seriously began to wobble.

Still, we tottered pointlessly on for a decade or so, mainly because I wasn't around that much.

When I left the Corps, a mate got me a job with a clandestine outfit which 'stabilised' warzone situations that were far too delicate for legitimate government agencies to dirty their hands with. You're thinking 'mercenary', amigo, aren't you? Well, I suppose you're right.

We were pretty good, too, taking down a handful of big players holed up in caves in the Hindu Kush that the CIA hadn't even heard of. Trouble was, they were so far off the radar that there wasn't even a price on their heads.

And then I took a bullet in the chest, three in the gut and one through my arse. Would you believe it … it was the first time I'd been shot? Everyone was so sure I was going to die that even Susie flew out to see me. Said we could patch things up when I got home. Hell … we could maybe start a family.

But I didn't die, and we didn't start a family.

When I got back to Blighty around a year later, I somehow managed to get a job on the Holloway Road lecturing on creative writing to undergraduates at a university so dreadful it was ranked bottom of *The Sunday Times*' 'Good University Guide'. No names, no pack drill, amigo. Doubtless I didn't improve it, but I'd used my convalescence to knock out two very average works of fiction, and that classified me as an author.

Then I got a little too friendly with Amy, my head of department.

So friendly, that when I was caught fucking her across her desk by the vice chancellor, I was invited to take a sabbatical. A very long sabbatical; one endorsed with a P45.

But then I had a stroke of luck.

In fact, I had three strokes of luck.

First, I managed to keep the whole sordid business hushed up.

Second, Susie put in for a transfer to her firm's Exeter branch, which was a gimme. 'Transfer me,' she told them, 'or I walk.'

We were both tired of London – don't buy that Samuel Johnson bullshit about when a man is tired of London, he is tired of life. Heck, my life was just about to begin.

And the third stroke of luck?

Well, you see, I kept on seeing Amy, at least for a while. She really was a terrific fuck as well as being a pretty good *Guardian* columnist. And she persuaded a friend at Falmouth University that I was what they were looking for. The whole thing worked seamlessly, except that I never saw Amy again after the move.

Don't ask me how, because although I claim to know many things, I would never claim to have even a rudimentary understanding of how the female mind works. But I knew that Susie knew, and the bastard who you'll come to know as Richie Malone wasn't quite ready to leave her yet.

Yeah, but what about you and Mandy? Isn't that what this chapter was supposed to have been about?

For sure. I'll get to that in a bit.

But right now, I've still got to figure out what to do with the girl on my bed.

FIVE

TODAY, 05.51

Okay, so how do you know she's dead?

Let me check back ... according to your narrative, you woke up at 05.45, and it's now 05.51. So, let me see ... that's around six minutes ago. Have you checked her pulse, maybe tried a spot of good old CPR? It's possible to survive for five to ten minutes – you should know that – before serious and possibly irreversible brain damage and then death occur.

Oh, she's dead all right.

Sorry – with all my trying to work the intricate details the fuck out, I must have neglected to mention that what actually woke me up was the lake of blood that slicked across the bed and onto my face.

Odd, isn't it, but for a soldier who's had to do more than a little bit of knife work in his time, I've never been that good with blood.

It was the smell that hit me as I opened my eyes. Like the smell of raw meat: a sweet, metallic pungency that's always made me want to heave.

I'm covered in it.

I make the mistake of rolling her over, and I see three things.

First, that her throat has been crudely slashed from ear to ear, so death wouldn't have been quick; and second, lying beneath her head, which for an instant I fear will become detached from her body, is the murder weapon.

My bread knife.

And the third?

Oh yes, the third. Good point. Her face … her face was a face I've never seen before. I'd have known if I had. Her eyes were shut, and that suggests to me the likelihood that she'd been drugged before her throat had been hacked open.

She must have been a looker, when she wasn't dead. Young, somewhere between twenty and twenty-five, perfect bone structure with high feline cheekbones that suggested Russian or Eastern European heritage, a straight nose and full lips that would have sealed the deal for me before they turned blue, straight jet-black hair with a bob, a little too shiny to be her natural colour. I don't need to be Hercule Poirot to confirm this – a glance at her lower abdomen revealed that what little hair she had in this region was blonde.

Oh … you didn't say that she was naked?

Well, she was.

Height?

Difficult to gauge a person's height when they're lying down, particularly when they're crumpled and dead, but she was tall. I'd say a good five foot nine, maybe even taller.

And her body type?

This sounds a bit pervy. I'm not one for giving marks out of ten to dead women, but she certainly would have been a ten. No doubt there; the body of a model … maybe her breasts were a little too full, so make that a lingerie model. Oh yes, had I come across this one while she still had a pulse, I'd have moved heaven and earth to bed her.

So, what did you do: call the police?

Be patient, I'm coming to that. Okay, this is too much, I think, so I kick myself into action and paddle though a pool of blood that has now seeped off the bed and is spreading across the floor towards the bathroom.

Do you know how much blood the average human body holds?

Eight pints, give or take … everyone knows that.

Actually, you're wrong: it's somewhere close to one point two and one point five gallons.

Ever spilt a pint of beer?

Well imagine spilling ten to twelve pints of beer. And then transpose it into the deep red, slippery plasma that we don't even think about, coursing through our bodies, keeping us alive. And most of this is now either on the bed or on the laminate floor where I'm slipping and sliding towards the shower, leaving a trail of crimson behind me.

I shower, water as hot as I can stand it, then dress and begin to mop up the blood. Christ, this is gross, and it takes forever.

How the hell were you ever a soldier?

Different ball game when someone's trying to kill you.

I'm sweating and covered in blood once more, so I shower again, bundle my blood-soaked shorts and T-shirt into a bin liner, then look at her one more time – fuck, what a waste, she really was a stunner – and then I cover her with a sheet.

***

So at this point, amigo, a couple of things occur to me.

First, I'm interfering with a crime scene. I'm not just interfering with it; I'm actually destroying it.

Yes, you're right, what I should have done was to have rung the feds the moment I woke up. For sure, they're not going to look any further for the murderer. All the evidence they need to convict me is right in front of them: the girl's on my bed with her blood all over it – or what I've not managed to dispose of. And why would I dispose of it anyway, if I'm innocent? She's been hacked to death by my bread knife and my prints are all over it.

Open-and-shut case.

But what about motive? If you don't know her, why would you have killed her?

Ah yes … my short-term memory loss. Possible explanations for this: maybe I've suffered an aneurysm … maybe even a brain tumour, a head trauma or concussion. The last two are highly unlikely as I have no pain. I'll rule out the first two, purely because of my machismo: Richie Malone's still stupid enough to think he's indestructible.

How about a seizure, epilepsy, heart bypass surgery or depression?

Nope, this isn't getting me anywhere. So that leaves the most probable cause: I've been a victim of, or have witnessed, a traumatic event such as a violent crime or accident.

And the second?

Second what?

The second thing that occurred to you after you did your best to dispose of or contaminate the crime scene. Get with it, Richie! Christ, man, you really are losing the plot.

SIX

NINE MONTHS AGO

I want to talk about Mandy.

Why? What possible bearing can that have on your present predicament?

Look, I've told you … by recalling intricate details from the past I *may* be able to trigger some fucking recollection …

Conjectural. I want to hear about the other thing that occurred to you as you were mopping up the blood of the woman you claim neither to have known, nor to have killed, and for whom you'll almost certainly do a life sentence in some Spanish dungeon unless you can get your shit together.

Overruled.

I'm going to talk about Mandy because, actually … I want to. This is my fucking narrative. And, since you ask, this strand of memory *does* have a bearing on my recent whatever-the-fuck-you-called-it.

I sigh, sit down at the dining table and light a cigarette. I've not smoked for years. Marlboros some bird must have left behind; always hated them, but that's how bad things are right now. I inhale and then think I'm going to die from a coughing fit.

Fuck.

Okay … Mandy and me and this big, dopey red setter of hers called Gordon – who the fuck would call a dog Gordon? – lived in something approaching domestic harmony until last November. Note harmony … not bliss.

I'd spent a bit of time in limbo after Susie hoofed me out, and then, after a year or so, on Mandy's say-so and just when I was beginning to believe that things may just fizzle out and she might even consider going back to Rwoopardo, I packed my bags and headed north. Probably the stupidest thing I've ever done, but do I regret it?

First, I rent this twee little three-bedroomed Victorian terrace in a village called South Cave, six miles west of Hull.

Hull, if you don't know it, is a fucking shithole … In fact – and I know this may well cause upset – in my opinion, most of the North of England ticks that box.

So finally, her divorce comes through. Rupert, the soft sap, discovers some backbone when the accusations start to fly and makes things as difficult as he can. Although, truth be told, I don't really blame him as Mandy had totally stitched the bastard up. Rwoopardo's only faults were to be boring, gullible and – anecdotally – to possess a dick the width of a pencil.

But even some pretty pricey silks couldn't save him from coughing up half of the one point five mil he declared each year from his architectural firm, half of the proceeds from the sale of the château in the Dordogne, ditto the chalet in Zermatt, and half of a pension fund that would have funded NASA for a decade.

And just for the record, because I like to tell it as it is, Rwoopardo's firm was based in London, not Hull, which is where he'd had the three affairs and numerous liaisons with prostitutes – correspondence bearing graphic details of which Mandy had entered into a 'fake' email account he didn't even know he had.

Mandy, in addition to being a terrific ride, was what can only be described as a scheming bitch; added to which, she was also a dab hand at those techy sort of things.

There were no kids involved, and the only thing Rupert and I had in common was that neither of us wanted the bloody dog.

So, their mansion in Hull got sold, and a year later, when I'd signed the book deal and had a nice little nest egg sitting in my Swiss bank account, I bought a small estate in a better (more rural) part of South Cave – which, to be honest, by now I'd actually begun to think wasn't quite such a shithole – and Mandy and dopey fucking Gordon moved in. And then the perfect order of my perfect life was turned on its head.

Living together, amigo, simply fucks things up. Trust me on this.

Well, a couple of years later I start spending more and more time abroad. I'd bought the villa in Marbella by then, and this had become my writing base.

Yes of course the climate was more conducive, but there was so much more to inspire me in Andalucía; remember I'm writing filth, and a writer needs inspiration – and there was certainly no shortage of it in Marbella and Puerto Banús. Hell, some of the Brazilian girls even carried their own card machines for home visits, so it was also tax-deductible. I won't bore you with the details here, but let me just say that paying for sex isn't such a bad idea. We all pay for it one way or another, anyway.

You actually paid for sex? Jesus … No, please … do bore us with the details.

Okay, if you insist. And it does have a certain relevance, to discover how easy, guiltless and downright convenient it is to pay to have sex with beautiful young women only served to fuel my sex addiction.

***

The first time I had sex with a call girl was certainly right up there as one of the best days of my life.

And how exactly did you find this … what do we call her, a hooker?

Hooker will do. Internet, of course.

Marbella boasts more high-end hookers, or escorts as they're generally referred to, than anywhere else in Europe – in fact, probably anywhere else in the world.

So eventually I found this website called Eurogirlsescort.com – not the most original name, but it does what it says on the tin.

I was still quite naïve back then, and I hadn't a baldy what some of the services they advertised were: 'Girlfriend Experience'? Did I want that? Fuck, no … a girlfriend experience is one where you face constant recrimination, curtailment of what you enjoy doing and endless nagging, so this was precisely what I did not want.

What I wanted was a prostitute experience.

Anyway, I picked out this Brazilian. Twenty-six years old, silicon boobs, bisexual, CIM – which I learned stands for cum in mouth, golden shower, anal if you want it …

We really don't need all this detail, thank you.

Well, you did ask for it.

Anyway, I remember the day as if it was yesterday. I awoke without a hangover, ran for an hour, then went to the gym for a heavy weights session, out-bench-pressing this big black fella wearing a Man United shirt.

Irrelevant detail.

Scene-setting, amigo.

I'd already decided what was going to happen later – or, in reality, I'd made a decision that would trigger a certain course of events – therefore I wanted to look my best for it.

So, I shower in the gym, put on my white wife-beater and stroll down to The Meeting Point, where I work on the book for a couple of hours. During this time, I'm messaged by four women who want to have sex with me – okay … I joined one of those dating sites purely for experiential reasons – but this cuts no ice, as

I have plans for later.

It's now six o'clock, I'm home and hosed, and she's not here yet. So I message the agency and ask where the fuck she is?

'On her way,' I'm told, then she texts to say she's stuck in traffic.

I'm actually quite nervous because this is my first real prostitute experience and I'm not really sure how it'll go … which is in fact the reason why I'm doing it. I did pay for the services of a hooker once before, but that was for different reasons which I'm not going to divulge as they have no relevance to the story. And before you even think it … it was a she, and one with all the right bits in the right places.

But I'm anxious because I don't really understand the etiquette for this sort of thing, and there's no way to learn it – even with the help of Mr Google.

I think about having a drink, but I decide against it for two reasons: a) I'm not sure if it will affect the Viagra, and b) I don't want her to smell alcohol on my breath, which I know is illogical because she wouldn't give a fuck.

So, she texts to say she's lost, and I have to go out and walk the streets to find her. I'm sorry, but shouldn't this be the other way around?

Ten minutes and twenty texts later, I clock her walking down the hill towards the sea and I have an opportunity to appraise my purchase.

And I know it's her because her tits should have their own postcode.

So far, so good … she's as described on the website – although, truth be told, I'm a little underwhelmed by the simple white dress. But I'm happy to forgive this because the difference between high-end escorts and street prostitutes is that the former don't need to advertise the fact that they're available for sex, whereas the latter do.

She's impressed with my villa, and we have a glass of wine on the terrace and engage in a little small talk. She says she's a lawyer but I very much doubt this as a) she couldn't find the street I live in, and b) when she leaves she can't work out how to open the gate.

I tell her that I'm a writer and I'm doing this so that I can get inside the head of my central character, who spends much of his time in the company of call girls. She doesn't, of course, give a flying fuck as long as I part with the cash, which is my next duty before the action commences.

I'm kind of hoping that she'll stuff the three hundred euro into her bra, but she counts the wad of cash and puts it carefully into her purse. She then signs my receipt and that gets the business out of the way.

Now, you may well – or then again, you may well not – be wondering two things: is this legal, and what does she look like?

Firstly, it is legal. I am paying for her time, and should I choose to clean my apartment in a clown suit while she sits and drinks Veuve Clicquot Yellow Label Champán con crianza on my terrace is no less legal than having sex with her.

Secondly, she is very, very good-looking.

Let me tell you a bit about her.

Lena – obviously not her real name – was built for sex.

As I've said, she's Brazilian – I was tempted to go Russian, but I'd decided I'd build up to that – around five foot six, olive-skinned with long blonde hair, green eyes and an arse you could land a helicopter on. If you're thinking Gisele Bündchen here, you'd not be far wrong. Maybe a tad shorter and with bigger tits?

It's actually her skin – I kid you not – that I find most attractive. It has the feel of velvet; her entire body is unblemished, and it goes without saying that it benefits from the absence of ink.

'Do we kiss?' I ask, and she responds by pushing her tongue gently between my lips.

'I only kiss men ... or women I'm attracted to,' she goes, and of course I buy this.

Now, amigo, I know this will disappoint, but I'm not going to go into the sordid details of our hour together. But let me tell you that it was one of the best hours of my life, and probably the best three hundred bucks I've ever spent.

Recent research suggests that eighty-five per cent of men engage the services of a call girl for oral sex, and I can now understand why.

For almost forty-five minutes this divine creature keeps me on the cusp of ecstasy. She is a pro in every sense of the word and controls the tempo of the engagement as expertly as Nigel Owens controls a

30

rugby international, and I don't even get penalised for a crooked put-in.

So when it's over, she showers – she even asks me politely if it's okay to piss in the shower … and no, amigo, I categorically did not want a golden shower – kisses me and leaves, and I'm left to reflect on my experience.

Do I have any regrets?

NO.

Do I feel any guilt or shame?

A categorical NO is again the answer.

There was no emotional connection; sure, it's likely that I'll book her again – which I do – because once you open a packet of crisps you don't just have one, do you?

And that's actually quite a good analogy because I felt a heck of a lot more guilt after eating half a tube of Pringles before I went to bed that night than I did for having an hour's sex with a hooker.

So what else was good about that day? Let me tell you.

Once Lena's gone, I shower, dress, drive into town and meet my good Spanish friends in the Moët.

We have a few drinks and I am on sparkling form. And why wouldn't I be? I've just contained myself for almost an hour in bed with a beautiful young woman, and she's offered me a freebie as a mark of respect for my (Viagra-assisted) performance – okay, I'll accept that this may be a little like a Boots loyalty card, but what the heck? I'm sharing a drink and good humour amongst friends, and no one but me knows what I've just been up to.

I feel that I've earned a steak, so I treat my good friend Maria and myself to a slap-up dinner in my favourite restaurant, The Orange Tree.

The meal costs almost as much as the sex but again it's money extremely well spent, and – please excuse the cliché – you can't take it with you, can you? We have a laugh and I drive home drunk and happy to eat Pringles and fall asleep on my terrace.

So, let me tell you something that may help to explain why that day was so great and the seismic effect it has had on my future thinking.

Relationships, amigo, are a total waste of time.

To pay for sex … terrific sex with one woman and to hang out with another woman, or maybe even other women, as good friends, is the way to go.

No commitment, no complications, no heartbreak and no recriminations. And there's neither 'happy ever after' nor 'not happy ever after', because there is no 'ever after'.

And so, I'm left wondering why on earth hadn't I worked this out decades ago? I would have saved me a fortune … if I may paraphrase George Best: the rest of my money I wasted.

***

So, back to Mandy.

It wasn't long until I realised that we were pretty much on the same rocky road as Susie and I had been.

And then another thing happened. Two years ago,

Mandy finished the book she'd been writing ever since I met her, got the red carpet treatment from Christopher Little – the agency who finally let Harry Potter out of his weird fucking cage – and, hey presto, her face is suddenly everywhere.

She's on the back of every bus, every hoarding; she's on telly being interviewed by Melvin Fucking Bragg, has been invited to appear on Loose Women (ironic, that one) and is suddenly bezzy buddies with Janette Winterson, who six months ago she'd said she couldn't fucking stand.

The highlight, though, was having her book big-upped as the most significant work of narrative feminism since Germaine Greer's *On Rage* by that ghastly woman who writes a column in the Saturday *Times* and still thinks it's cool to wear cut-off jeans over black tights; certainly not what someone in their late forties should be seen dead in.

Tell me I don't detect a hint of jealousy here?

Fuck, no – anonymity does it for me. To hell with celebrity.

I don't believe that.

Whatever.

Anyway, I'm going to digress for a moment and get on my soapbox.

Is this really necessary? Remember, the clock's ticking.

Yes. Fuck it … yes, it is.

I light another Marlboro and manage to take it down without violent protestation, my body welcoming the nicotine this time.

I always think it's so bloody unfair how women writers always get the nod over men. I know this to be true, because the filth I write is published under a female pseudonym. As I've already said, you'll know it, of course. And who do you think suggested this? The publisher, naturally.

Have you ever read that dreadful book by Paula Hawkins, *The Girl on the Train*? You know, the one where there are about four different narrators, and not only are they all unreliable, but they all have the same voice to the extent that you constantly have to keep referring to the start of each chapter to see whose point of view you're reading? And to top it off, even a total dullard could work out who dunnit after thirty pages. I ask you: how did that ever get into print, let alone become a bestseller?

And then there's the little wizard himself. If I ever feel a pang of regret that I've not had kids, it's instantly extinguished by the surge of relief that I never had to read that shit about broomstick hockey and disappearing railway platforms to them at bedtime. But if *I'd* written that, it would have stayed where it belonged – on the slush pile.

Okay, doubtless J. K. Rowling is proud of that shite in the same way that I stand by the porn I've written and – God willing – will continue to write. But only a woman could have got that load of utter tosh into print.

And then there's *Fifty Shades*. E. L. James – go on, have a guess … man or woman?

There, you see, my point entirely.

***

The thing about Mandy was that she was the only woman I've ever known who could walk into a room and every man without a white stick would instantly want to fuck her.

Well, apart from her gay hairdresser, of course. Even old Dicky in our local, who couldn't piss further than his slippers, would have wolfed down a couple of Viagra if he'd had a sniff of a chance. You could describe her as brazen, but I think 'dirty' is a better fit.

In all honesty, she wasn't actually that great-looking. Strawberry blonde – or that's how she liked to call her hair – good body, nice carriage and a mischievous rather than beautiful face which centred on her top lip. A friend once said that she had the perfect cocksucker's mouth, and who was I to argue?

But she oozed sexuality in a way that Ian Paisley oozed Free Presbyterianism. It was utterly magnetic. She was totally incapable of walking into a bar without flirting, without being the centre of attention. At the beginning it sort of bothered me, and then I realised that it was just the way she was – and, in any case, jealousy is the most unattractive facet a partner can have.

So, of course, I flirted back; flirt and counter-flirt. It never led anywhere – until, that is, I copped off with her best mate one night, two years ago. Ha! You never knew about that, Mandy, did you? To tell the truth, it wasn't really worth the effort.

And then, last November, she dropped the bomb, and that was it.

Look, this is all very interesting, but can we please *get back to the other thing that occurred to you as you were destroying the crime scene?*

SEVEN

TODAY, 05.58

Oh yeah, that.

Okay.

This is going to sound a bit weird, but let's face it: the day hasn't got off to a start that you would call entirely normal, has it?

Well?

Well … it just occurred to me, it's odd how all this stuff's come to the forefront of my mind when I should be wracking my brains for some recollection of last night.

So?

So, it's almost as if someone wants me to recall this shit, wants me to trawl through my past recollecting intricate detail after intricate fucking detail.

What are you suggesting?

I don't know … look, I know this sounds fantastical, but it's almost as if someone's somehow implanted these memories, maybe embedded some sort of … I don't know … chip? So that everything I remember reinforces who I think I am, whereas in reality this isn't me at all.

Maybe I'm not even Richie Malone?

And, tell me, what would be the point of that?

Maybe the point of it is that I've not got to the critical bit yet. Maybe this memory implant, or whatever the fuck, is like a train journey where you just jump on a random train … maybe in some weird place like Poland, where you can't understand a fucking word because everything's formed entirely with Zs and Xs, and the staff who should be there to help you are all washing cars in the North of England. You don't check where it's going, and then, when you realise you're headed in totally the wrong direction, you have to figure out how to get back.

Maybe when this memory implant plays to the end, what happened last night will be in there and of course I'll remember who she is, what we did …

And probably how you killed her?

Probably. Possibly. I don't know.

I'm beginning to feel defeated as well as anxious-slash-borderline scared?

Sounds highly improbable to me, like something out of James Bond. Feel your head, man, look at it … can you find any evidence of your 'implant'? Or maybe you were hypnotised? Wouldn't have been the first time you've fallen asleep in the Moët, would it?

The Moët? I was there last night? How'd you know that?

Oh, just a wild guess. Or maybe because – like the homing pigeon after crumbs of pussy that you are – you end up there virtually every night.

You know what I think?
I think I've been drugged.

EIGHT

NINE MONTHS AGO

Okay … so I'm going to talk about how Mandy and I split up.

Is this really relevant to the narrative?

Yes … it fucking well is. And you'll see why later.

I sit down at the desk in my writing room, open my laptop and select the file titled 'Journal'. I'm not a habitual diarist, but there have been times in my life – and this was one – when it seemed like a good idea to chronicle events, my thoughts and my emotions.

The first entry was from towards the end of November last year. It may seem like a pretty random place to begin, but there's a reason for it.

Wed 25 Nov

M gets back from a meeting with her publisher that had to involve an overnight stay, even though it's, like, only an hour and a half away.

Said she wanted to meet a few friends. Fine. Meets me in Costa in Hull early as I want her to see a house

I'm considering buying to let (got to park the filth money somewhere) and says she's got something to tell me. I know it's not good. We have a coffee, she looks anxious, and I know it's very definitely not good.

It's something she wants to do, she says, but hasn't done yet. Intriguing.

Actually, as it turns out, she has.

She says she connects with Lucy (her agent) in a way she doesn't connect with me and wants to have sex with her and possibly a relationship.

Fuck. I'm floored.

Says she will not have sex with me until she has finally decided. I'm totally stunned; didn't see this coming, although we had joked about the old bisexual 'possibilities'.

I feel it's a bit unfair – the not-having-sex bit.

And then she says she's already been snogged and 'fiddled' by Lucy, and she liked it. Wouldn't be fair on Lucy, to have sex with me, she says.

Quite, I mumble, but now think this is doubly unfair, as this revelation just makes me want to fuck her more.

I text her later. Flippantly, I put: *Have us both, we'll share you*. I then suggest, in a pervy way, *Lucy, when I'm not around. When I'm in Spain.*

Good idea, she texts back; an interesting departure. But I'm expecting this to blow over.

I make the mistake of thinking we both are.

Thur 26 Nov

Phoney war begins.

I know this sounds fucking crazy, but I offer her a vacant apartment I own in Hull for Saturday night, so if she wants to try full-blown lesbian sex with Lucy, go for it. How much more generous can I be?

Well actually, it's not being generous; it's sort of exciting and may shore up a bit of a drab patch in our relationship. It may even give me something to write about, as I'm currently a bit floored on the next work of filth.

We joke about cameras etc. I even make the bed and change the sheets, no trouble; maybe sniff them afterwards. It's all still very flippant and a bit of a joke – no indication that this is relationship-threatening.

Fri 27 Nov

Emily, M's mate and sort of PA, who is what we might call a confidante – and who I happen to know has had a threesome herself, but it was a bit of a disaster – talks her down, telling her she is not a lezzer; definitely not. Don't be stupid and don't risk jeopardising your relationship with Richie, she says.

Why not try his idea of a bisexual prossie in London? Fuck … did I suggest that? Mid-morning, M meets me at home and says, 'I'm sorry, I got it wrong.'

And me?

I'm happy with this. Move on. Maybe do the bisexual prossie thing. I'm well up for that.

All looks good.

Now, this is with hindsight: a wonderful thing.

Shouldn't I have fucking well asked why? And what was so wrong with our relationship that she turned her attentions to someone else, male or female? But I just didn't realise what was coming next.

Sat 28 Nov

M goes out this evening to straighten things out with Juicy Lucy.

Yep, by now I'm starting to hate this woman and I feel threatened. M says she will tell her it's sort of got out of hand … she's been flirting, and she's sorry she led her on.

I stay in.

She gets back at 11ish, and I can tell immediately that things have not been straightened out.

She's quiet and in a very strange mood. I know her moods well enough by now. Not that I'm dead sensitive; they're just that obvious. And this one is as obvious as a red wine stain on the carpet, embossed with dog shit.

Talking of which, I'd taken Gordon for a walk round the village that afternoon, and for some reason wandered into Goldsmith's and briefly considered buying an eternity ring. Why? Good question: perhaps just to put something on her finger that represents a commitment. Do I feel threatened by Lucy? Hell, yes.

Sun 29 Nov

Sunday morning dawns.

Gordon shits, tea is made and I'm right: M tells me she wants to have a relationship with Lucy at the expense of ours. There is no place in it for me; that's it for us.

Almost twelve years gone in the blink of an eye.

Still wants to be friends. Fucking great. Okay … my heart is bursting inside, but if this is what she truly wants, then how can I talk her out of it?

That ghastly cliché 'if you love someone, let them go' comes to mind, but in fact, therein is a truth that's hard to fight.

Maybe, she says, it'd be better if she moves out until this is all sorted out. So, she's going to stay with Jodie for a few days, a slag mate who sells posh underwear and would fuck a lamp post if she couldn't find anything with a pulse, to 'mull things over'.

Our relationship, when we met, was stellar, cataclysmic, something that broke all records and boundaries of my expectations of life, sex and feeling connected to someone in a way that I'd never imagined could be possible. This was true love, and now I was truly devastated.

I go to the gym, blank out an hour with a spin class then register on what I consider to be a civilised dating website.

Hang on … if you love her, why do you do this … and so soon?

I don't know? Maybe because I want attention

and affection, I suppose, not just sex … although if I'm not going to get sex with M, then what? I can't go to Spain every time I want a shag; I'd never be off a fucking plane. And maybe because suddenly there's this yawning chasm in my life?

But … actually, you know what? Sex isn't my prime motivator. I guess, being Richie Malone, I just want someone attractive to put a little affection my way and pump up my ego.

And then there's the woman thing; it's okay in theory being dumped for a woman, but in practice it's as much a brick wall of rejection as if she'd left me for another bloke.

Only then I could have gone round and punched his lights out.

I feel dead empty.

Both dead and empty.

So what do I do? I ring Maria in Marbella, a Spanish girlfriend who I've – you've got to trust me on this – never slept with, and tell her M and I have split up. She's not surprised. She always told me she thought it was a toxic relationship. Says she has no agenda, but I'm best rid. Of course, I reply.

I eat Sunday roast in the Fox and Coney, barely registering what's on my plate, and consider life without her.

Then I go home alone and watch rugby.

Life, Jim, but not as I'd known it.

Mon 30 Nov

And so, it's all change (again). M's got it wrong … again.

There's other stuff going on in my life, which is probably a good thing.

I'd put in an offer for the Hull property. After trying to out-bid two other parties, I leave it at £162k. Not worth any more as a BTL.

On the positive side, my latest work of filth has just hit the top ten bestseller list.

And then, at teatime (Northern expression), day one of my single life is surprisingly railroaded by some unexpected sexting.

Below is a summary (not the entire transcript):

Her: *I'm on the train from Manc. Pik me up? Do u like wet pussys?*

Do bears crap in the Vatican? I think.

Me: *yes yes yes. How long you going to be??*

Her: *20. See u at stn. Go for a pint then to yours for a fuck?*

Me: *Coolio!*

So I pick her up, we have a quick couple of drinks in the Fox (I can tell she's already had a few on the train), then home. Awesome; her knickers are so wet you could make tea out of them.

Tue 1 Dec

M's in London.

New book, different publisher. I know she's with

Lucy cos she set the meet-up. I'm not ecstatic about this, but, hey-ho, she's her agent and life goes on.

We do a lot of texting about the 'new life' each of us may be facing … take your time and decide, I say … ball's in your court.

Wed 2 Dec

And then it's all change once again.

We'd arranged to meet for a drink in the Lion and Key early evening, after my spin class.

But M's not there.

This is because she calls in with Lucy and has sex with her.

She tells me later that Lucy licked her out and she came, but that she wouldn't touch her. This isn't going to work then, is it? I think. Oh … and Lucy's tits weren't anything to write home about, either.

I have a beer in the Lion, and phone Nig, my sport-addicted friend, to talk about rugby.

Pissed, and pissed off.

I need a couple of days away to sort my head out.

Mon 7 Dec

I booked a room in the Black Swan in Ravenstonedale, one of our favourite places and one with a large bank of good, wholesome memories.

Ideally, I'd have gone for two nights, but they only had a room for the Monday. Fuck knows why …

thought everybody had their heads up their arses with Christmas gunning at us from around the corner.

I drove north in torrential rain, wondering if this had been such a good idea. It could have been a lot worse; I almost crashed on the M6 when the Aston aquaplaned. Scary.

Arrived at around 1.30 p.m., had soup and a sandwich, put on lightweight kit, buried my phone and torch in plastic bags at the bottom of my rucksack, and set off.

Ran for two hours; showered and lay on the bed, recovering from the unaccustomed exertion of a long, hilly run and a wrist that was fucking killing me from a fall down a scree slope.

M sent pic of us in Zermatt five years ago. Memorable, happy times, but can't dwell in the past.

With that I discover, to my surprise, that the Black Swan has Wi-Fi. It never used to. And the texting begins. Once again, what follows is a summary, not an entire transcript:

Her: *It's been crazy ... I feel I was railroaded by the idea but not the reality x*

Me: *And for the record: you broke us up on Sunday ... fucked me on Monday ... broke it off again on Wednesday; so, let me see, Tuesday was a fairly normal uncomplicated day. What's Saturday/Sunday going to be like?*

Her: *U denied me the emotional attention I needed. All you care about is yourself. You're a selfish misogynistic grumpy bastard. U let me go ahead. U cud have said dont do it. I was honest with u. More fool me ... And u use my ideas for your writing ... all of this, it's all a fucking mess.*

Me: *Selfish: guilty. Grumpy: only when provoked. True, I have neglected you emotionally and for that I can only apologise. I wanted you to have the freedom to do what you felt you needed to do. Material? Don't go on the offensive about that cos everyone uses everybody's ideas. I have a lot of faults, that's true. Not denying that. Okay, here's what I think we should do: put things on hold for a week/10 days. Carry on as normal; I still want you to come to my b/day. If you feel you want to resume a (better more communicative) relationship and have relayed this to Lucy, when we'll talk about it. Fair?*

Her: *Richie i am not a lezzer. I am sure now.*

Me: *Look, let's just have a cooling off period and review in a week or so. We can still talk etc. I really, really don't want go through this again, and I have a suspicion that when you tell her it's just bezzies without the pussy action ... it'll be back to sq 1.*

And then it goes a bit downhill. That – I'm sorry, amigo – I am keeping to myself.

I go down for dinner around eight, have a reasonable steak, two pints and a couple of brandies to numb the pain which is now pulsing through my wrist like I'm holding an electric fence.

I take a couple of codeine and fall into a deep, dreamless sleep.

Tue 8 Dec

Still raining; start of the floods where whole villages get

49

flushed away. I have no dry clothes, so I put on my wet ones, go for another run then drive home.

Except I don't go straight home … I take a slight detour to Harrogate to meet this bird I'd been 'speaking to' on the dating site.

I was in and out of this fucking Harvester quicker than anyone over the age of six who'd accidentally strayed into a Justin Bieber concert. Clearly, she'd sent her granny.

Sat 12 Dec

I'm bored.

Nothing from M since my night in the North York Moors.

Maybe 'cool it' means 'cool it'.

So I call this Sarah who I'd also been 'talking to' on this dating site. Her real name isn't Sarah, but she won't tell me what it is until we meet, as she says she has a very 'high-profile' job. Bullshit – so do I, but she's certainly not finding out about that.

I'd gone to Leeds to watch Carnegie play Doncaster – big local derby, Carnegie won. We appear to have a lot in common, 'Sarah' and I, although I can tell she is stratospherically above my intellectual level. Maybe she's MI5 or something? Coolio.

I'm intrigued.

We agree to meet for a coffee.

Wed 16 Dec

Jay and Simon arrive for my birthday.

Ate in the Fox. M didn't come. Well to be fair, I didn't ask her. Seems like we're playing 'who blinks first' at the minute.

Thur 17 Dec

My birthday: got up, gym, into Hull (fuck knows why?), lunch at The Minerva (not bad, truth be told) then a bit of a pub crawl around town, as being pissed is the only way to truly appreciate Hull, followed by dinner in 1884 Dock Street Kitchen.

M actually turns up – and yes, I know, this sounds a bit bitchy, but the spotlight was *totally* centred on her: the new book, Loose fucking Women, the Caitlin Frigging Moran column … blah-de-fucking-blah.

I cheer myself up by hosing down virtually a whole bottle of Howard Park Abercrombie Cabernet Sauvignon 2011. At a hundred quid a pop, it's seriously overpriced, but it's my birthday, and I'm paying for it with the wages of filth and anonymity.

M goes home, and we go clubbing. Club Valbon, which was dead, then Spiders and finally Fuel.

I'm almost ready to sound the bugle of retreat when I go to the bar and get chatting to this bird called Sam. The name's not the most promising start; I'm always a bit suspicious of those could-be-birds-could-be-blokes names. But she's hot, although I'm guessing around forty, so she's nudging the top end of my age range. Tall, green eyes, shoulder-length blonde hair worn straight with a seductively provocative curl at the bottom; a little on the skinny side, but good shoulders, a decent rack and arse, and a face I could certainly bear to wake up next to.

Says she's a barrister, divorced, no kids. I perk up. I buy her a drink, we dance, we snog, I get her number.

Things are looking up.

Fri 18 Dec

Post-birthday recovery.

Nothing from M.

Hull being Hull, she's probably already heard about Sam. Wouldn't surprise me if Jodie, the fucking ride, nailed under some poor bastard in a shady corner of Fuel, hadn't copped us, antennae on warp factor nine.

Sat 19 Dec

Meet Sarah for coffee in Hull. Talked for ages.

Says her real name is Daisy (I'm not buying that either) and she does work for the intelligence services. She's not, like, a field operative; she works in something called 'strategic assignment'. This, I imagine, is deciding which fundamentalist MI6 are going to execute next. She's not got much of a sense of humour, though, because if I'd been her, I'd have found it hard to resist the old cliché: 'I could tell you more, but if I did, I'd have to kill you.'

Yeah … we do have a lot in common, but although she's attractive, I can't see myself in a relationship with her. Reminds me a lot of Susie, only taller and with shorter hair. And I keep thinking of Sam. Despite the name, I really want to ride her, whereas … I don't know – I'd want to read a book beside a roaring fire with Sarah-slash-Daisy.

I also find myself thinking that I wished I'd never started this, but bizarrely I feel I'm owed this freedom.

We part, agreeing that we'll keep in touch. She says she's met a couple of people through the dating site that she's made friends with.

Whatever.

It's not a commitment, but it leaves me feeling good after what I've been through.

Mon 21 and Tue 22 Dec

Cornwall.

Running away again. Need more time to think.

Life's a bit of a rollercoaster right now.

Why Cornwall?

Oh … didn't I tell you? Another bird I met on the Internet. Enter Jenny from Liverpool who's a lorra lorra laughs. We went for a drink, must have been sometime last week … yeah, Tuesday.

We met in Manchester, and I'd had the presence of mind to book a room in Malmaison.

Good plan.

A quick drink followed by a faster meal than

McDonalds can throw at you, and we adjourn to the bedroom. No preliminaries. And we're talking banging like the proverbial privy door when the plague's in town here.

So … Cornwall.

Jenny's idea.

Stupidly, I let her choose the hotel, so she opts for this bijou spa retreat right on the beach in the middle of fucking nowhere that costs five hundred notes a night. It's supposed to be near Padstow, but it turns out to be a forty-five-minute taxi ride away.

She's a mate of Rick Stein's so we trot off to his gaff for lunch. The great man's there himself, and, it has to be said, he gives us a tremendous welcome.

Now, I don't know much about chefs, but I've worked out that he specialises in fish … mainly because a) it's right on the coast, and b) there's loads of fish pictures everywhere, so his face looks like it's been slapped by a dead turbot when I ask him if I can get a decent steak here.

Decided to turn phone off as there's no signal in Cornwall in any case.

I told Jenny that M and I had split up months ago, so in case she decides to ring me, it'll go straight to answerphone.

Wed 23 Dec

Home from Cornwall.

Switched on my phone on the way back and there

are six messages from M, each sounding more desperate then the last. Will I phone her please? She wants to talk. What the fuck am I playing at? Then ... what am I doing for Christmas? Funny ... never really thought about that. Then her next message ratchets up the tension to defcon three, and I decide I'm not going to ring her but text and suggest we meet instead.

So when I get home I do this, and we meet in the Fox.

This, it transpires, is a totally stupid thing to do, as is telling her that I'd 'met' someone ... just for a coffee. Who is she, and how did I meet her? Internet, I say ... dating site.

She goes totally fucking ballistic and suddenly everyone in the pub is looking at us. There isn't even a jukebox to zone her out.

'I see,' I say. 'So it's okay for *you* to terminate our relationship and move in with your "lover"' – and I actually do the inverted comma thing with my fingers, which only serves to fan the flames – 'but not okay for *me* to go for a coffee with someone I have no intention of ever seeing again.'

'That's not the point,' she screams. 'Lucy and I "happened". Yours was premeditated.'

'My what?' I answer, knowing I'm never going to win this. 'My coffee? Nothing happened, nor is it going to.' Which, of course, is true. But Sam ... well that's a very different kettle of fish, and I'll be keeping very quiet about that.

'I *was* going to suggest we get back together,' she

says. 'I am definitely not a lesbian, and I've told Lucy it's over. But you can forget that now,' she shouts, and walks out. 'Fuck you, you bastard … I hate you and you're going to pay for this,' she screams before slamming the door.

All eyes in the Fox are trained on me in that ghastly English accusatory manner wherein you are condemned without recourse to forevermore wear the badge of Bastard.

Thur 24 Dec

M calls first thing and asks if I'll look after Gordon for a few days. Excuse me? It's like last night never happened. Did it? I think.

She's going away for Christmas. Got a last-minute booking but they don't take dogs. I should tell her to put the big, dopey fucker into kennels, but I don't because Gordon connects me to Mandy, and that's better than being a hated bastard who drinks coffee with a total non-connect.

Less than twenty-four hours have passed. Last thing, I was a bastard; now I'm a dog-sitting bastard? I don't ask her who she's going with, because I know; after I'd finally snuffed out my slim chance of reinstating of our relationship, she simply changes her mind once again, just like in that ghastly Billy Joel song.

I don't dredge it up. Of course I'll have Gordon, I say.

Ironic. I never liked the fucker in the first place, but now that she's setting up home with Juicy Lucy, I'm the only friend he has, and he's the only friend I have. So we'll have the Last Waltz, two sad lonely bastards together.

I think … no, I wish I were either a dog, or maybe even gay? It would make life a hell of a lot simpler.

An hour later she drops Gordon off with a barely audible thanks and disappears into the winter gloom, and out of my life.

Dog walk. Got soaked … feel shit.

That's the last time I saw her.

Fri 25 Dec

Happy Christmas to me.

Happy Christmas to me.

Just Gordon and me, dancing around the Christmas tree in our party hats; okay, maybe that's one visual metaphor too far.

Nothing from Mandy. I check my phone a thousand times. Not a dicky bird.

I wrap up a Bonio, give it to Gordon, eat my M&S Christmas Dinner for Single Sad Bastards and settle down with Gordon and a bottle of brandy to watch *Shaun the Sheep Movie*, with an emptiness inside that borders on physical pain.

NINE

TODAY, 07.08

I close the journal.

I know this has got some bearing on the dead girl, but for the life of me, I just can't figure it yet.

I'm grasping at straws here; the drowning man, desperate to save himself, attempting to hold onto any floating object, no matter how small.

I'll think of something.

Anything.

And then it hits me. Shit, why didn't I think of this before?

The one woman still talking to me with no axe to grind – maybe that's not a particularly good metaphor in the circumstances – who would really know if this is who I am.

Maria.

I have to phone a friend.

TEN

TODAY, 07.09

Maria picks up at the third ring.

'Hey, Malone, can you not fucking sleep?'

This kind of reassures me but in itself is not enough. What's worse, I've not entirely figured out what I'm going to say to her. Probably telling her there's a dead girl in my bed isn't the best way to begin the conversation.

'Yeah ... no, just woke up.'

'Well, this had better be important. I've got a night shift later, remember?' In fact, I don't remember; right now, this information isn't even halfway to registering on my give-a-shit-ometer.

But there's another reason for ringing Maria: she's the senior traumatologist at the Costa del Sol Hospital. A traumatologist is what the Spanish call someone who puts nearly dead people back together. Okay, she may not be able to bring the girl back to life, but she may be able to throw some light on how she got dead, other than the obvious. It doesn't occur to me, of course, in my confused state of mind, that inviting her to conduct an impromptu, unofficial autopsy – the evidence for which would be hard to conceal – may not overly enhance her career prospects, let alone distance her name from mine in the very short shortlist of suspects when I finally trigger the CSI investigation.

'Yeah, well it is. I'm sorry, babe, I know it's early, but I've got a bit of a problem.'

'Hey … how many times do I have to tell you not to "babe" me, huh?'

'C'mon, you love it really.'

She laughs. A dusky, sexy laugh; but I wouldn't go there, amigo. It's not that I don't want to. I *won't* … yeah, even Richie Malone lives by certain principles that a lesser human being would refer to as rights and wrongs, but which shape the consequences of our actions.

And this particular consequence would be one complication too far and cost me the only woman I can genuinely call a friend.

Oh, she's a looker all right. Tall, brown hair, hazel eyes, slender, full-breasted – her own, she claims; but why should I care, as from a semantic point of view, once you've paid for them, ownership is indubitable? Think Marta Etura with a smaller nose, add ten years; although, to be fair, she looks less than the sum total of her fifty-four summers.

So, one night we came to within a fag paper's width of doing the wild thing and then I nuked the moment by referring to her as the sister I never had, and as a consequence she wouldn't talk to me for ages.

There you go, amigo, a prime example of actions and consequences, not rights and wrongs.

'So tell me, Malone, you got some bimbo in your bed who won't go home, and you want me to pretend I'm the cleaner?' This, amigo, is in fact closer to the truth than she thinks.

Ask her where you were last night.

'Hmm … look, this is a bit embarrassing, but I seem to have some sort of short-term – I don't know, maybe it's not short-term, but, like, memory loss. Do you happen to know what I did last night?' Where I was?'

Silence.

'Was I … like, with anyone?'

'You seriously don't remember?'

'No – I totally don't remember. I think I may have at some point fallen over, maybe banged my head? Last night's a kind of a blur.'

'Hangover, more like.'

'So … do you know anything or not?'

'You really don't know?'

'Nope. Last thing I remember yesterday was …' I search my brain for something, anything that would time-frame my memory loss. Nothing. 'Come to think of it, I can't remember a single bloody thing about yesterday.'

'I better check you out. You may have a concussion. I'll be there in ten minutes. Lie down. Don't, under any circumstances, do anything to exert yourself. And definitely no sex.'

Fat chance of that.

NO ... no, not a good plan.

Perhaps. Okay, I see where you're coming from.

'No, babe ... look, I'll come round to yours. I need ... I need to pick up some cigarettes, in any case.'

'You don't smoke. Oh my God.'

'Get dressed, babe, I'll be at yours in twenty.'

I hang up.

ELEVEN

NINE MONTHS AGO

It's the day after Boxing Day. I've been on my own for over two days, and I'm climbing the walls.

So, an idea occurs to me. I decide to ring Sam, except I can't find her number, and I'm on the point of giving up when I notice Gordon chewing something that looks suspiciously like a business card.

I try to extract it from his mouth but he's not minded to give it up, and I can see her name and number are about to get pulped into oblivion along with my chances of a post-Christmas gloom-lifting shag.

I extract the Bonio I always carry for such eventualities from my pocket, fling it across the room and, hey presto, the business card is abandoned like a Tyrannosaurus dropping a Velociraptor when he spots something bigger.

I smooth it out and key in her number.

Hang on; aren't you supposed to be going round to Maria's? What the hell are you talking about this right now for?

Oh, because for one thing, it'll take her fifteen

minutes to put her face on and she won't let me in until she's done, and for another, this *does* have some relevance to what I'm about to tell you, so shut the fuck up for once and just listen.

Hey! That's no way to talk to me.

Whatever.

So, I'm about to hang up when she answers.

'Hi, Sam … ah … did you have a good Christmas?'

'No, it was shit.' Pause. 'Who the heck is this?'

She's got a ridiculously sexy telephone voice and I can feel the stirrings of a boner until Gordon nudges me in the groin on the quest for another biscuit.

'Oh, sorry. Richie … Richie Malone. Remember, we met in that club, what was it … Fuel? A few nights ago?'

Silence. Fuck, have I become this instantly forgettable?

'Yeah, I remember you. The writer. The writer who's only had two books published that went pretty much nowhere. I googled you.'

Ouch. That hurt. The curse of being the scribbler who writes under a pseudonym strikes again.

'Yeah, well, like I said, I've had others published but not under my own name, for various reasons, such as I didn't particularly want to get murdered by one of my principal characters.'

Another silence.

'They all say that.'

I'm left wondering how many writers she knows. But she's a lawyer, so I'll buy it.

Okay, this isn't going well, and I'm about to accept that even Richie Malone can't win them all, when she comes right out and says it:

'Okay, you weren't a bad kisser, so I suppose I can at least forgive you for part of the horseshit …'

'It's not horseshit, I promise.'

'Whatever. I'm fed up with Christmas.' Another pause. 'I may just go into the office. Unless you want to come round for a fuck?'

Does a bear wear a big hat in the Vatican shitter?

I hit the wine cooler and grab a couple of bottles of Dom Pérignon Vintage 2009; not the shitty stuff – the Tokujin Yoshioka Limited Edition variety I'd ordered from Harrods for my birthday but forgotten about. I'd got the distinct sensation from my brief meeting with Sam that here was a woman it pays not to go cheap on.

I needn't have bothered, and I'll tell you why in a minute.

Twenty minutes later I park the Aston where she can see it – yes, I know this is childish, but the vitriol about my writing still hurts – close to the front door at the head of a quarter-mile-long gravelled drive leading to what would appear to be an Edwardian rectory set amid several acres of manicured, horse-filled fields. Nice. Nicer than my gaff, actually.

She lets me in.

'Nice car,' she says.

'Nice tits,' I reply.

I open the champagne, pour two glasses, we snog, we fuck. That's the thing about sex. No matter who you are, no matter what your status is, no matter how you look, dress or smell, almost everything else in life you could be doing is worse than having sex. Even bad sex.

Except this sex isn't bad.

If this had been the National, Mandy at her peak would have only beaten her by a head, and yes, I mean that in the allegorical sense as well.

If you ask me, for a porn writer you're lacking a little in engagement. Can't you do any better? You know, embellish it a bit? Add a splash of colour? Go beyond the basic facts? I mean, isn't this your chance to shine under your own name and emerge from that cloud of anonymity?

Heck, no. I don't write about my own sexual experiences. I may *draw* from my own sexual experiences, but I sure as hell don't write about them. Ethics and all that. In any case, when it comes to filth, I happen to like the cloak of anonymity; I wear it well. Other than it makes it harder to get laid sometimes, Sam being a case in point. If she hadn't been a complete hound, I'd never have even got close to getting between those beguiling thighs. And yes, before you ask, this is part of my motivation to write a bestseller in my own name. Charisma and good looks alone, amigo – on some rare occasions – simply just aren't enough.

Anyway, at your insistence I'll fill in a few of the blanks.

So … we did it in her living room – sorry, she calls it the drawing room – on an expensive-looking rug by the fire. Then we did it on the spiral staircase, and then we went at it – pardon the cliché, but hammer and tongs would be an appropriate summary – in her king-sized canopied bed for several hours, until hunger and my need for more alcohol drove us down to her kitchen where I bent her over the Aga and we did it again.

By now I'm well into the second bottle of bubbly, and I notice that she's not touched her glass.

'Not a fan?' I ask, holding up my glass.

'I don't drink,' she replies.

Of course, I'd like to ask her why because I have a deeply entrenched prejudice – which I inherited from my father – about people who don't drink … although his prejudices were also extended to people with beards, dirty shoes and anyone who drove either a German or a Japanese car. But now is not the right time; that's a question for another day.

The champagne and a turkey sandwich help to shore up my strength but, truth be told, I'm feeling my libido beginning to flag. Yes, even with industrial quantities of Viagra fuelling the foundry.

I'm guessing she senses this and retreats to her closet, from which she emerges moments later in some pretty sensual apparel and proceeds to set up an expensive-looking camera on a tripod facing the bed.

I'm beginning to think that I'm not entirely sure I like where this is going; besides which, my old man is starting to feel as if it's been through a mincing machine.

But being an old-fashioned sort of guy, I don't want to disappoint the lady. Besides which, the charcoal hold-ups and Victoria's Secret lingerie accentuate the deliciously curvaceous sophistication of her body, fanning my dying embers into flames, and soon we're at it again, rutting like white-tailed deer.

Still, the camera, which has one of those remote things so you can set it to shoot at will (pardon the pun), clicks every few seconds, and this unnerves me; and not just in the performance anxiety department.

So, after round sixteen – let's just say, as I've lost count by now – I drain the last of the champagne, she lights up a joint and I ask the question:

'Ah … just what exactly do you intend to do with those, um … photos, by the way?'

'Oh, I dunno.' She offers me the joint. 'Want some?'

'No. Thanks. I'm not being sanctimonious, I just never got on with the stuff.' I kiss her shoulder, play with her bra strap. 'Anyway, you haven't answered my question?'

'Maybe sell them to the *News of the World*.'

I laugh. Is she for real, or is it that anything below the *Financial Times* is off her radar?

'It doesn't exist anymore. It was shut down in 2011 or thereabouts. And oddly enough, the reason for this was that it somehow acquired a reputation for exposing celebrities' drug use, sexual peccadilloes, and setting up journalists in disguise to provide photographic evidence. In fact, just the sort of thing you're doing now.'

'Really? I didn't know that.'

'Well, you should do; after all, you're a lawyer.'

'Then you've got nothing to worry about, darling, have you?'

I hate it when a woman calls me 'darling', especially

after the first fuck. It takes tacky to a new level, and they only do it to annoy.

'I'm a lawyer and you're a little-known, inconsequential writer, so I'd hardly class myself as a blackmailer, and I'd barely class you as a celebrity.'

She knows how to wound, this one. She even outscores Mandy with this ego-scything woman skill.

'What about the Aston?' I ask, knowing as I say it how lame this sounds.

'Oh, I've got plenty of clients with Astons, Bentleys and Ferraris who haven't a pot to piss in. Anyway,' – she takes a drag from the joint, inhales deeply – 'I'll email the best ones to you. Then you'll have plenty of masturbational fodder for those cold, lonely winter nights.'

I don't know whether it's 'masturbational' or 'fodder' that triggers the thought, but I suddenly remember that Gordon is alone in the house, and aside from the probability that he'll have shredded all my significant paperwork, including an annotated work of filth my editor sent back for my approval, he'll be dying for a shit. If, that is, he's not already had one.

'Got to go,' I say, leaping from the bed and throwing on my clothes.

I kiss her on the forehead to repay her for calling me darling.

'That was great. Let's do it again sometime,' I say, searching for my car keys.

I'm halfway down the stairs when she goes: 'And don't forget that possession is a two-way thing, Malone.

Make sure you keep those images to yourself, darling, or I *will* see you again. But it'll be in court.'

As I gun the Aston's V12, the thought hits me that I'm probably at least four times over the drink-drive limit. Still, the urgency to remove Gordon from the house and rescue my MS outweighs any moral responsibility or the threat of a possible custodial sentence, and I fire the thing down the drive and head towards South Cave.

I get home to find that Mandy has let herself in and taken Gordon. As he is no longer here, there can be no other explanation. Besides, a faint scent of Chanel Chance still lingers. Not my favourite, but better than the aroma of dogshit.

No note of thanks, flowers nor chocolates, but at least he hasn't crapped everywhere, and my MS is still intact; although I could have sworn it isn't precisely where I'd left it. My undercover stints in Northern Ireland taught me to be especially analytical if you know that someone, particularly someone whose intentions aren't entirely altruistic, has been in your living quarters.

***

There's a very simple way to avoid becoming embroiled in a toxic relationship: don't have a relationship.

And this is precisely how Sam and I conducted our sexual peccadilloes for the next six months. Although, to be fair, peccadillo is somewhat of an overstatement as there was nothing immoral, illegal or unethical about it.

It couldn't even be classed as misconduct, although some of the stuff she persuaded me to try would have raised an eyebrow or two; it certainly would have interested *News of the World* readers – had it still existed – even though she was just a lawyer and I was a little-known, inconsequential writer.

Still, it was good shit I could use in my next 'inconsequential writer's' work of filth, and for that alone, I will be eternally grateful to her.

And I know what you're going to ask, amigo, because I'm beginning to understand how your mind works. You want to know about the pictures?

Of course. Well?

Well, two days later the email arrives. There are about fifty images and they are pretty, I don't know … graphic?

That's it – just graphic? Is that all?

Graphic will do. How do you suggest I categorise highly pornographic images?

Anyway, let me ask *you* a question for once? What's the point of taking and sharing highly pornographic images of you and your partner having sex?

Um … like she said, masturbational fodder?

No … well not entirely; superficially, maybe. The point is to make you want to fuck her again. And again … and again. And it worked.

Our first coupling was the one and only time I visited her house; the rest of the action took place in my gaff. She said it was so I could have a drink without risking my licence, but I think it was perhaps to prevent any form of emotional attachment on her behalf. It didn't bother me. I prefer home fixtures anyway, and there was absolutely no way I was going to fall in love with her. She was no Mandy; there was no emotional connection whatever. Heck, we didn't even bother trying. I could count on the fingers of one hand the number of occasions we said more than twenty words to each other of an evening. I wasn't interested in getting to know her, and she wasn't even remotely interested in getting to know what floats my boat. It was just sex; nothing more. But very good sex. Amazing sex, actually.

So, what happened? Why did it end?

Ah, that … the end of our non-relationship? Well, that was down to Mandy.

Hang on; I thought you said you never saw her again?

I didn't. This is how it happened, amigo … listen and learn.

One day about three months ago it occurs to me that Mandy still has a set of keys to my gaff, so I text her and ask her to return them.

This is the first communication between us since Christmas – she's just blanked me out of her life. Two days later she replies: says she'll drop them in the letterbox next time she's in the area. No how are you? No maybe we could meet for a coffee? Not even a belated thanks for having Gordon. Nada. She's seriously pissed off with me, and I don't really know why. After all, it was her who started fucking someone else – hang on, do you refer to having sex with another woman as fucking her?

Christ, you're the porn writer. You don't know? Still, if you ask me, I'd say any form of vaginal penetration defines it as fucking ... such as a rabbit, or a—

Yes, okay, okay ... I get the point. Anyway, I still don't know why she's so angry just because I met someone for a coffee. What's the big fucking deal about that?

You just don't get it, do you? You joined an Internet dating site looking for someone to have more than coffee with, at the precise moment that she wanted you back in her life. It's a double whammy. Man ... you really have no idea how the female mind works.

Very little, I'll grant you that. Anyway ... she does drop the keys off, but not before she's finished what I bloody well know she started when she picked up Gordon after Christmas.

Which is?

Which is having a damned good root around my house to find out exactly what I'm up to. And find it she does.

Why I hadn't changed the password on my laptop, heaven only knows, but the next morning, around seven, she calls and says that she's got all the images Sam sent me on her flash drive. Gross and depraved, she says. Pot, kettle, black, I'm thinking, and then I remember the ones where Sam had inserted this black dildo into an orifice it probably wasn't designed for while I'm banging her from beneath (at least in this shot I'm not identifiable) and I'm thinking, okay, you probably have a point.

She then rants on for about five minutes: how could I? I'm going to pay for this … I've humiliated her (I've no idea how, as no one else knows anything about it, unless she's hired a private eye – which I wouldn't entirely rule out).

Her voice is rising to a pitch that only dogs can hear, when suddenly she stops and calms the fuck down. Then she says it: I stop seeing Sam, or she puts these photos all over the Internet. She doesn't go into the specifics of how she's going to do that, but I know enough about her (post-Rwoopardo's unfortunate demise) to know that she is capable of creating some serious fucking fallout.

And then I'm thinking that from my point of view, as a little-known, inconsequential writer, this may not be such a negative as there's no such thing as bad publicity. Of course, this will not be the case for Sam, but being the selfish bastard I am, I don't see that as being my problem.

Once this filth is in the public domain, her clients will drop her faster than Ben Kay dropped the ball over the Australian line in the World Cup final, which would trigger the end of her career. Again, not my problem, amigo.

And then she drops the biggest bomb since the day she told me that she likes another woman licking her pussy: she knows it's me who writes the filth that has almost residential status in the top ten bestsellers' list (and she actually has the audacity to call it filth). She almost spits the pseudonym, pronouncing each syllable with what I can only describe as measured female rancour. And as she says it out loud, I feel a bolt of terror hit my heart, and for a minute I'm waiting for the crushing chest pain, the shortness of breath, the collapse to the floor followed by imminent departure from this mortal coil.

But this doesn't happen, and for an eternity there's just silence as I take in the implications of what she's just said and she basks in the sepia-tinged satisfaction of my pathetic predicament.

So … how does she know this?

Because, remember, I left the annotated MS of my work of filth on the desk in my study. Okay, it doesn't have a name on it, but she reads *Viagra Falls* on the title page; one click on the Internet takes her to 'Coming Soon in Books', and a second takes her to my publisher's website, where she can pull up the synopsis and match the first chapter with what's in front of her.

Why the hell did you leave it lying around?

Because, for one thing, my brain was absorbed in calculating how much Viagra I should take to ensure that Mr Floppy wouldn't come knocking while I'm pleasuring Sam, and for another, I wasn't expecting an intruder. But you're right, amigo, it should have been in the desk under lock and key. Basic schoolboy error.

And, anyway, didn't she already know the name you wrote under?

Absolutely not; one of the conditions of the initial three-book contract was that I took this to me grave. Okay, I've told a couple of people … two writing friends of mine who also use pseudonyms – a sort of swapsies, if you like – but certainly not Mandy.

So, anyway, back to the story … then she says that if I ever contact Sam (to be fair, she doesn't actually refer to her by name but by a string of obscenities which prefix the word 'bitch'), let alone see her, she will share this information with the national press, in addition to plastering it all over the Internet.

If I ever even contact her again, she repeats, be assured that this is precisely what will happen. And I know how much anonymity is valued by my publisher as well as me. He will drop me quicker than Shane Warne dropped Javagal Srinath to rob Damien Fleming of a second Test hat-trick, and this will leave me in precisely the same canoe without a paddle, drifting up shit creek, as Sam will find herself in.

And I don't know how I know this, amigo, but I know how fucking devious and downright nasty this woman has the potential to be, so I am left in no doubt that this is precisely what will happen.

Game over.

TWELVE

TODAY, 07.25

I park the Porsche outside Maria's apartment and take the lift to the fourth floor.

It's already warm, but the prospect of a beautiful early autumn day spent lounging on the beach and a leisurely lunch in Chiringuito Pepe's Bar is as remote as me writing a literary masterpiece.

I'm about to ring her doorbell when I hesitate. Once I tell her, I involve her, and do I really want to do this? Is it fair to implicate her? You see what a magnanimous bloke I'm now becoming?

Anyway, this particular tale of redemption lasts less than five seconds before I ring the bell, and she opens the door almost at once.

Mr P, her bisexual, racist chihuahua, is there behind her wagging his stumpy tail and grinning at me like Jack Nicholson in *The Shining*.

We know he's racist because he only ever barks at black fellas and when he does she has to practically blindfold the little fucker to prevent him from going mental.

And before you ask, Maria is convinced that he's bisexual, but in my book this is perfectly normal because all dogs are bisexual. They're dogs, for fuck's sake, therefore they have no moral compass. And just to prove it, he sidesteps Maria and starts humping my leg.

She ushers me into her beautifully designed and sumptuously decorated penthouse apartment overlooking the sea and the Casco Antiguo.

Without thinking, I take out a cigarette and am about to light up.

'Hey … don't fucking smoke that thing in here, Malone. Get your ass out on the terrace. What's all this smoking about, anyway? You fucking hate smokers.'

I oblige, and she fetches an ashtray. I don't bother to explain because, in truth, I don't know why I'm smoking either.

'Coffee?'

'No … actually, yes,' I reply, 'and stick a large brandy in it, will you?'

Last night … last night? Ask her about last night.

I light a cigarette, park my arse on a wicker chair and prop my feet on the table.

She returns with the coffee.

'Let's start with last night,' I say.

'Hey … feet off the table, Malone. Christ, you really have bad boy written all over you this morning. Just cos you're fucking some bimbo half your age, doesn't give you the right to behave like a total asshole.'

It usually does – much to her amusement – I think, but that's not a subject I want to debate right now.

I do what I'm told.

'So, tell me about last night. Was I with someone?'

'You seriously don't remember her?' She takes out her phone. 'This bring back any memories?' She shows me pictures of the girl and me in fairly intimate entanglements; we're in the Moët, and it's her, all right – the dead girl … the dead girl who's lying in my bed. There's no mistaking it. 'You know who she is?'

'Yes … and no,' I reply. 'She's the girl in my bed, okay … but I don't know who she is.'

'What, you just walked out and left her there? What you say … "Going to the shops for more condoms, cariño,"?' She laughs. 'But I doubt it if she speaks Spanish anyway.'

'She didn't really say anything,' I reply. There's no good way to move this along delicately, so I just come right out and say it. 'She's dead, actually.'

'Dead! Jesus Christ! What … you having a laugh, Malone? Don't fucking fuck me around, you fucking fucker.'

But through the veneer of a smile so forced I can see the perfect symmetry of her face strain with effort, I know that she knows that this, for once, isn't one of Richie Malone's trademark bad taste jokes.

'Shit … you're serious, man, aren't you? She better not be fucking dead. You don't know who she is? Don't know or can't remember? And how you know she's dead anyway?'

'I really have no idea who she is. I have no memory of her or anything about last night, so if you know anything at all perhaps you would be good enough to fill in the blanks?' I stub out my cigarette and light another. 'And I can guarantee she's dead, unless she's somehow developed the ability to carry on living without blood in her veins.'

I swallow a mouthful of coffee. 'There's no brandy in it.'

'You're going to need a clear head, Malone.' She sits and stares out to sea. 'The girl is Natasha Nikolaeva. She is the daughter of Alexei Nikolaev. You know him?'

'Nope. Not a baldy. Sounds Russian, though.'

'Oh, he's Russian, all right. Head of the Russian mafia in Puerto Banús, and not the sort of man whose path you'd want to cross … or whose dead daughter you'd want to find in your bed.'

'Oh fuck …' I say. 'Fucking … fuck.'

Hard to make a bad day any worse.

THIRTEEN

TODAY, 07.30

Maria's idea of an HIA, or head injury assessment, is thankfully more concise than I expect.

By now, she has pretty much concluded that – apart from the fact that I've taken up a habit that hitherto I had considered to be repulsive – I'm not exhibiting any of the more serious indicators of cerebral trauma.

The only 'severe' symptoms I report are 'difficulty remembering' and 'confusion'. I score 'moderate' on feeling like 'in a fog', 'irritability', and 'nervous or anxious', but for very good reasons. I don't even register on any of the physical symptoms, so I score a modest 30/132, which pretty much puts me in the clear.

Nonetheless, she ploughs on with the Orientation, Immediate Memory, Concentration and Delayed Recall protocols. This is the test used in professional Rugby Union, she tells me, to determine if a player is fit to continue. I tell her that I would consider this test to be wholly inappropriate as most of the players are so thick these days, they would struggle to pass it before they got kicked in the head.

Anyway, I fly through the test, although one part of me is slightly disappointed as it would explain a lot, and maybe even suggest that I'd imagined the whole thing.

'What I don't understand,' I say, 'is how I can recall intricate shit from months ago – you know: times, dates, names, places – but I can't remember anything about last night. Any ideas?'

She shrugs.

'That, Malone, is what we're going to have to find out.' She stands, picks up her phone and hands it to me. 'But right now, we need to call the police. *You* need to call the police.'

Oh, hurrah for that with bells on. Finally doing what you should have done the moment you woke up.

'No!' I yell. 'No … at least, not yet. I need more time to figure this out.'

'Figure what out? There's a dead girl in your bed, for God's sake. You claim to know nothing about her. Maybe you do, maybe you don't. But if I were you, I'd rather be in police custody than sit around waiting for Alexei Nikolaev to come knocking on *my* door when he finds his daughter's missing.'

'Yeah, well, that's a chance I'm going to have to take.' I light another cigarette and inhale deeply. I can see why smoking is so addictive. For one thing, it helps you concentrate, and the only thing that's going to get me out of this shitstorm is to focus on how I inadvertently got into it in the first place. I put her phone back on the table. She picks it up.

'Well, if you aren't going to call 112,' she says and turns towards the terrace doors, 'I am. You've involved me in this, Malone. By coming here and telling me about it you've made me an accessory, and that means I could go to jail, lose my job … all of this … lose my fucking life. Thanks very fucking much.'

Not only has she the right to be seriously pissed off with me, she's also right, of course.

All I can figure out is this: whoever did it wasn't the Russian mafia, unless it was some disenchanted foot soldier who was prepared to put his own life on the line for an extreme act of vengeance. And if this were the case, Nikolaev wouldn't have much difficulty in tracking him down.

But Maria is right: he would naturally come knocking on my door first, as it wouldn't take much for him to establish that I was probably the last person to see her alive. I'd like to know why I was with her, of course, other than what was evidenced by Maria's photography. But then, for reasons I'll share with you shortly, that doesn't stack up either.

Was it a random encounter in a bar, or was it a planned meeting? And why was I all over her like flies on dogshit? And in public? Apart from anything else, it's not my style. This would be helpful to know, but to judge by Maria's snaps, if it were the latter then the meeting had gone pretty much off the rails by that stage.

So, whoever killed the girl certainly had a grievance, but that grievance had to be either with Nikolaev or with myself … or perhaps even with both of us, and I haven't the faintest idea how I'm going to find this out. But at least I now know who the girl was and the sort of shit that will be coming my way.

And so ... maybe a police cell isn't such a bad idea; at least, until I can get my lawyer to figure out where this is going. My lawyer? Shit, that's ironic, for reasons I'll divulge shortly.

Of course, there is also the concern as to how many of the cops are in Mr Nikolaev's pocket, and that doesn't bear thinking about.

I can hear Maria talking on the phone in the lounge and so I light another cigarette and prepare myself for the inevitable.

FOURTEEN

THREE MONTHS AGO

The first thing I do when I get off the phone that morning is to ring Sam.

I actually felt quite – I don't know, maybe sad? – about giving her the bad news. Not because I felt anything for her, but simply because we had such a good thing going, and it certainly hadn't been on my agenda to put an end to it.

I explain what has happened, and that I couldn't see her again. I was expecting that, with her passive-aggressive personality, she would simply say 'Fuck you, Malone,' and ring off. But how wrong could I be?

She actually … like, cries?

Cries … why?

Yes, cries.

It turns out that, initially anyway, this was precisely the relationship – or non-relationship – she had been looking for, and then somehow it had grown into something more than that. Fuck knows how; if we were to play a game of 'Mr & Mrs', neither of us would get a single question right.

But she knew that I wanted a liaison without commitment or complication, and so it was easier to say nothing, as to tell me how she really felt would risk me bailing.

Short answer: she's in love with me.

Now this should have been my cue to let the curtain drop and leave the stage with a bow to rapturous applause, but something in her tears and in Mandy's downright viciousness awakens the stubborn steak in me.

And so I do the complete opposite.

Of course, I wasn't in love with her, so all I planned was a goodbye fuck. And that would be that.

We would meet at a hotel well away from Hull, have a drink, go up to the room and spend a couple of hours fucking each other's brains out. Then I would simply tell her that we couldn't do this again, and set sail into the sunset.

Except it doesn't work out like that.

So, what did happen?

Amigo, let me tell you something. A goodbye fuck is never a good idea, for so many reasons.

Top of the list: there is always one partner who won't let go, and on this occasion it was both of us. She was in love with me – fuck knows why – and I loved fucking her. And so both of us had motivation sufficient to continue the non-relationship, which by now was a non-relationship on one side only. But she could live with that because, like anyone who is in love and whose love is unreciprocated, she believed it was as inevitable as day would follow night that one day, I would come to love her.

And so, the game resumed again; only this time we played by different rules.

We would meet at a hotel, maybe once every ten days or so. And because I would choose the venue it would have at least four stars and a decent restaurant. We'd have a drink – and I didn't drink alcohol when we were together, which made the pre-dinner sex even better. So we'd have dinner and then go at it properly until one of us fell asleep. It was a totally different ballgame; having dinner together meant that we talked, and I found that she had much to absorb me.

So … I don't get it. Why the personal interest now? I mean, you could just have continued as before, the only difference being that you met at a hotel. You didn't even have to have dinner together, did you?

Yeah … no, you're right. We didn't. But she works long hours and … a piece of advice, amigo: a woman isn't at her best in the bedroom department when she's ravenous. And I dislike room service as much as I dislike editors who defile perfectly acceptable prose with a heavy pen.

So, we would make an evening of it, and it's difficult to do that without some form of conversational engagement.

And how did the transition from twenty words per night to the candlelit romantic dinner work?

Okay, I can smell sarcasm from a very great distance, amigo.

Let me tell you that there *was* a certain awkwardness when we first sat down and stared at each other across a dinner table. Sure, it felt unnatural, but it also felt good. Mandy had wanted to put an end to this, and here we were, playing our own game.

It must have seemed like a blind date?

Yes, in some ways it did. But when you know that you're going to spend the rest of the evening, and most of the night, having steamy sex, it takes the sting out of the chatting-up process, as there essentially *is* no chatting-up process.

No small talk?

None whatever. We'd already established that neither of us was interested, so we went for it and dug in deep.

Our first meeting, post-Mandy's intervention, was in Manchester – the Principal. Decent hotel, although the cuisine was a little short of my expectations, but I wasn't that hungry, and neither was she; and so, with a combination of disinterest in the food and an unexpected interest in my dinner guest, the maître d' dodged a bullet.

So she comes straight out and tells me her life story.

Now remember, this is a woman who's 'fessed up to loving me and I've confessed to nothing, so this is a seriously big chip to play at our first 'proper' meeting.

Heck, you could almost call it a date.

As Hank Moody – who incidentally, could learn a trick or two from me – said: a date is defined as two adults, generally, but not always, heterosexual, meeting for the explicit purpose of sexual engagement after seven o'clock at night. And that, I suppose, regardless of past history, was exactly what we were doing.

Anyway … her backstory.

Her parents moved to London from Warsaw in the seventies, so she was born in England. Her father was a well-known film producer – Jan Kieślowski – and a big mate of Roman Polanski's. He'd managed to piss off the Soviets to the extent that he was no longer the darling of mainstream film production companies and had to ply his trade with the lesser independents, where budgets were so small that he couldn't get his stuff out there. And then his anti-Soviet sentiment earned him death threats, and he decided it was time to get the hell out of Dodge.

Unfortunately, he never got much of a chance to flourish in England because both he and Sam's mother died in a road accident when she was eight, and so Sam was brought up by an aunt who lived in Peterborough.

But it wasn't a total tale of doom and gloom, as her father had inherited well and set up a decent trust fund for her, so she ended up reading law at Oxford via Haberdashers' Aske's School for Girls.

Then, just as a hard luck story looked to have been averted, disaster struck again; she got pregnant by some guy she was seeing while working as a pole dancer in a nightclub during her first-year summer vacation.

So, she took a year out. She had a daughter, and the father fronted up and took on the kid so she could finish uni.

Didn't she consider having an abortion?

89

She has Polish ancestry, amigo, therefore she's a left-footer, and the Catholic Church's stance on abortion couldn't be clearer on the matter.

So that's all I know; she wasn't that keen on elaborating, and I didn't want to press it, but I get the impression he was a lot older than her and had maybe made what sounded like a considerable fortune by less than legitimate means.

Anyway, she finished up with a first, and she would have been a QC by now if she hadn't developed an addiction for keeping big-time scallies out of jail.

So, what bought her the estate in Yorkshire? Surely not the salary of a defence counsel?

Oh, she's pretty well paid, but it also seems that daddy's trust fund was something approaching a bottomless pit. I get the impression that she wouldn't have to work if she chose not to.

And she still goes by the name of Kieślowski?

Heck, no. That went when she lived with the aunt, who changed her name to Sloane.

Anyway, back to the narrative. By now things had changed big-time between Sam and me. In addition to dining together, we were sleeping, yes, actually sleeping together; not just satiating our carnal desires. So it meant that we woke up together, and therefore, before I knew it, our non-relationship had become a relationship.

Of course, I only realise this when I break my no-alcohol rule and have a little too much to drink one night, and ask her to stay with me in Marbella. She has the audacity to tell me that she'll think about it, and I wake up the next morning and find myself not only not regretting the invitation, but also wondering when she'll make her mind up and hoping she'll answer in the affirmative.

She does, and spends a week at my gaff, which, I'll be honest, is unexpectedly amazing.

I take a week off writing, much to my editor's chagrin as the next work of filth is already almost a month behind the scheduled publication date, and we actually do stuff together.

We go to Sevilla, we go to Ronda, we go for long walks along the Paseo Maritimo, we go up into the hills and stay overnight in this cute little *parador* where the food is fantastic but the service is dreadful, even by Spanish standards. We lay close like young lovers, holding hands and staring into each other's eyes on the beach, and we eat in my favourite restaurants and share honest laughter into the small hours.

I introduce her to my friends, and she is charming and radiant, relaxed and erudite in their company. They adore her; well, apart from Maria, that is – but any woman I'm stupid enough to introduce Maria to gets a glacial reception and is treated with the sort of distain a mongoose treats a cobra with.

But above all, we talk … and we talk … and we talk. And I find a great and unexpected pleasure in this because she is intelligent, amusing and self-deprecating – and that's when I realise that this is a very different game we're playing.

And so, I ask about her abstinence from alcohol.

'I used to drink at school,' she tells me, 'then it got out of hand during my first year at uni, and that summer I lost myself in alcohol and got pregnant. So part of the deal with the child's father was that I went into rehab, and I've not touched a drop since.'

What? So she was an alcoholic when she was twenty? Is that possible?

Now who's being naïve? There are a heck of a lot of people younger than twenty who attend Alcoholics Anonymous, you know.

'I just happened to be tub-thumping for so long before I finally broke; and when I did, I found myself … hmmm … I hate to say it, but I'd come round and find I was engaging in risky sexual behaviour in semi-public places.'

Like what? Go on, I'm interested.

Okay, it's not really relevant to the story of our burgeoning romance, but she told me she once gave a guy she didn't know a blow job on the settee at a party.

Anyway … back to the story, if it's okay with you, amigo?

So, late one hot summer's night, she lies with her head on my lap as we rock on a hammock on my terrace, and I find myself pondering what it might be like to live together.

I marvel at the reflection of the moon dancing on the sea, as I often do, and then I realise that, as night follows day, the inevitability of her love becoming requited is but a hop and a skip away.

She returns to England, and I stay on for a month to finish the book.

Now, normally a day of productive writing is rewarded by a night of debauchery and lascivious antics, either with one of my tax-deductible Russian beauties, or by the good old-fashioned method of using my looks and charm to peel a looker away from her mates in a bar and entice her back to my villa.

I actually like the balance, you know?

Heck, it's not about saving money, because you can learn a lot from Russian – or even French – hookers, and none of this intel ever gets wasted.

But I also like the thrill of the chase.

And then, one day, I don't know … maybe two weeks after she's gone, I find myself thinking of Sam, and I realise that I've not slept with anyone since she left.

Maria, with her nose for observing my 'affairs' has detected this too, but I can't work out if she's pleased or annoyed at this unpredicted deviation.

So Maria thinks she's in with a chance of a crack at The Greatest Lover on Earth, does she?

Amigo, there's really no need for that sardonic twisting of the knife, now, is there?

No … Maria knows that becoming anything other than what we are would ruin everything we've got. Okay, occasionally I used to regale her with salacious titbits of my 'adventures' that she found highly entertaining, and the well from whence came this source of amusement has now dried up.

And so, in short, I'm suffering the longest period of celibacy since I was eighteen, and it's then that I realise I'm in love.

And there's a certain irony in that this is all Mandy's fault; none of this would have happened without her malicious and thoroughly nasty intervention.

FIFTEEN

TODAY, 08.25

I drive back to my gaff with a heavy heart, and we wait for the Policía Nacional to rock up with their helicopters, sniffer dogs, CSI, forensic team and handcuffs.

We'd been instructed to await their arrival at the gates (I'm not that optimistic about them finding the perpetrator of this crime if they can't find my villa, as it's as easy to find as Heathrow Airport is for a Londoner) and that they would arrive within fifteen minutes.

So it's no surprise when three plain-clothed officers roll up in an unmarked car almost three-quarters of an hour later, get out and light up. Why anyone would expect the police to arrive on time in Spain is beyond me? The one who's clearly in charge – let's call him Robocop, as his human nature has clearly been bypassed – appears to be more interested in finishing his narrative than investigating a crime, and a further three cigarettes get smoked before they finally turn their attention to me.

Will the body be beginning to smell, I'm wondering? Will the corpse be infested by maggots already? I ask

Maria these questions while we're waiting for them to approach, and she simply shoots me a disdainful look and tells me to shut the fuck up unless I have something important to say. And let her do the talking, even if they speak some English.

With the introductions and pleasantries ultimately complete, we walk up the drive and into my gaff.

Where is your 'gaff', and what's it like? I'm sure we'd all like to know, wouldn't we?

Okay, amigo, this is holding up the narrative, but I suppose it has some bearing on what happened.

My gaff is a five hundred square metre six-bedroomed and five-bathroomed manor right on the beach, wedged between the La Cabane Beach Club and Javier Bardem's pad. I must say, by the way, what a very nice person Javier is, and so is Penelope; I've had them over to dinner a couple of times, and they've reciprocated. Very genuine people ... not Hollywood at all, and excellent company.

So, back to the villa ... it's got the obligatory infinity pool, a gym, cinema, four-car garage, is the pinnacle of luxury, and I think that's about all you need to know.

Let's just say that if I wanted to rent it out – which I don't – I could get maybe twenty thousand euro a week? The only problem is that you have to drive everywhere, and I do like going out. There's a chic little *chiringuito* a five-minute walk away which is very popular with the beautiful people, and I eat there a lot, but I'll usually drive into Marbella and get a taxi back. Or, more often than not – if I'm still sober enough to get the key in the ignition – drive back. Okay, that's the TripAdvisor bit done … happy now?

Deliriously.

But as to how I got back last night, I have got absolutely no idea, and I somehow know that this will be one of the first questions out of Plod's notebook.

SIXTEEN

ONE MONTH AGO

So ... along with the realisation that I'm in love comes a dreadful apprehension that I don't deserve her and the almost certain knowledge that I'm going to let her down.

To be in love with a woman, amigo, means that you commit to her totally, and total commitment is something for which I have a poor track record.

And sadly, this is indeed how things turn out. Here is no tale of redemption; no happy ever after.

Except that I don't tell her this. We carry on as we had done for the past two months, but somehow I know that she senses the little spark that lit the flame has been extinguished.

When a woman continually tells you she loves you, a positive response is expected; and I have no Equity card.

Sounds to me as if you wouldn't know what love is if it slapped you in the face.

Amigo, you could well be right, although I'm not so sure. I thought I knew, but it turns out that – at least in Sam's case – I was just in love with the idea of being in love. It's the old, old story. With Mandy it was different. God, how I loved that woman, and now I wished that I'd loved her more and not let our relationship slide into that same quagmire where the bond between Susie and me withered. But with Mandy, my love peaked precisely when she fell for that bloody pussy-licking bitch of an agent. It was a case of wanting – almost to the point of obsession – what you can no longer have. Is that love? Tell me?

So, what happened to trigger this emotional turnabout? No, let me guess – your celibacy came to an abrupt end in that knocking shop you drink in called the Moët?

Right about the first part; wrong about the second.

You know, I actually thought I could do it? I really, genuinely believed that this was it, that here was a woman I could spend the rest of my life with. I had managed to convince myself that I still only looked at beautiful women from a purely aesthetic sense of appreciation. Monogamy was staring me in the face.

You mean you stopped flirting?

Of course I didn't stop flirting. Heck, you can take the man out of the bog, but you can't take the bog out of the man.

But I stopped converting flirtation into strategic manoeuvres; until, that is, I had to go back to England for a weekend.

It was a trip I'd been dreading for a while, and it turned out to be worse even than the sum of my darkest fears. The catalyst for my reluctant visit was a mate's sixtieth birthday bash in suburban Liverpool – yes, there is in reality such a place. I've known Johnny for a long time; he's also a writer, and a huge fan of mine (one of the very few I'd trusted enough to reveal the name I write the filth under).

But by nine we were being press-ganged into participating in line dancing, the Guinness was dreadful, and I'd had enough. So I call a cab and sneak out of the drab little function room where the party's being hosted.

Twenty minutes later and I'm seated at the bar in San Carlo's, five minutes' walk from my hotel, 30 James Street. This was once the headquarters of the White Star Line, who famously rained down paper strips with the names of those who'd perished on the Titanic onto apprehensive and disbelieving relatives. Nothing very 'woke' about that, was there?

Fascinating. But that's enough of the history lesson. So, what happened?

So, what happens is, I'm sitting at the bar contemplating what to do and feeling slightly bad about bailing from Johnny's Big Line Dancing Bash, when in flocks this throng of garishly dressed, pissed-up Scouser birds who proceed to populate the table next to me. Seriously, amigo, the last time I saw a bunch of critters this scary was under a big top.

And then something flicks that 'twat' switch in my brain … you know, the one I mentioned earlier? And before brain can control mouth, I'm telling the most outrageously dressed one how wonderful she looks in that dress. I kid you not, if an animal in a safari park was discovered sporting colours so luridly offensive, the gamekeeper would shoot it.

Anyway, I tell her that I'm not hitting on her … that she's way too young (bullshit) and too pretty (more bullshit) for me and turn back to the bar, when one of her mates says something like, 'Hey, mister … don't I know you from somewhere?'

Now this usually fills me with a deep sense of dread, but it's a very long time since I'd had sex with anyone either in or from Liverpool, and so I treat this as a positive.

'Hey … you're that fella from off of the telly, ain't you?' asks a bird dressed in what I can only describe as camouflage get-up.

'I be he,' I say, knowing that at some point, if this is to go any further, I'm going to have to elaborate a bit.

'The writer,' she says. 'I saw you interviewed on the telly.' Well fuck my old boots … you could have knocked me off my bar stool with a feather. Someone actually knows who I am.

She's not bad-looking. Maybe thirty-five, but I'm guessing closer to forty as women have a hard life in these parts. Her face, not entirely smothered by make-up, is a curious mix of Eastern European and Native American and unusual to the extent that I find her attractive. And the one thing the camouflage trouser suit (or is it a onesie? It's best to know these things in the event of necessity for urgent removal) does for her is to accentuate the shapeliness of her body.

There's no need for me to peel this one away from her mates, because she does it herself. I'm sitting on this stool, remember, and seconds later she's got her legs pressed against my knees and one hand on my inner thigh and the other round my neck. She's clearly the leader of the pack, and I know this for two reasons: her mates realise that none of them stand a chance of copping off with someone from off of the telly and go back to sniffing around for lesser male prey, and I instantly know that we're going to have sex.

And this is in fact what happens, and that's all I'm going to share with you, amigo; but let's just say that my brief period of celibacy-slash-monogamy came to an end in spectacular fashion.

SEVENTEEN

TODAY, 08.35

So by now, Robocop and his mates have reached the front portico, but one more cigarette is required before entering. God knows how these guys would ever get on a plane.

I'm thinking this is purely to add to the suspense and push me towards some sort of ledge from which I jump into a full confession before they've even surveyed the crime scene.

But I don't acquiesce, mainly because – as far as I'm aware – I'm not guilty, and eventually we enter my villa. I offer coffee, tea, water, alcohol, but all are declined, and it's all I can do to stop myself from diving into the drinks cabinet and wolfing down half a bottle of brandy.

The formalities are agonisingly bureaucratic and slow.

What is my name, my date of birth, my nationality, my passport number, my NIE, my occupation, UK address, and so the list goes on ... and on. Heck, the girl will have decomposed before they even get to look at the body. What about getting a pathologist out here? I ask.

'Shut the fuck up, Malone,' says Maria. 'What did I tell you, man?'

All of these questions are addressed to me in Spanish, translated by Maria, and my responses conveyed back to Robocop and his team in similar fashion.

And then, fifteen minutes later, satisfied that all the information has been collated, he asks two key questions: when did I discover the body, and how did the girl get here? I answer the first question truthfully, and Robocop makes no attempt to hide the fact that he's noting the time that elapsed between discovery and report of the death.

My answer to the second question calls for a general raising of eyebrows and an exchange of sceptical looks. I don't know, I tell them, who she is, what she's doing here or how she got here.

And it's then that a strange thought hits me: are these guys actually real cops? I have no experience of Spanish cops (other than the ones I bribe to fend off speeding tickets) so I have no knowledge as to whether this procedure is normal. But there is something that seems not quite right here.

Why the elaborate build-up? Surely they would want to see the body first? And why isn't a Crime Scene Investigation or a forensic team combing my estate for clues, dusting the place for prints?

I don't buy the idea that I'm already charged as guilty based on one phone call. And these clowns don't even look like cops, so my paranoia deepens.

I mean, even by Spanish standards, there is absolutely no urgency about proceedings, and that is when another question enters my mind: Maria made the call ... can I really trust her? A negative answer is unthinkable, of course. We've been close friends for ... I don't know ... certainly three years? When we met pretty much coincided with my purchase of the villa, so that would be about right.

But could she possibly be in on this? She does, after all, have a set of keys to the villa, codes for the security system and knows how to disable the cameras. And could she be in bed with these bogus cop bozos and whoever carried out the murder?

But why? Surely if Maria had an axe to grind, wouldn't she have called the real cops, as having me in jail, fitted up for a crime I didn't commit, would certainly be punishment enough for whatever it is I have done to upset her. And then I get to thinking – this being the case – what exactly could I have done to deserve this?

Well, maybe she's just so much in love with you that it simply becomes too much for her when you're finally in a relationship that looks like it's going somewhere. Instead of, you know ... what did she call it ... just fucking bimbos?

Yeah ... no, you're right. That's what I'm thinking, too. And even in her darkest hour, would she risk becoming involved in a plot that could jeopardise her entire career and livelihood?

Before I have time to deliberate the matter further,

Robocop announces that he will now inspect the murder scene, and could I please advise him where to find it.

'Allow me to show you,' I say. Maria translates.

'Thank you, no. That would involve possible further contamination of the crime scene, so simply direct us to the bedroom,' he replies through Maria's mediation.

How did they know the murder scene was a bedroom? I'm thinking. But even if Maria had mentioned this, it would have made little difference as to establishing their validity. 'You can wait here until such time as we have finished our initial investigations,' goes Robocop.

So I give them directions, and off they head.

I sink into the settee, light a cigarette and put my feet on the coffee table. I shoot Maria a challenging look: my house, I can smoke and I can put my feet where I fucking well choose. Then, I wonder, had not that thread of groundless suspicion entered my brain, would I have given her that same look?

She reads it.

'Well?' she glowers at me. 'Why you look at me like that, Malone? You think I want the cops crawling all over your place? We had no fucking choice, man.'

'No,' I say, '*You* had no choice. I would have liked more time to try to figure out how she'd got here and who's who in this fucking pantomime.' But the truth is that I don't really know what I want, and I suppose she is right; but this acorn of illogical suspicion has started to expand, and I'm not good at concealing my unease. As I say, I have no Equity card.

'You think maybe I have something to do with it?' Christ, how is it that women can read my actual fucking thoughts? Am I that transparent?

'Of course not,' I lie. It's just that ...' But my words tail off as I hear the sound of urgent footsteps hammering down the wooden staircase and along the marble hall. I prepare myself to be handcuffed and frog-marched out of my villa; possibly for the last time.

And suddenly all three hombres are standing in front of me in a power triangle, with Robocop glaring at me, arms folded.

For an age, no one speaks.

'You think this is some sort of joke, señor Malone?' So the bastard *can* speak perfectly good English.

'I'm sorry?' I don't bother to remove my feet from the table; I take a long drag from my cigarette and stub it out.

Robocop says nothing and continues to stare at me with a hostility that strikes me as a little excessive, even towards a girl murderer. I wouldn't particularly want to get on the wrong side of this fucker, bogus cop or not.

'Perhaps you can tell me why I would want to make a joke out of this?' I ask. 'An unfortunate young woman, with whom I have no acquaintanceship, has somehow got into my bed and has been murdered by a person or persons currently unknown who broke into my property. And it would appear that I had been drugged, as I have absolutely no memory of anything that took place yesterday. What could possibly be remotely amusing about that?' I realise how lame this sounds as the words leave my mouth.

'I should charge you with wasting police time.'

What the fuck is he talking about? I'm thinking.

'There is no dead girl. No dead girl in your room. No dead girl in any other room. We have searched the entire house and she does not exist. She is a figment of your imagination, señor Malone. Maybe she is a fantasy for one of your novels. There is no girl, dead or alive, here.' He shoots Maria a frosty look by way of telling her that it would be stretching the point to call her a girl.

I'm floored. If I hadn't been seated, I would have collapsed.

Instead of which, I jump up, run along the corridor, up the stairs and into the master bedroom where I stare incredulously at the bed.

He's right. There is no dead girl.

She's gone.

I search all the other first-floor rooms, knowing I'm going to find nothing. Robocop, for all his lack of urgency, is thorough; that much has become clear. And two other things have also become clear: he's a cop, all right, unless this is some over-elaborate double bluff, which lets Maria off the hook.

And secondly – and of greater importance – have I somehow dreamed this whole thing up? Has my mind been playing games with me?

And if so, how close am I to the asylum there they will lock me up, feed me industrial quantities of Prozac and throw away the key?

EIGHTEEN

TODAY, 08.59

Eventually I regain enough composure to get myself downstairs and face the vitriol and aggression that Robocop will no doubt continue to hurl at me.

But there's just Maria to fix me with a condescending-slash-borderline withering stare, as Robocop and his two stooges have left; their departure no doubt hastened by the urgent need for nicotine.

'What the fuck is going on, Malone?'

I shrug, sleepwalk to the drinks cabinet and select a bottle of Torres Gran Reserva, remove the top, and belt down as much as I can until my stomach is on fire.

'Fucked if I know,' I reply.

I notice my hands are shaking. It's not even nine o'clock; I've taken up smoking, and now I'm drinking brandy for breakfast.

'She was there, Maria … I know it happened. I'm not making this up, you know? I swear.'

'So tell me, why would someone go to the trouble of killing the girl to frame you and then remove the evidence?'

I take another belt of brandy and sit down, cradling the bottle.

'And you'd better take it easy on that stuff cos you've got to drive me back to town.'

I should be feeling, I don't know … some sort of relief that I'm not en route to el Penitentiary Málaga? But any deliverance is tempered by the knowledge that I am either going mad, or I'm part of an elaborate hoax and there is worse to come. I know what I woke up to was real, as is everything else that has happened since then.

'That's what I have to find out. And why I still can't remember anything about yesterday.'

'Put the bottle down, Richie,' she says gently. Heck, there's almost tenderness, almost compassion in her voice, and with that I know she believes me. 'It's not helping.'

She's right. I really need a clear head because I know this isn't going to be the end of it. The vultures are circling.

My phone vibrates in my pocket. I take it out and clock the name. Rwoopardo.

Shit, I haven't heard from him in, I don't know … maybe two years? I don't even know why I have his number in my phone, as neither of us ever had anything to say to each other.

So what the fuck can he want? I think about ignoring it, and then curiosity gets the better of me and I decide to answer. Maybe Mandy's been run over. I'm not sure how I'd feel about that right now. But not for one moment do I connect the call with my present predicament, so what he has to say comes as something of a shock.

'Rupert?'

'Hi, Richie.' The wetness of his character almost drips through the earpiece. 'How are you?'

'Get to the point, Rupert. I'm sure you didn't wake up this morning all concerned about my health.'

'Oh, but I did.'

Pause.

I light a cigarette.

'Well, perhaps you could enlighten me?'

I get the distinct feeling that the bastard is about to tell me something … something that, for the first time since I've known him, will challenge the subordination he has always felt towards me since I relieved him of Mandy.

But he's not ready to give it up yet, and I have to grudgingly admire how he's twisting the knife.

'How are things in la-la land this morning? Sun still shining? It's cold and grey here.' In addition to a personality you could wring out, he has a manner of speech with a total absence of steel.

'Get to the point, Rupert. I have a busy schedule this morning.'

'Oh, what's that then? Writing third-rate novels? Lying in the sun and fornicating with under-age girls?'

'It's a dirty job, but someone has to do it,' I reply. 'And I have a very strict age code when it comes to women: nothing outside the parameters of twenty to forty, so I'd be very careful where I spout that allegation if I were you, Rwoopardo, unless you want the courts to relieve you of any remaining assets that they didn't direct Mandy's way.'

I'd say that makes it about fifteen–all.

'I don't suppose you've heard that Mandy and I are back together again?'

This revelation doesn't quite rival the dead girl's disappearance, yet it shocks me profoundly. But nothing would surprise me about Mandy, and it would come as no shock to learn that she was no longer interested in pussy.

But to get back with Rwoopardo? No, there has to be some ulterior motive here.

'Congratulations. When's the wedding? Oh … I see – you want me to be the best man? Well, that would certainly be appropriate.'

He laughs that insipid, reedy laugh reserved for the celebration of occasional small triumphs that always used to annoy the hell out of me. And now, on this particular morning, it is the last thing I want to hear.

'Except that *I'm* the best man. And as you're just a bad memory she wants to erase, you certainly won't be getting an invite.'

Christ … so they are getting remarried? What the heck is Mandy playing at?

I struggle to keep my dignity, but keep it I do.

'Well, like I said, congratulations.' Ouch, that hurts. That really hurts. 'No, seriously, when are you getting remarried?'

'Christmas. We're holding the ceremony in the Dominican Republic on Christmas Eve. Nothing elaborate … just around a hundred and fifty guests, invited at our expense, of course. Oh, and partly funded by *Hello!* magazine who are covering the wedding.'

'Have you just rung me to gloat, Rupert? Because, if so, I have better things to do this morning. Like take a shit and a shower.'

But he's not finished yet.

'Of course, we would have set the date much sooner, but Mandy's flying out to Australia next week. Have you heard she's been invited to take part in "I'm a Celebrity"?'

'Nope … again, that's missed my radar, Rupert. I can only express my deepest sympathies to her fellow contestants, and of course the indigenous insects and reptiles who will be compelled to share intimate personal spaces with her.'

The reedy laugh again.

'So … is there anything else you'd like to chew the fat about, old buddy, or am I free to go about my daily business? As I said, I *do* have things to do.'

Pause.

'Have you ever heard of someone called Tom Dempsey?'

My blood runs cold … literally cold.

It's as if someone has just injected antifreeze into my veins.

This time it's me, the writer with verbal diarrhoea, who's lost for words.

'Stupid question, really,' he goes. 'Course you have … you wrote a book about him, didn't you? What was it called? Oh yes … something like *Whiskey in The Jar*. There or thereabouts. Only you wrote it under the name of Cecil C. Wingfield. How very grandiose. Except that a little bird told him who really wrote it, in exchange for a lucrative deal to write his actual memoirs and not some emasculating flight of fantasy that made him the laughing stock of the Republican hierarchy. And that little bird happens to be the beautiful woman who became an overnight literary sensation and will soon be my wife once again.'

'Mandy,' I murmur. 'Jesus Christ.'

Maybe this is starting to make some sort of sense now.

'She,' he goes, 'she who was once fleetingly yours but is now mine again, repentant for the machinations she invented and the damage that she caused to my good name and, of course, my bank account. But that's all in the past now.'

'How very Indiana Jones, Rupert; still not an original bone in your body? So … as you and I could hardly be described as "bezzies", is there a particular reason why you're sharing this information with me?'

'That's a good point, Malone, a very good point. But strange as it may seem, I don't hate you; in fact, I pity you. I don't know what Mr Dempsey is planning for you but it will not be pleasant, and, as a consequence, I thought – as a sporting fellow – that I should give you a head start.'

'Well that's mighty magnanimous of you, Rupert. And I suppose I should be grateful for the heads-up, but may I remind you that I have considerable experience of dealing with, shall we say, hostile Irish activity in general, and Mr Dempsey in particular?'

I know as the words leave my mouth how unconvincing this sounds. And what's worse, Rwoopardo knows it too.

'That was a long time ago, Malone. And you are one man ... one ageing man, used to the good life, against many.' He laughs that insipid wheezing, nostril-snorting chuckle, and I would wholeheartedly give everything I own just to punch him.

'Anyway,' I say, 'he's in prison. And last I heard, he won't get a sniff of a review for at least another three years.'

Take that to the bank, Rwoopardo.

'Ah, yes. Well, that *was* the case until he engaged the services of a top criminal defence barrister. Ironically, she's English, and, even more ironically, she lives in Hull, and I believe that you may even know her. How's that for irony?'

Fuck me.

Sam? Surely not.

Jesus. I knew she defended scumbags ... but Dempsey? Why? Of course there'd be a massive payday for her, but could she know about my connection with the bastard?

'And she hired the services of a top forensic accountant who persuaded the Dublin Court of Appeal to take the case back to the Supreme Court. And they ruled … I've got the newspaper report here, so I'll read it for you … here you go: "that the alleged financial indiscretions that Mr Dempsey had been incarcerated for were attributable to an offshore company to which he had no ties, nor knowledge of its existence."'

I picture the bastard's smug face at the other end of the connection.

'So, he's a free man. Walked out of Mountjoy Prison last Friday; and I believe that he's either back in Spain or will be there shortly – besides the business he wishes to conduct with your good self, he has a little matter of proprietorial criminal activities to discuss with a certain Russian gentleman who, shall we say, appropriated his throne in his absence. And now he wants it back.'

The proverbial penny is dropping now, and this is starting to make a lot more sense … although not in a good way.

But he's not done yet.

'Oh, but I have one piece of good news for you, Malone …'

Pause.

He's going to have the last word. I know it. It's fifteen–forty, and my first serve has just gone wide.

'You're killing me with the tension, Rwoopardo. Do you want a drum roll?'

'Killing you?' Again, the sneery laugh. 'Well, that's the good news. Whatever he has in mind for you, Malone, Mandy has obtained his word that he will not kill you. So, you have at least a little more life to look forward to, even if it's spent sat in a wheelchair.'

'This is indeed good news. Marbella is very wheelchair friendly,' I say, but I have a strong suspicion that death itself is rather less to fear than anything that Dempsey may regard as suitable payback for what happened and the clown suit I made him wear.

'And you really should be grateful to Mandy for the compassion she has demonstrated in this matter.'

I've had enough of this.

I take another belt of brandy, Maria scowls at me and I throw the bottle as hard as I can at the window. The triple-glazed pane remains intact, but the bottle does not.

'Fuck off, Rwoopardo, fuck off and die. And if you have any money left in the bank, I'd invest in a cock extension so Mandy doesn't have to send for the black houseboy on your wedding night.'

Pathetic, I know, but there's not much left in the locker right now.

I ring off, stare at the phone and then decide to throw it at the window too.

Fuck it.

NINETEEN

TODAY, 09.09

So, I suppose you're going to ask about Mr Dempsey?

Yes, a bit of background would certainly be helpful.

Okay. I was coming to that.

Tom 'Bear' Dempsey was once regarded as the world's most dangerous man.

Dempsey was – and possibly still is – the Chief of Staff of the Provisional IRA, and as hard a bastard as I've ever come across.

But like Al Capone, nothing he had 'allegedly' done would stick until he was finally tried and sentenced to ten years' imprisonment for tax evasion.

I only met Dempsey the once, but that meeting was what you might call memorable.

So memorable, in fact, that I still wake on occasions in a cold sweat with the vivid imprint of our acquaintanceship etched into the tapestry of my worst nightmares.

I ran into him back in '88 when I was working undercover for the Special Reconnaissance Unit – the SRU – in South Armagh: a unit attached to 14 Field

Security and Intelligence Company known internally as 'The Det', so secret that it wasn't supposed to exist. Dempsey owns a farm complex that straddles the border and was once probably the world's best location for smuggling; an activity which next to Gaelic football was Dempsey's preferred recreational pursuit, and how he amassed the tens of millions he stowed beneath his mattress.

One of our guys was getting close to him and had even managed to infiltrate his inner circle before he went off the radar, and I was tasked with tracking him down.

It was a pointless exercise, as everyone knew he would be decomposing in some Monaghan bog by now, but this was the protocol ever since that idiot Robert Nairac decided to take on the IRA single-handedly in their own local bar.

Anyway, I managed to get close enough to conduct surveillance on the farm complex before a sniper spotted a glint from my binoculars on the one sunny day of that summer, and before I could leg it, I was surrounded.

Another stupid schoolboy error?

Correctomundo.

I spent the next twelve hours believing them to be my last, blindfolded, gagged and bound to a post in what Dempsey called the Bear Pit, a vast ten-by-five-metre chasm dug deep into the floor of one of his outhouses. This was where he managed dogfights and bare-knuckle boxing; other recreational pursuits that filled the empty hours in between directing terrorism and watching Gaelic.

But before I'd resigned myself to the certainty that this was where I would die, I'd been interrogated and beaten senseless. Don't ask me to list the extent of my injuries, but amongst other, more trivial ones, such as broken teeth and a smashed jaw, they broke my left ankle, right arm, smashed five ribs and punctured a lung.

So how the hell did you get out of there?

Oh, simple enough. I used my charm and charisma, just like I do with women.

I don't buy that.

Oh, trust me, amigo, trust me; it worked. It worked … or I wouldn't be here today.

You see Dempsey, for all his durability, had one major weakness: he could never resist a challenge, particularly if it was a physical one.

And since I'd been dragged into his barn by three hombres dressed in khaki and brandishing AK47s, I had not said a single word.

I had always believed that to take a vow of silence in a situation such as this – one that I'd not experienced before, but one that I had mentally prepared for countless times – would give me a slight advantage. For one thing, your captors cannot exploit the pathetic timbre of your voice; they cannot prey on your fears.

I'd been interrogated for several hours, each round of interrogation leading precisely nowhere other than to frustrate my captors and inflict more physical pain on me. But during this time I had located a small object that was to save my life: a nail protruding slightly from the post to which I was bound.

I noticed it because between the pounding my face and body was taking, I felt it digging into my hand, and bit by bit, over the hours, I used all of my strength to wiggle it loose and eventually to free it and to clasp it in my clammy palm. It was the width of my clenched fist, which I knew would be more than sufficient to inflict significant physical damage, should the opportunity arise.

Amigo, this sense of purpose, although I had no idea where it may lead, was the one thing that got me through those hours. I never thought of giving up – that would have been too easy. I bore no hatred, no emotion whatever towards my captors; my entire concentration was absorbed in gaining possession of that nail.

That nail to me was life or death because I held onto the belief that if I could somehow work it free, I would find a way to use it to turn this unfortunate sequence of events around, which otherwise would certainly lead to my extinction.

So up to this point Dempsey had not made an appearance.

The most senior of his henchmen was a man who went on to hold high political office but is now dead. One other went by the name of Micksey McVeigh, and he eventually became what was laughingly referred to as a supergrass. He now lives the life in Canada, under British Intelligence Services protection and funded by Her Majesty's government, thanks to the fact that he turned several of Dempsey's inner circle over to the Brits. I don't know the identity of the third man.

But all of this was in the future.

So, when they could get nothing out of me and I was battered, bloodied but not entirely broken, the Politician sent for Dempsey.

And this, amigo, was the only time in my life that I have felt real fear ... a fear so profound as to paralyse me to the extent that for a brief period my fingers, now numb and bloody, almost released that nail. And that would have been my one-way ticket to oblivion.

Let me remind you that I was blindfolded so I could not see Dempsey, but my silence had enhanced my hearing so that I could make out all that was occurring in the Bear Pit with an unprecedented clarity, hence I knew the identity of two of my captors. Lose one sense, amigo, and the others, over time, become enriched. With my breathing slowed, despite the pain I was able to step out of myself and become silent, a trick I had leaned many years before from a Navajo Indian friend.

And before long I could see with my ears.

The Politician tells Dempsey that they have tried everything, but there is nothing they can get from me. Nothing ... I have not said a single word. Waste of time, he says. I'll shoot him and dump the body, he offers, as if he's proposing to remove a car from a packed driveway.

Silence.

I hear Dempsey approaching.

For a large man, he is light on his feet. I know that he was an athlete, a footballer of note and an amateur bare-knuckle fighter to be feared. But now he spends time counting his money rather than sweating for it, so the leanness of his youth has departed, and he will not be as sharp as he once was. I know if I can engage him in combat, I can turn his weight to work against him.

'So … you've lost your tongue, fella?' he says in that slow, mild border-country manner that I know he likes to use to conceal both his malice and his intelligence.

He is standing within a metre of me now. He can sense my fear, and I can sense the excitement that killing me will give him.

'Gi'me the knife.' The order is barked at McVeigh, standing behind him on his left.

The weapon is transferred wordlessly, and I hear the click of the safety switch then the release as the blade is ejected. It's an Out The Front model, and for a moment I allow my mind to be distracted, contemplating how many times it has been used here, in this death chamber where good dogs and bad men had died before me.

'If you're not gonne use your tongue, we might as well remove it for ye.'

He's closer now.

My hands are bound but my feet are free, and for an instant I consider using my legs as weapons but quickly reject the idea. With my hands tied, it would lead nowhere. I need to lure him in, to get him to release me, and I have just one bargaining chip to achieve this: my tongue. My silver tongue that has lured so many women into my bed will now be put to a less trivial pursuit.

He removes the gag.

I try to speak, but my voice crackles after the arid hours of silence.

'Water,' I mumble.

'So he can speak, after all.' Dempsey.

'Give me water,' I say, 'then I'll talk.'

A bottle is put roughly to my mouth. It's glass, and it hurts the stumps of my teeth, but I drink it down and almost heave when the liquid, combined with congealed blood, hits the pit of my empty stomach. I realise it is lemonade, sweet and sickly mingled with the blood, but at least it's fluid. The bottle is pulled away from my mouth, and I feel the blindfold being removed. The room is dark, but what light there is stings my eyes and they take an age to adjust and turn the shapes before me into objects.

'Do I detect a wee Belfast accent, my friend?'

'I am not your friend,' I reply, my voice firmer now. I know I must do what I can to show strength in my voice; to hide the fear that I feel.

'Brave man, aren't ye?'

'Certainly braver than a man holding a knife in one hand and a gun in the other to the head of a man tied to a chair.'

He laughs. We all laugh, and suddenly it's like the scene from *Pulp Fiction* where they all share a joke before the violence begins. Except the violence started a long time ago, and now nothing is funny.

'Tell me who you are, who you work for and why you're here, and I'll finish you quick.' McVeigh lights a cigarette and throws the packet to the Politician. 'Tell you what … I won't even cut your tongue out. Can't say fairer than that, can I?'

The three stooges are finding this hysterical. If I could free my hands, I figure, I could take Dempsey, and then a thin ray of optimism begins to brighten my dark world.

'I'd say … if I didn't know better, that you're SRU. But of course, we all know it doesn't exist, does it … so ye can't be.'

'I'll tell you what, Dempsey,' I say, mustering an illusion of self-confidence that's just a veneer. 'Untie me, and let's you and I go at it. Just us two … man to man. Put down the gun … you can keep the knife if it stops you pissing your pants. You win, and I'll spill my guts … tell you everything you want to know – then you can do what you like with me. But if I best you, I go free. And if I do, I give you my word, I'll never breath a word about what happened in here.'

Silence.

Long silence. I can smell the tension in this dank death pit.

Then laughter. Soft and uncertain at first, then Dempsey laughs and the laughter becomes near hysterical.

We're back in a Tarantino movie.

'Let me see if I've got this right, fella.' Dempsey wipes his eyes with the back of his hand. 'Jeas … I have ne' laughed so much since pussy got stuck in the washing machine.'

More laughter.

I join in, although, truth be told, I find little humour in my predicament.

'You want te fight? You want to fight *me* in yer condition?'

'That's right. That's what I said. You won't get anything from me unless you earn it in a fight. Ask them.' I nod at the Politician, McVeigh and the other comedian. 'These useless cunts have been at it for hours, and what did they get out of me? Huh? Sweet fuck all. And that's all you'll continue to get. Other than the satisfaction of killing me. Think about it.'

Silence.

'Untie him.' He nods to McVeigh.

'No … *you* untie me.' That's part of the deal. 'This starts right now.'

I need him to put the Glock down where I can get hold of it the instant I disable him.

This is a big card to play, but he buys it.

'Okay,' he says. 'Watch him,' he orders the others. 'I don't trust this cunt, mangled as he is.' My heart sinks as he shapes to lob the gun to McVeigh but he's busy lighting another cigarette, so he places it on the earthen floor of the chasm, a metre or so to my left.

Perfect. I'm left-handed.

I calculate the time I'll require to carry this out as he moves behind me and begins to cut the rope. I have now transferred the nail into my right hand, and I grip it tighter, smothering my right hand with my left as the rope loosens to ensure he cannot see it. Suddenly my hands are free, but I'm still bound to the post.

I feel the blood coursing through my wrists and buy valuable seconds by reiterating the terms of our agreement. He grunts approval, and sufficient sensation returns to my hands before I issue my next order.

He doesn't know it … none of them know, but I am now in control, and it is only a matter of time before this is all over.

It's like when you look at a beautiful woman and she returns your gaze. You're holding her with your eyes, and she probably doesn't know it yet but she has already decided that she will sleep with you.

Of course, there's still the probability that this will go terribly wrong, but I push this thought to the dark recesses of my mind.

'Now, untie me.'

Like a lamb to the slaughter, Dempsey begins to loosen the knots, and suddenly the rope falls away. I make sure I will not become entangled by it when I make my move. I shake my legs to get the blood moving. I know how difficult it will be when I try to stand, so I'm happy to wait for him to make the next move.

I check out the three stooges at the other end of the pit. Predictably they have relaxed, relieved of their responsibility now that Dempsey has assumed control.

I calculate the time I will require. Three … maybe four seconds, depending on how accurate I can be with Dempsey. That is the key. And as I'm assuming the safety will still be on and the Glock will be unarmed, I need to allow another second for these procedures.

And then I estimate that it will take a similar time for the Politician, McVeigh and the other bozo to react and ready their automatic weapons to take me out. It's not an exact science but, if the cards fall the right way, I calculate that the odds are slightly in my favour. There's no alternative.

It's time.

'Okay if I stand?'

I don't wait for an answer and rise slowly from the wooden chair that has become a part of me. I have no idea of time, but day has become night and is now day once more.

I take the brunt of my weight on my right foot, but my left ankle is so badly twisted and broken that it serves no purpose other than to provide some sort of balance, in return for which spasms of pain shoot through it like an electric current.

I cast my eyes at the Glock in such an obvious manner that Dempsey latches onto my gaze.

Suddenly aware that I may try to reach it, he moves to his right and shapes to kick the gun towards the Politician.

This is my cue, what I have planned for.

His back is turned now, and as he goes to kick the gun, I lunge at him and plunge the nail as hard as I can into the soft tissue at the back of his right knee. He screams and drops to the floor, releasing the knife as he grabs his knee with both hands.

I body-roll beyond him and grab the Glock, releasing the safety and chambering a round.

The pendulum has swung so quickly that the three stooges haven't even started to react, and before any of them can ready their weapon, I have plugged a bullet into McVeigh's left knee, another into the Politician's right shoulder and put a third into John Doe's brain.

So, you're wondering, why didn't I finish the others? *Indeed.*

Well, that's a good question, but I suppose ... truth be told, Dempsey and the Politician were what the Intelligence Services referred to as 'untouchable', and McVeigh was on the radar as a possible informer.

Better the devil you know. Take them out, and you may end up with less despotic but better organised adversaries; not so easy for double agents who didn't get killed to get close to.

So now I have the whip hand.

I grab the knife, flick the blade back into its sheath and seize the three AK47s. I remove the magazines and toss them into a corner. Doubtful if the two men squirming wretchedly on the floor would be capable of using them, and also unlikely that they have any additional weaponry, but I keep the Glock trained on them as I turn my attention to Dempsey.

He's writhing on the floor. All three are making the sort of noises you'd expect to hear in an abattoir, and I have to admit that I derive a certain satisfaction from this turn of events.

'Shut the fuck up, you two,' I say, and for good measure put a bullet into the Politician's left foot and another into McVeigh's other knee.

By the way, if you're ever in Vancouver and notice a man with long, greasy hair, a droopy moustache and a pronounced limp in both legs, that's probably him.

Meantime, Dempsey is squealing like a baby and trying to remove the nail from the back of his knee. I use the foot beneath my shattered ankle to push it further in, which – believe me – hurts me almost as much as it hurts him.

'You'd better fucking kill me,' he goes, cos if ye don't, I'll find ye … and I swear to the fuckin' Almighty … ye'll be begging me to kill you for hours before I do it.'

'Leave the Almighty out of this,' I reply, cos he's got fuck all to do with what goes on in this shitehole of a country.'

I can't resist one more stamp on the nail before I go, irrespective of the pain it causes me.

'Okay,' I tell him with as much of a smile as I can manage, 'I think that's probably nailed it. I'll be seeing you around, Dempsey.'

Fifteen minutes later, I've disposed of the automatic rifles and dragged myself to the nearest lane.

This is a three-car-a-day road, so I'm exceptionally lucky when a farmer in an ancient Land Rover comes into view some twenty minutes later.

The Glock persuades him to stop and to drive me to Dundalk hospital, where I call my unit and tell them to get a bodyguard detail over here pronto before I'm anaesthetised and taken into surgery to have my ankle reset and various other bits of my battered anatomy patched up.

And I think that pretty much sums up my meeting with Mr Dempsey.

TWENTY

TODAY, 09.17

Okay ... so I'm sitting here all dewy-eyed, reminiscing about Dempsey, when it hits me like a very hard thing slamming into another thing that's soft and stupid.

I have, again, become the victim of meticulously calculated and callously executed female treachery; I have been undone by another world-class piece of womanly manipulation.

To fall prey to this once could be deemed as unlucky, but to cop for it twice on the same day – and remember, amigo, most people aren't even out of bed yet – could only be considered as calamitous.

I'm thinking back to The Morning After the Night Before.

This particular morning was that which followed the night I spent with Liverpool Paula, whose combat gear, incidentally – as I'm sure you'd all like to know – *was* actually a trouser suit.

In all honesty, it was a pretty good night. The girl really knew how to show me a good time, and although it involved spending an absurd amount of money –

one that would be considered life-changing to most Scousers in shell suits – it definitely beat the hell out of line dancing and sitting alone in a bar.

First, we hit the Cavern Club, but it is still early and it's pretty dead. We down a couple of cocktails and move on to the appropriately named Rude Gentlemen's Club, then hit Heebie Jeebies, but we only have one drink here as I clock the phrase 'eclectic DJ nights' on their promo board, and as I loathe the word 'eclectic' (even when it's used correctly – which it isn't here) I really can't countenance giving them any more of my money.

So, we move on to The Zanzibar which is rammed, and that's when my memory becomes a little blurry; although I do remember some of the sex, which I have already told you was pretty amazing.

I'm afraid that here you'll have to use your imagination, but let's just say that Paula, Sam and Mandy have now become a three-horse race in the bedroom department, and the bookies have announced that all bets are off.

***

So, we wake up five minutes before breakfast closes and, romantically, I slide my hand between her legs.

But she's having none of it and announces that there will be no further action until she's been fed; ergo, nanoseconds later we're seated in the dining room with the waiting staff scowling at us. Remember my advice about bedroom performance when a woman is ravenous, amigo? Well … here is a prime example.

I'm seated opposite her, but she ignores me; her interest is purely focused on food. Do good-looking women in Liverpool starve themselves all week then gorge on Sunday mornings at someone else's expense? I'm wondering.

Oh, she's a looker all right; there's no doubting that.

Tall … maybe five ten, willowy with long blonde hair and delightful Eastern European high, symmetrically sculpted cheekbones and pale green eyes that give her an exotic aura of classical mystique. If you're thinking Joanna Krupa with a splash of Native American here, you wouldn't be far off the mark.

It's always nice to wake up next to a woman you copped off with when inebriation was fairly well advanced and find she's not a total swamp donkey. Believe me, amigo, this *has* happened … yes, even to The Great Richie Malone.

I realise that I haven't a baldy what we talked about last night, so it's like meeting her for the first time, but she must have stayed fairly sober because it turns out she knows me pretty much inside out. A little too inside out for comfort, truth be told.

And she also knows a little too much about Mandy and Sam. Okay, they both have a pretty high profile, so it wouldn't have been hard to google some of this information, but then she talks about stuff that only I could have told her, and I'm quite surprised by this because even when I'm not in total command of my mental faculties, this is the sort of intel that stays where it should do – inside my head.

And then I notice something in her eyes that I never like to see in a woman: malicious intent, and that's when I know that this brief liaison is not going to end well.

So she has now consumed half her body weight in the deep-fried cholesterol-stuffed fodder that passes for a full English, and I'm pushing a sausage around the plate, feeling deeply uncomfortable with the situation.

It goes without saying that any further sex is now off the agenda, and suddenly I just want her out of the hotel and out of my life.

And then she comes right out and asks the question:

'Are you in love with Sam?'

My first instinct is to tell her that this is none of her fucking business, then it occurs to me how dangerous she could be, and this is a game that requires careful adherence to the rules.

'Maybe,' I reply, non-committedly, 'but I suppose if I were, I wouldn't have slept with you, would I?'

'No,' she goes, 'nor would you be packing large quantities of Viagra and condoms for a weekend away, would you?'

Okay … being the gentleman that I am, I offered to use a condom – actually, several condoms would have been required – an offer which happily she declined; but how did she know about the Viagra?

My Viagra consumption is something I keep to myself, on the basis that this information should be shared on a need-to-know basis and no one other than me needs to know.

Well, everyone knows now.

Yes, but as it has some bearing to the narrative, amigo, that's a price I'll have to pay.

So, the point is that she's obviously had a good root through my stuff while I was asleep, and, it turns out, that was not all she got up to while I slumbered; but I'll come to that in a minute.

She's finished eating but she's showing no intent to move, and the waiting staff are looking seriously pissed off now.

I'm guessing what's coming next and so it doesn't totally surprise me.

'I want a hundred grand. In cash.'

'So do I, love,' I reply lamely. 'But money doesn't grow on trees; it has to be earned.'

'Oh, I've earned it, all right.'

Pause. I always hate it when my instincts are right.

'So, let's be clear; which occupation is more prominent on your CV – blackmailer or prostitute?'

She doesn't flinch, so I guessing she's done this before.

'Don't take it personally. Actually, you weren't that bad in bed.' She smiles. 'I've had worse.'

I don't know what affronts me more – being blackmailed or being close to the bottom of this particular customer satisfaction survey.

Why is she blackmailing you? I don't get it.

Hold on … I'm coming to that.

'High praise indeed. Now, tell me: why on earth would I even consider giving you a hundred grand?'

'Oh … I forgot.' She passes me her phone.

Fuck.

'How did you take these pictures?'

'That doesn't matter. Let's just say I had an accomplice.'

'That's a big word for a Scouser.'

She laughs.

'I'm not a Scouser. I'm Ukrainian.'

'Same difference,' I reply. 'Well, extortion is another big word you may want to learn. But you'll have plenty of time to improve your vocabulary, as you could be looking at up to fourteen years behind bars for this. So … if I were you, I'd maybe rewind the last five minutes, delete those photographs and get the fuck out of here. That way, this never happened.'

And so … what was in the photographs?

Do I really need to spell it out? The same shit as was in the photos Sam took, only worse. I can't even remember doing most of this stuff. Maybe she slipped me some sort of drug that wipes your memory but leaves you on autopilot in the bedroom?

'Well …?' she goes.

'Well, I don't know much about blackmail, but doesn't a blackmailer have to make some kind of threat … you know, define the use to which he or she is going to put the illicit materials that they have obtained dishonestly?'

I didn't have to ask; I know where this is going.

The staff have cleared all the remaining food, and are now forming a line of solidarity by the buffet table and are glowering at us. If we'd been having a normal Sunday morning sort of conversation, I'd have called the manager and complained about this overt harassment.

'Oh ... good point,' she goes. 'Well, I thought Sam Sloane might like to see them.'

'Ah ... she's got plenty of pictures of me already, thanks. So I really doubt if she'd want any more. Now, if you're finished, I suggest we go as I've got a plane to catch.'

'So you're not going to pay ...?'

'Is the correct answer.'

Silence.

'Fifty grand?'

'Fuck off.'

She sighs.

'Okay. Well, then it looks like I'll be sending these to Sam.' She edges closer, elbows on the tables, steeples her hands and fixes me with her eyes. 'Question is, do I send them to her business email or to her personal account? Personal, I think ... it's a bit more intimate. Oh ... and I think I'll copy Mandy in as well. She's probably still interested in what you get up to.'

'I very much doubt it.'

This is getting worse by the minute. I don't know what Mandy's reaction would be, but I do know she is capable of bearing a serious grudge for a disproportionate length of time, so it would be like poking the proverbial bear with a stick.

'You know what … I quite like Mandy. I think we could be good friends. Maybe even more. Did I tell you last night that I'm bisexual?'

'Congratulations.'

'No, seriously; I'd like to get to know her better. I'm sure we'd have plenty to talk about.'

'Send those to anyone,' I say, with a confidence I don't feel, 'and I will go straight to the police. I promise you.'

'And I'll deny it … I promise you. I've done this before, so I know exactly how to make this untraceable. You won't have a shred of evidence.'

She gets up to leave, and I follow her wretchedly out of the dining hall as the staff move to our table like vultures to carrion.

***

I check out and have four hours to kill before my flight.

Under normal circumstances, I'd probably have gone back into the city or maybe had a nosey around Albert Dock, but instead I drag myself back to San Carlo's, where I met Paula, in the hope that someone may know something about her.

I know it's a forlorn hope, particularly as I've not got a photo of her; and even if I did, and even if someone did know her, they would keep it to themselves. That's how things work around here.

This, of course, is precisely what happens, so I have a beer, and then another beer, and I contemplate precisely how my life is going to disintegrate if she carries out her threat, which I have absolutely no doubt that she will do.

TWENTY-ONE

TODAY, 09.31

I'm pulled from my reverie by a disturbance in the far corner of my living room.

For a moment I'm lost in time and space as I'm utterly focused on What Happened Next, and then I realise that the commotion is simply Maria cleaning up after my brandy-throwing episode.

I should be grateful, but I'm not.

'Leave that … the cleaner will sort it out tomorrow.'

'Don't be such a slob, Malone,' she goes. 'The room fucking stinks like a fucking brewery anyway.

'A distillery.'

'A what?'

'Doesn't matter.' I give up on literalism and turn my mind back to that Sunday lunchtime in San Carlo's.

I'm sitting on the bar stool, waiting for my phone to ring and for the torrent of abuse that will surely follow, and debate whether I will answer it or not when the time comes.

And then something else hits me: an emotion that I'd only ever heard about – one that I had never felt in my entire life before – and it takes me a while to figure it out, but by the time I've put away my fourth beer the realisation has dawned on me that I actually feel guilty?

I actually care about hurting Sam.

So, I do the only sensible thing I can think of and I ring her. Confess my sins ... get my plea for absolution in first.

Why the hell would you want to do that?

Okay, amigo, fair point ... as I saw it at the time, there were two ways of dealing with this situation: the first is my normal approach – to deny everything, no matter how unbelievable my denial may initially be. Let me tell you a story: the Larry Gorman Bus Ticket story.

Is this really necessary? You see, there you go, holding up the narrative once again.

Yes ... fuck, it is. Since you ask, it is necessary.

I went to school with this bloke called Larry Gorman. I kid you not ... that was his real name. Not a bad rugby player, but not a big hit with the girls.

But that was partly because he had chronic acne, and partly down to the fact that there wasn't a whole lot left worth bedding after my best mate and I had run out onto the park.

Anyway, the summer after we finished school ... it was one of the hottest summers in Northern Ireland I can remember ... one day, he cops a load of his next-door neighbour sunbathing naked in her garden from his bedroom window. And rather than do what most spotty teenaged boys would do and masturbate furiously, he decides to do something about it.

So he goes round all innocent, claiming to have locked himself out of his house, and blow me ... maybe it's the heat, but she has the hots for him, and before long they're doing the wild thing in her bed.

And then they hear hubbie pull up on their gravelled drive. Larry manages to get dressed but there's no escape, so she shoves him beneath the bed, which is precisely the first place the cuckolded hombre looks when he bursts into the bedroom. Wifey, meantime, is showering in the en suite, all sweetness and light. So hubbie drags Larry out by an ankle and is about to pound seven bells out of him – when for some reason he asks him what he was doing under his bed?

Larry, by now, has resigned himself to the fact that he's about to get a pounding that he probably deserves, and one that will serve as a salutary life lesson; but then this idea pops into his head, and he tells hubbie that he was looking for his bus ticket.

What kind of fucking stupid story is that? goes hubbie. Is that the best you can do ... you expect me to buy that? And anyway ... what the fuck was your bus ticket doing under my bed?

This buys Larry some time, and so far the hombre hasn't inflicted any physical damage, so he then he says that wifey had asked him to fix the blind in the bedroom and that he would find a screwdriver in the box under the bed ... which is where he must have lost his ticket.

And then wifey comes out of the bathroom all innocent and asks what's going on ... why is hubbie strangling Larry? By now he's got him by the throat. Hubbie tells her that Larry claims to have lost his bus ticket while looking for some tools, and she starts laughing and says that she'd told him the toolbox was in the spare room, which was where the blind was that needed fixing, and it's all been a huge misunderstanding.

Hubbie still isn't convinced and – I have to say, I'd be with him here – tells Larry that he doesn't buy into this bullshit and that if he 'fesses up, he won't beat him up too badly; but if he persists with this lie, he will kick the proverbial shit out of him.

It should be added here that not only was hubbie in the RUC, based at Castlereagh where he'd been well trained in the art of obtaining confessions, he had also played rugby for Ulster. I'm guessing that wifey probably had form for this sort of thing and hubbie hadn't been able to nail down a confession just yet, so here was a golden opportunity.

But Larry sticks to his story, no matter how ridiculous it sounds.

And then he starts to cry … says that the ticket was for a bus from Belfast to Dublin where he's going to see U2, and he can't afford another one; and then, minutes later, hubbie – the daft sap – is actually under the fucking bed looking for the bus ticket, and when they can't find it and they'd looked everywhere, you know what he does? He gives Larry a fiver to buy another one and asks if he wants a lift to the bus station.

So, amigo, that's the Larry Gorman Bus Ticket story – the boy should have got a fucking Oscar for that.

And you actually believe it?

Oh, but I do, amigo … and I'll tell you why.

About three years later I have a party for my twenty-first in one of my old man's warehouses. At about one in the morning, Larry's mum turns up to take the Spotmeister home, and I have a slow dance with her and somehow manage to cop off. A quick snog as the DJ plays 'Rocket Man' – which is quite appropriate – then we then go outside for a fag, and soon it's time for a boy to become a man and fuck a proper woman. She's a fine thing, Norma Gorman, late thirties and fit, and so after I've taken her to Jupiter and back behind the warehouse, she tells me the story about Larry and Belinda her neighbour, who also happens to be her best friend. That's how I know it's true, amigo.

You couldn't make shit like this up.

Anyway, I haven't gone all philanthropic here, as there's another reason why I decide to come clean with Sam.

The photographic evidence?

Correctomundo.

As she's about to receive – if she hasn't already done so; although I'm guessing not, otherwise I'd have heard by now – some pretty debauched images, I'm thinking even the Spotmeister couldn't lie his way out of this one.

So anyway, I key in Sam's number, order another beer and wait for Armageddon to meltdown.

Truth be told, she takes it rather well. Says something like it was only sex without emotional attachment, so it's no different to sleeping with a prostitute – which, in effect, it was – and she doesn't have a problem with that (and this in itself is very good news for me) – ergo, it doesn't challenge our relationship, and I did the right thing by not paying up. Says she's feeling particularly horny this morning, and she'd rather like to see the pictures anyway.

I'm feeling a huge sense of relief, but at the back of my mind something's not quite right. Also, I can't help wondering if perhaps she may have 'accidentally' slept with someone, and that could be why she's taking this unfolding drama so well. And with that thought, I ask myself a question: would I care if she had? And the answer comes back with unexpected clarity – yes, I fucking well would. I would feel jealousy similar to that which I felt when Juicy Lucy started noshing on Mandy.

Let me tell you something about how a woman's mind works, amigo – listen carefully and learn.

There are two types of womanly reactions to this sort of thing. The first is where the woman goes into meltdown straight away. This is normal, and it's also how a bloke should react if the situation was reversed.

She calls you every name under the sun, swears vengeance and it's relationship-ending stuff, until days later when she calms the fuck down and looks at the collateral damage in a more balanced light, and so she either forgives you (but never forgets) or she throws you out.

On the other hand, some women are what I call

slow burners ... they have a long fuse – sometimes, a very long fuse. Once lit, an explosion is guaranteed to follow, but there's an analytical process that has to be worked through first. Mandy was one of these and, it turns out, so is Sam.

Is there a point to this?

The point to this, amigo, is that if a woman accepts, or should I say, appears to have accepted your fallacy and human fragility, it is only a matter of time before she has overanalysed this to the point where she concludes that a) you have done this before, b) you do it all the time, and c) you will almost certainly do it again. Then it becomes either relationship-ending, or you live under an ever-darkening veil of suspicion, and I can promise you that this type of reaction is by far the worse.

And if you're with her in person as she works through this process from acceptance to paranoia, you can actually see the fuse burning.

It begins with questions, some of which are almost collaborative – she may even pry for details about the 'inconsequential' sexual encounter itself.

Beware, though: these questions may appear innocent, but they are not, and they will not go away. In fact, they will intensify, and the explosion (and you can see it coming) will be prefixed by a comment along the lines of: 'What I don't understand is why you had to ...', and that's when you know that you're about to be left steeped in your own blood.

***

You may remember – or then again you may not – that way back at the beginning of this sorry narrative, I made the bold claim that all women are basically the same.

And while I stand by that statement, I would add the caveat that what separates the best from the worst is how they lie.

You're one to talk.

Amigo, I fully accept that … pot, kettle, black and all that … guilty as charged.

But there are different sorts of lies, and while I accept that there is no honest justification for the web of deceit that is my past, I would say in mitigation that I lied to avoid causing hurt and that I also lied by omission because of necessity. But I have never lied with malicious intent.

Now I'm sure there are some good women out there who would find this thought abhorrent – and if you are one and you're reading this, then for this sleight on your character I humbly apologise. But, with the possible exception of my ex-wife, I have yet to meet one.

And certainly, neither Mandy nor Sam fall into that category.

For the first couple of weeks after my Liverpool trip, things tick along fairly normally. I didn't see Sam as she's in Hull, but our correspondence seems to be untainted by the Ukrainian Incident. I invite her out to Marbella, but she says that she's just taken on a high-profile client so this is occupying pretty much all of her time.

I asked who he is (we always assume the villain is a he, don't we?) and then she gave me the old client confidentiality bullshit. I know it's bullshit because she has never held back on this intel in the past, and I have the distinct feeling that in some way I am connected to her client and that somehow there is a connection between this client and the Ukrainian Incident, and boy … how right do I turn out to be?

And then, just as I'm recollecting this and before the penny begins its slow and painful descent, my phone rings.

It's Sam.

Nothing unusual here. We generally phone each other once a day.

This is what's called communication, and I understand that it's customary in a normal relationship. When you're just fucking someone, you don't bother; your communication is purely functional. You really don't give a shit about what they've been up to, who said what to whom or what they're planning to have for dinner that evening. It's all just static, and – both of you know this – it's purely about checking-in and making arrangements for further sex.

I've got to be honest here and say this is certainly one thing I don't like about relationships – pointless phone calls.

Ah … but I seem to remember you saying that both of you hated small talk?

Correctomundo, amigo. Oh, we do. But there's a huge difference between sitting over the dinner table on the second bottle of Domaine Loubejac Pinot Noir, and talking inconsequential piffle on the phone.

What about texting?

Either perfunctory or dirty. Nothing in between.

Anyway … now it's *you* who is holding up my narrative.

Just checking. That's what I'm here for.

So, before I answer, I already know pretty much how the conversation will go. You see, that's precisely how pointless phone conversations are. Nobody ever says anything important over the phone.

Hang on. Didn't you call her to say that you were about to be blackmailed, and provide sordid details of your intimate encounter with the Ukrainian hooker/ blackmailer over the phone?

Okay … that was different. And that's the exception that proves the rule. That was done out of necessity, or what I incorrectly perceived as necessity at the time. So, if you'll just kindly shut the fuck up for one moment, I'll tell you what happens.

Okay, Richie … the stage is yours.

Thank you.

So this is how the conversation will go: she will tell me about what she's been up to – she'll have mucked out and fed her horses; she'll have been for a hack; being a Sunday, she'll be meeting a girlfriend for drinks at her local, followed by a Sunday roast; then she'll be doing some work focusing on the 'big-time' villain whose identity she's being pretty coy about. And then, just to keep me interested – as she knows I hate talking on the phone – she'll possibly spice things up by telling me that she masturbated this morning or that she's planning to masturbate later – or perhaps even both – and will probably do a little scene-setting here just to indulge my fantasies and sweeten the pill of a totally pointless phone call.

And that'll pretty much be that.

So, I'll tell her about my day so far.

I'll begin by telling her about finding a dead girl in my bed; about being interrogated by the Spanish Gestapo; about finding that there was no longer a dead girl in my bed, but learning from that invertebrate ex-soon-to-be-remarried tosser who Mandy still apparently associates with that I will shortly be enjoying life from a wheelchair, courtesy of the former Chief of Staff of the Provisional IRA. And not only that; it's not even ten o'clock yet, and I've taken up smoking and have drunk half a bottle of brandy before I've had breakfast.

Of course, none of the aforementioned will pass my lips, but just as these thoughts are running like cheetah-chased wildebeest across the featureless savannah that passes for my mind, and I'm about to swipe the answer option, another thought strikes me.

Of course.

The archetypal penny has finally dropped.

I now know exactly who her high-profile client is, because Rwoopardo has just let the proverbial cat out of the bag, and I've been too dumb to figure out why she would agree to represent a certain Mr Dempsey.

My jilted lover's fuse has finally burnt through to the powder keg.

TWENTY-TWO

TODAY, 09.42

I answer.

There's cordiality, but there's also something in her voice that warns me that this is going to be as far removed from the dialogue I've just imagined as gun control is from American legislation.

Okay, maybe I'm paranoid here, because I know what's coming.

'I've a couple of things to tell you, Malone,' she goes.

'Why, Sam?' I whimper pathetically. 'Why? Why did you get that bastard out? You've no idea how fucking dangerous he is; and now he knows who wrote that bloody book, he's coming after me.'

She ducks the question. Clever, that.

'First …' She takes a deep breath, and for the second time in less than an hour I have the distinct sensation that the person at the other end of the line is deriving a disproportionate amount of pleasure from my wretched predicament. 'And just for your information,' she continues, 'I never received those photos … although I have seen them.'

Pause.

'Your Ukrainian friend didn't send them. Whatever threats you made must have been enough to put her off. Or maybe she thought about it and was more scared of what the person who was going to receive them to might do to her. And I know this, because she told Mandy.'

My mind actually boggles. I never knew what that expression meant until now, but it has literally vaporised and folded in on itself.

'*What?* Mandy? How the fuck ...'

'Do I know? Strangely enough I got a call from Mandy about three weeks ago. My first instinct – after the threats she'd made to us – was to tell the bitch to go fuck herself. Which is precisely what I did. But then, when you confessed about your little accidental Ukrainian episode, I decided to call her back to hear exactly what she had to offer.' There's a real hardness in her voice now; one I've definitely never heard before. This isn't the Sam I know. When we were just fucking, and then after that, when we were in a 'meaningful relationship', never once had I experienced the clinical and calculating frostiness with which she's speaking to me now.

It's like I'm in a third-rate seventies horror film where aliens invade human minds; hers has been appropriated, and mine is about to be taken over. And I wish they'd hurry up and do it, because at least that would release me from the bludgeoning fiasco of this reality.

'Go on.' I light a cigarette and wish I hadn't thrown the brandy bottle at the window.

'So, I called Mandy back, and she told me about Dempsey. I'd never heard of him.' Why does this not surprise me? Is someone who didn't know that the *News of the World* has been defunct for over seven years likely to know that the Godfather of the IRA is in prison for tax fraud, let alone know who he is?

'She told me that this woman called Paula, the Ukrainian prostitute …' She pronounces the word as if to say it too quickly would detonate a bomb in her throat.

'Blackmailer,' I interject, as if it makes a difference.

'Whatever. Anyway, the devious bitch sent the photos to Mandy instead of me.'

'What's devious about that? And why on earth would she send them to Mandy?'

'Oh … she's done her research well. She hacked into your laptop while you enjoyed your post-shag slumber and found the photos of us …'

'What, the ones you took?' I knew no good would come of that.

Amigo … never, ever, no matter how stimulating it may appear at the time, allow a woman to capture and store a photographic record of your sexual shenanigans.

'Yeah.'

She lets this hang to allow me to digest the fact that Mandy now has two different sets of incriminating photographs, and I'm left wondering who this is going to be the most ruinous for.

'Wait … why would she send those to Mandy? She already has them.'

'Fishing trip … she wouldn't have known that. But more importantly, she'd also had a good rummage through your laptop and found a file that included a full transcript of your journal – you know, the bit you showed me – and she figured that this would wind up Mandy sufficiently for her to blackmail me as an identifiable target, so she sent her this as well.'

Fuck. I'm lost for words. Did I really show her my 'journal'? I don't remember that. This just gets worse and worse.

'Mandy then told me,' she continues, 'what she has in her possession. So what? I said. Why would I give a fuck? I asked her. She now has two sets of the same photos of you and me, and one of you with the Ukrainian slut, so what's she going to do? Set up a hardcore porn website? So, then she told me what else the Ukrainian sent.'

'I still don't see how … or why she's going to blackmail you?'

'Ah … you just don't get it, do you? Come on, Malone, how did you ever manage to plot a novel? It was that diary that pushed her over the edge. Let me give you a piece of advice: next time you want to keep a record of all the women you've fucked and your other extra-curricular activities in Spain, it could be an idea not to flag this up by naming the file "Journal", with a password on your laptop that a retarded monkey could crack. Mandy didn't give a flying fuck about the photographs, but when she read your diary she went mental. Not only did you provide intricate details of your intimate liaisons with her and your sordid little incursions into cyber-sex, but – and this is what pissed her off the most – you logged detailed transcripts of every meaningful text that passed between you two over the period before you finally split up. And, not only that: she's convinced that you're going to publish them. Maybe it wouldn't have mattered so much if she hadn't been rocketed into the media spotlight, but it sure as hell does now.'

Pause.

'Are you still there, Malone?'

I am, and I'm trying to fathom how Sam knows so much about Mandy. It's like she's her fucking secretary all of a sudden.

'Yeah. But what's that got to do with you? Why doesn't she take it up with me, instead of you?'

'That's what I thought at first. But when she told me what she was planning, it was clear that she needed me. If I refuse to cooperate, she told me, these photos will be plastered over the Internet, as well as being sent to my boss.'

'So? She's threatened that before, and she didn't do it.'

'Yeah, that's what I thought as well. But she said that was just a warning, and the secret to being a good blackmailer is similar to being a good poker player – to keep your ace in the hole until you really need to use it. And now that time had arrived, and that ace would coming out if I refused to cooperate.'

'And …?'

'And that's when she mentioned Dempsey. She told me that she'd had a meeting with him and they'd done some sort of deal. His legal team had constructed a tenuous case to get his sentence quashed, but they didn't have the clout to convince the judge. And that was where I came in; it wouldn't cut any ice without someone with my experience and reputation. And the fact that I'm English, licenced to practise in Ireland and I'm representing a key Republican player would give them even more clout.'

I feel the need to interject.

'He's not a player; he's a sociopathic cunt.'

'Maybe he is. Actually, what really persuaded me to act for him was a series of anonymous phone calls where the caller detailed my every move and told me how easy a target I would be if I didn't play ball.'

'Why didn't you go to the police?'

She laughs. 'You know why? As a defence counsel, I have first-hand experience of how useless they would be. Anyway, having me on board, he'd said, would appeal to the Americans, who would put pressure on the Irish judiciary. If Mandy could get him released, not only would he commission her to write his official memoirs, but he would come after you for writing that book and it would be a happy-days-slash-win-win-situation for everyone. Apart from you, of course.'

'You know about the book?'

'Of course I know about the book. Mandy told me; she even lent me a copy.'

Pause.

'Why the fuck did you write it, Malone? It wasn't even funny. To be honest, I don't blame him. Particularly after what he had to endure in Mountjoy as a result. Mind you, it does sound pretty convincing. You sure that didn't happen?'

'No. It didn't happen. I promise.'

'Oh ... a Richie Malone promise. How very dependable.'

Neither of us says anything for an age.

'I thought it was quite good, actually. And so did my publisher.' However hopeless the situation, I hate to have my ego bruised. But I'm guessing you know that by now. 'And it sold pretty well. You know what's going to happen to me, don't you?'

'Yeah ... look, I'm sorry. I didn't have any choice. But to tell you the truth, you bloody deserve what's coming to you. You fucking bastard.'

'I thought you weren't upset.'

'Christ, Malone ... for all your philandering, you know so very little about women.'

There you are, amigo ... see, slow burner – what did I tell you?

'Look, he's not exactly going to kill you, is he? Mandy made him promise that. He'll just slap you around a bit, maybe break a few bones, then get you to own up to the book, issue a public retraction and everything will be hunky-dory.'

Mandy: my saviour. How grateful should I be to you, you bitch? But I'm left wishing I'd never written that bloody journal, let alone the book, and I'm left wondering which is going to cause most damage.

'And where does that leave … us?'

She laughs, but ignores the question.

'There's something else you should know.' But her voice is a little softer now, a quantum shade more like the Sam I know and – trust me – I actually care about.

'Go on.' I'm not sure I have the capacity to take on board any more bad news without further alcohol, so I shuffle to the drinks cabinet and find a half-empty bottle of Jameson's, from which I take a long pull. The spirit sets my stomach on fire.

A thought occurs to me: 'You said you saw the photos. How … if the Ukrainian hadn't sent them to you?'

'I was coming to that. When I was at Mandy's. By the way, she's moved into this *huge* manor house just outside South Cave. It's lovely. She must have made a killing from that book.'

'And …?' Set against my immediate life prospects, Mandy's residential status holds little interest for me.

'They're actually quite titillating.' She laughs. 'Not as good as the ones I took. Mine are more … hmmm … artistic; the Ukrainian's are really just a catalogue of your actions, and you don't even seem to be enjoying it much.'

'That's because I was drugged, which was why I was even there in the first place.'

'No, you were there in the first place because you're a sex addict and you find it impossible to resist temptation. I know you, Malone. Anyway, the other piece of information I have for you concerns Mandy's new partner.'

'Yes, I know about that. She's remarrying Rupert. He told me himself this morning. And, to be fair, he warned me about Dempsey's release.'

She laughs.

'And you bought that bullshit? I thought Rupert was the only one stupid enough to believe that this is actually going to happen. It's just a sham. She's using him ... I suppose, as she used me, and as she uses everybody.'

'At last – some good news.' My curiosity gets the better of me. 'Go on, then ... so, who's her new partner? Let's start by establishing whether it's male or female?'

'Oh, very definitely female. She seems to have taken rather a shine to your prostitute-slash-blackmailer. Paula's moved in with her. She didn't get a bean from her attempts at blackmailing, so at least she's got some compensation for her efforts.'

Despite the situation, I manage a smile. Sam reads my mind.

'Don't even think it, Malone.'

TWENTY-THREE

TODAY, 09.59

I ring off.

I suppose things could be worse, but it's hard to imagine how.

Even if Dempsey doesn't leave me in a wheelchair, I'll still have the fallout from fessing up to that bloody book to deal with.

At the very least, I'm going to be the object of ridicule to the pseudo-literary world I tangentially belong to, and any hope of publishing anything in my own name will have gone west.

Worse still, Mandy knows the name I write the filth under, and that particular threat hasn't even been laid on the table yet.

And then there's still the matter of the dead girl. That certainly isn't going to go away.

'So, what was that all about, Malone?'

It's Maria. I'd forgotten she's still here. She places a mug of coffee in front of me.

'Drink that. And no – I am not putting any brandy in it. Nor anything fucking else, for that matter.'

'Your language is a disgrace, Maria,' I go. 'There are over one hundred and seventy thousand words in the English language, and you seldom rise above the banal communicative utterings of a guttersnipe.'

'What the fuck is a guttersnipe?'

'There, you see? My point entirely.'

Okay ... so leaving Maria's language aside, I'm sure we'd all like to know exactly what was in this book that has caused such a furore.

I'm coming to that. Be patient.

'You should eat something,' she says. 'You want me to cook you nice omelette?'

'Maria, I hate omelette. You know that.'

She sighs. 'Okay ... well maybe you run me home now? I've got things to do, and I'd like to get a couple of hours on the beach before fucking work.'

I'd like a couple of hours on the beach, but that possibility is as remote as decent service in a Spanish restaurant.

'So, what was all that about?' she repeats.

'I'll tell you in the car.'

I drink my coffee and look for the car keys. I usually throw them into a pot on a shelf in the entrance hall, but they're not there, and I'm about to initiate a search when my eye is drawn to a large brown object that's been pushed beneath the front door.

It's a manila envelope – you know, the sort used for the delivery of important documents – and instinct tells me that what's inside it is unlikely to be good news.

I pick it up, gingerly unpick the seal flap and tease it apart with the tip of my thumb and forefinger as if I'm expecting something venomous to emerge and bite me.

And this is exactly what happens. My blood literally freezes.

But before I can conduct further examination of the contents, I'm aware of Maria behind me. I put the envelope behind my back and turn to see she's dangling my car keys.

'Malone … Christ, man – you look like you seen a fucking ghost.'

Which, amigo, is precisely what I have just done.

TWENTY-FOUR

TODAY, 10.13

I'm in the garage searching for something to hide the envelope in, as if to conceal it would render it less real.

In the end, I give up and bury it beneath an assortment of beach crap in the boot of the Porsche. I'm probably in what people refer to as a state of shock, but my years of dealing with shit like this kick in, and I focus.

I back the car out of the garage and swing the passenger door open for Maria.

It's a glorious late September morning, and I think about lowering the roof just to get some air and clear my head, but then it occurs to me that drawing attention to myself is the last thing I should be doing.

Talking of things you should be doing – should you be driving?

Funnily enough, that's what Maria asks, and the answer is categorically yes. What's the worst that can happen? I get stopped and breathalysed and end up in a cell? At least then – in theory – neither Dempsey nor Nikolaev can get to me.

Anyway, the contents of the envelope have dissipated any lingering effects of the alcohol.

'You goin' to tell me what that call was all about or not?' she asks.

I'd rather not tell Maria anything, particularly as she's done her best for the last few months to completely blank out Sam's existence, but I feel I owe her some sort of explanation.

And so I tell her pretty much what Sam has just told me, omitting the Paula connection and further extraneous information that would only serve to paint a blacker picture of me; if indeed that is possible.

'So, what's in this book? Why is this Dempsey – how'd you say … pissing his pants about it?'

'It's not really him who's pissing his pants, actually.' I reply. 'It's me.'

I tell her about my one and only meeting with Dempsey, which in itself had left him salivating for revenge, although – and if I'd had the good sense to just leave it at that – I probably would have dropped off his radar by now as I was pretty much untraceable. That was one of the two things the SRU was really good at: burying the identities of their agents. The other was the anonymous burial of their dead agents.

Dempsey would have had more important things to worry about, in any case. And with the Good Friday Agreement, there was a fair amount of burying the hatchet by both sides. That said, I've heard he's got a pretty long memory, and had I been unlucky enough to bump into him, he would have been certain to try to even things up. Even before I wrote the bloody book, I'd humiliated him in front of his inner circle, and that's not the sort of thing a man like him is likely to forget easily.

'So why is he coming after you now, after all this time?'

'Well, first of all he knows who I am. Thanks to that bitch Mandy, not only does he now have the name of the man who left him squealing like a pig on the floor of his barn, but he also knows that it was me who wrote the book that shattered his ultra-hardman image and made him a figure of total derision.'

'How did you do that?'

Yes … we'd all love to know. Do tell.

Okay.

About five years ago, I tell Maria, I was running a little low on ideas for the works of filth and, truth be told, I was getting a bit bored of trotting out the same old shit; I was in danger of becoming the archetypal one-trick pony.

So one day, over a long boozy lunch, I drop this idea on my agent. It came fresh out of my head and I'd not got around to a fully worked-out proposal, but he liked it enough to take a punt on it and told me to go ahead and write it.

Of course, the same branch wouldn't publish it, but this is a huge publishing house we're talking about, so he figured he'd place it with another, more relevant division of the company.

'So, what was it about?'

'Essentially it was about my meeting with Dempsey, and how I beat the bastard and his buddies in their own backyard.'

'Fucking hell, Malone? Why would you want to write that?'

'Oh ... vanity, I suppose. I wanted to hurt the bastard; remember, he was what was called an untouchable, so he could operate within his own fiefdom pretty much with impunity. He'd been responsible for the deaths of good men I'd come to regard as friends, so I suppose I wanted to remind him of how I had humiliated him. But remember, it wasn't published under my name, and the only one to know the author's identity was my agent, so I figured I'd be safe.'

'Fuck me, man. You sure love fucking with fire.'

We're on the AP-7 now, and I clock a cop car behind me. I'm in two minds whether to slow down to the speed limit or to floor it. I decide on the former, and off he fucks.

'It's called playing with fire ... and I had no idea that it would come back to bite me like this. There was no way he could have found out who wrote the book if Mandy hadn't raided my laptop.'

'So, first you tell him that what happened in that barn remains a secret, then you write a book about it? No wonder he's pissed off.' She shakes her head and sighs. 'And why'd you leave your laptop where Mandy could find it, and why you not protect it with a password she couldn't guess? Christ, man, you are fucking stupid or what?'

'It gets worse.' I drop the window and light a cigarette. Twenty-four hours ago, if someone had lit up in my car I'd have stopped and left them on the verge. Maria scowls at me but says nothing. 'I wasn't content with just giving the bare facts of what really happened, so I made up a different version of events.'

'Which was?'

'Which was that instead of challenging him to mortal combat, I told him I had a different proposal that may be of interest to him, but if he wanted to hear it, he must first clear the room. This was for his ears only.'

'And did he?'

'Of course. Remember, I'm tied to that chair and he's holding a knife in one hand and a gun in the other, so he hardly needs backup. So once they've fucked off, I offer him sex.'

She makes some weird snorting noises, and for a moment I wonder if she's having some sort of seizure.

'You offer him sex? Fucking hell, Malone, I never thought you were a gay.'

'I'm not. Remember this is fiction. I don't have a problem with homosexuals, although the thought of having sex with another man turns my stomach. I don't even like writing about it, but sometimes you have to consider your audience, and so maybe if a MMF threesome is somehow relevant …'

'Jesus, keep to the point, Malone. I don't want to hear about that sordid … obscenity you write, especially on a Sunday.' She actually crosses herself, and I realise that

I've accidentally disgorged more information about my covert filth writing to her than I have to anyone else other than Johnny.

'Why you offer him sex?'

'Okay ... but remember this is fantasy. Because I'd figured that a boy who'd grown into a man living with his mother, and who is constantly surrounded by men, had more than a little potential to be a closet shirtlifter. So, I said that I found him very attractive, that he had a kind of aura about him – which, in fact, he did – and that I would spill the beans about my clandestine outfit and hand over any other intel he asked for, if we could have sex. Of course, I would then feed him a load of utter bullshit, and he would then have to pretend that I somehow had beaten the shit out of him and allow me to crawl back to my unit. But our little bit of physical intimacy, I fictionally told him, would be a secret that I would take to my grave. And so – in the book, remember – we went at it like bonobo monkeys in the carved-out chasm of his barn for a couple of hours before he let me go, but only on the promise that I would make myself available for further sexual intimacy as and when he fancied it. I'm not sure if this could be classed as infiltrating the enemy, but that's how it was billed in the book.'

'Jesus, Malone, that's way too explicit to be made up. Man, you really are one, what you call it? One sick puppy ... you sure that's not what really happened?'

'I can assure you that it most certainly did not happen. And I can honestly tell you that writing it nearly made me heave. But my agent and the publisher loved it, and it got pretty good reviews. Chiefly from the inmates of Mountjoy Prison, who would have given him a particularly hard – pardon the pun – time.'

'No fucking wonder he's after you.'

'Honestly … I had absolutely no idea he was going to jail. I probably would have got away with it otherwise.'

I pull up outside Maria's apartment block in the Avenida del Mercado. She air-kisses me and gets out.

'Malone,' she says. 'You take care, you hear?'

'My situation, Maria,' I reply, 'is beyond care. But thanks anyway. Oh … okay if I use your parking space?'

'Sure, darling. Give me a ring later, if you're still alive. What was in that envelope, by the way?'

'It's better you don't know, babe.'

'And don't fucking "babe" me, Malone.'

I pull out into the street, vibrant with the bustle from the municipal market six days a week but quiet on a sleepy Sunday morning. I glance in the rear-view mirror and cop a large black Mercedes limo a hundred metres back pull out in unison. I clock two guys up front, one in the rear; men in black wearing the obligatory and somewhat clichéd Aviators.

Paranoia kicks in and I drive a circuit of town. They're still with me, not even making an attempt to conceal the fact, until I take a left back towards the AP-7 and they turn right towards Puerto Banús.

It's only a matter of time, I know; a matter of time before the goons in the Merc will want to do a little more than tail me.

TWENTY-FIVE

TODAY, 10.40

I park the Porsche in the underground car park beneath Maria's apartment block.

In the boot I find a copy of Thursday's Spanish national newspaper *Sur in English*, conceal the manila envelope within its pages, and stroll down the hill to the row of cafés and bars beneath the municipal market, where I do most of my drinking, some of my writing and – until recently – a not insignificant amount of my womanising.

I take a seat at the back of the Pata Negra, next to the toilet and opposite the tapas bar, where I have a good view of the street and from which I'm fairly inconspicuous.

Maria's right: I need to eat, so I opt for the *desayuno inglés*: fried eggs swimming in a lake of oil, translucent grease-coated bacon and what literally translates as mouldy toast, a *café con leche* and an orange juice. I could kill for a proper Ulster Fry – maybe, amigo, in the circumstances, kill isn't the right word, but you know what I mean.

It's quiet as the Sunday crusade for paella is still a few hours away, and my breakfast comes almost at once. It barely touches the sides, and I feel marginally better. I fancy washing it down with a beer, but I heed the second piece of Maria's advice.

'*Qué tal*, señor Malone?' goes Pablo, the owner, as he clears my plate and I order another coffee.

I light a cigarette and mutter a response in Spanish.

'*No sabia que fumas, amigo?*' He frowns. '*Lo siento, pero … no puedes fumar aquí, señor Malone.*'

You can smoke virtually anywhere in Spain, where the boundaries between indoors and outdoors become conveniently opaque, but for some reason Pablo's got a downer on it this morning.

'*Perdón*, Pablo,' I go, and take another drag on my cigarette before chucking it into my empty coffee cup. The froth sizzles it out.

Okay, amigo, because you like to savour the setting, here's the TripAdvisor bit:

The Pata Negra is very much a locals' establishment; tourists rarely venture in, and no one speaks much English. It's also a staunch bastion of bullfighting, and although the sport – if you can call it a sport – has been banned in Andalucía, if you crave reruns of classic contests between man and beast (or indeed, on occasions, woman and beast) the Pata Negra is the place to go.

The three huge wall-mounted televisions serve two purposes only – either to screen Spanish football (which I find almost as distasteful as bullfighting) or highlights of legendary one-sided matadorial contests.

So, there you go. Happy?

Deliriously.

And the subject of one-sided contests gets me around to thinking of Dempsey and my own sorry predicament.

Pablo brings my coffee, nods me a wink to apologise for telling me to extinguish my cigarette and fucks off to pull himself a surreptitious beer, which he conceals beneath the bar counter.

I take the manila envelope from the newspaper, prepare myself for what I'm about to see and look around the café to check I'm still alone. I am. There are a few hombres sipping early San Miguels, laughing and smoking in the area Pablo technically defines as 'outside'. My only other companion is to my right; between the framed photos of bullfighters is the huge wall-mounted moth-eaten head of a bull killed in action, a look of doleful resignation on his face. I know pretty much how he must have felt.

So, the envelope? Go on ... share – we're all dying to know.

Be patient.

From the briefest of glimpses in my hallway, I have ascertained that these are more bloody photographs, and therefore more bloody threats or more bloody blackmail; more bloody retribution. Only, after closer inspection, this time the hue of my despair is tinged with the slightest hint of optimism.

I don't see much cause for optimism?

Oh, but there is ... I'll get to it in a minute.

I pull them gloomily from the envelope, clutch them to my chest and count: ten ten-by-eight-inch glossy colour images of life and death in my bed.

The dead girl and me.

But there are two other photos which don't really go with the murder scene, and for a moment I'm lost as to why they've been included.

And then it hits me.

And they are …?

They're not great photos, as they've been shot from a distance and the light is poor, but they show the girl and me sitting together in the Moët, and for a moment it looks as if we're sharing a moment of intimacy. But then I look a little closer and note that she's actually slumped against me, and both of us have our eyes closed.

And then it strikes me that there's something else not quite right about these photos, but for the life of me I can't quite put my finger on it.

So I examine the pictures carefully, nausea driving the grease-generated acid reflux from Pablo's eggs back upwards from my oesophageal sphincter.

They are sickeningly vivid – earlier, in the heat of the moment, I hadn't realised just how gross a scene it was – and now it's laid out in front of me, I know that I'm going to heave. I bolt for the toilet, first taking care to gather up the evidence, position myself over the bowl and vomit violently.

Some soldier you must have been.

You've flagged that one up already, amigo.

When I'm done, I douse my face with cold water, take five deep breaths and reassemble as much of my dignity as I can muster. I sit down as Pablo places an ashtray at my table, his face a mask of concern.

'*Estás bien* ... No?' he goes. '*Fumas si quieres,*' he says magnanimously, and gratefully I light up. He wanders off, presumably to have a word with the chef about the breakfast that has made me heave noisily in his toilet. The nicotine settles my stomach, and I re-examine the photos. This time, believe it or not, they don't seem quite so bad.

So, now a couple of things strike me:

First – and I can't tell you how I know this – I have definitely not had sex with the girl. Every photo is basically the same; they just reveal a slightly different aspect of the same undiluted horror. But I'm unconscious and she's dead, so there's hardly going to be much in the way of action.

Then there's something gnawing at me about how I'm lying. At first, I can't quite put my finger on it ... and then it strikes me – I'm lying on my left-hand side with my back to her and my knees pulled foetal-like to my chest. And this is something I would never do, and I'd never do it for the simple reason that it hurts like hell if I lie on my left. I have a titanium pin and the remnants of an inoperable bullet in my left shoulder, and no matter how drunk I may be, if I go to sleep in this position I will wake up in agony and roll over. And I certainly never sleep in a curled-up position – my normal sleep position is spreadeagled – and this suggests that I have taken something that has upset my stomach, and this points to the probability that we have both been drugged.

Why are you so sure you've not had sex?

Because I wouldn't have distanced myself from her as I have in the photos. When I have sex with a woman who stays in my bed, amigo, I repay the fact that we have had physical intimacy by continued physical proximity. It's my way – what is recorded in the photos is not.

And then I examine the backs of the photos – I don't know what I'm expecting to find. My parents always used to write the place and date of the photo on the back, so maybe the person who took these will have done so too?

I hardly think so.

No, neither do I. Nothing, amigo, no surprises here – until I get to the last one, and then there it is: the blackmailer's big mistake. There, embossed, is a stencilled message:

TIME TO PAY UP. YOUR A MARKED MAN MALONE YOU BASTURD.

You see – had I killed the girl, I'd hardly have written a message to myself, would I? And if I had, it wouldn't have been spelled so badly.

Could easily be a double bluff – you set a smokescreen to divert attention elsewhere?

Okay … answer me one question, amigo – how the

176

fuck could I have taken photos of the dead girl and myself if I'm lying comatose in bed?

There are ways. But I'll admit it's unlikely.

Thank you.

I gather up the evidence of the murder I now know I definitely did not commit with a girl I definitely did not have sex with, stuff them into the manila envelope and place it back inside the centre of the newspaper. And as I do so, my eye is drawn to the piece that occupies the centre pages:

THE BOYS ARE BACK IN TOWN!

THE COSTA DEL SOL HAS LONG BEEN A HOTBED FOR INTERNATIONAL CRIME.

Irish, Turkish, Chinese and South American gangs are amongst the hundreds of groups operating here.

But it is once again the Russian mafia, armed with AK-47 assault rifles, who now have the strongest grip on the region once known as the Costa del Crime.

Sometimes referred to as the Bratva (Russian for 'brotherhood'), their members started moving to sunny Spain in the 1990s.

Over the years, Spanish investigators have discovered how they established a network of hundreds of companies in the country, which formalised real estate and then resold it many times at an increasing price through shell companies.

Simply put, they sold everything to themselves – the definition of money laundering.

Meanwhile, any 'pure' money was sent to Panama and Liechtenstein.

However, more recently Ireland's mafia groups, believed to be headed by former IRA Godfather Tom Dempsey, had seized control of organised crime on the Costa del Sol and had relegated the Russians to the lower leagues, forcing them to compete with the Turkish, Chinese and South American gangs.

But that all changed in 2015 when Dempsey was sent to prison in Dublin for tax fraud. Bitter infighting resulted within the Irish ranks, and this allowed the Russians to step in and resume control of Irish-held rackets.

However, following a successful appeal headed up by top English defence counsel Samantha Sloane, in which the Irish Supreme Court ruled '… the alleged financial indiscretions that Mr Dempsey had been incarcerated for were attributable to an offshore company, to which he had no ties nor knowledge of its existence,' Dempsey is back on the block, and a bloody turf war between the Irish and the Russians is on the cards.

Alexei Nikolaev, who is believed to head up the Puerto Banús-based Bratva, has alleged that Dempsey and his cohorts are feeding information about their activities to the Spanish authorities charged with investigating organised crime.

And just a few weeks ago, based on information

anonymously received, the Spanish Police launched Operation Oligarch, and the owner of Marbella FC, Alexander Grinberg, was arrested alongside ten other Russians.

They were all suspected of laundering at least €30 million through the club, believed to have been siphoned from illegal activities in Russia.

According to sources, all suspects had links to two Russian crime gangs, the 'Izmailovskie' and 'Solntsevskaya'.

During Operation Oligarch, eighteen searches in Mijas, Marbella, Estepona and Puerto Banús revealed large amounts of cash, electronic data storage devices, twenty-three luxury vehicles – including Bentleys and Ferraris – and an entire arsenal of firearms and ammunition.

In addition to handguns, numerous automatic rifles, submachine guns, assault rifles, silencers and night viewers were also seized.

Nikolaev, whose daughter Natasha recently published her first book, My Father and Other Animals, *a novel about organised crime which is thought to have caused considerable discord in the Nikolaev household, has not been implicated in any illicit activities.*

Neither Mr Nikolaev nor Mr Dempsey were available for comment.

Suddenly this sorry mess begins to make some sense. This is Dempsey's work, and it's not just the dreadful spelling on the back of the photo that tells me this.

And then another thing strikes me: I remember exactly what I was doing with Ms Nikolaeva last night.

TWENTY-SIX

TODAY, 11.02

I decide to go to the beach.

Fuck it … I'm not just going to sit around here and wait for the inevitable.

Shouldn't you be going to the police instead?

That thought does cross my mind. If I were in the UK and I was dealing with a less volatile agent of law enforcement than Robocop, this, amigo, is exactly what I would do. But I simply do not know how he would react if I show him photos of the dead girl and myself in my bed – the bed which he had found empty when he inspected my residence.

I suspect he would accuse me of some sort of publicity stunt and wasting further police time. And, in any case, I know this will not go away until I have somehow faced down both parties who are seeking retribution.

Besides which, I don't trust him.

So, I head back to the car park to deposit the photos and grab my beach gear, and then it occurs to me – for the second time this morning – that I really need to talk to someone I can trust to try to straighten this out in my head.

She's not going to like it, but there's only person I can trust.

And it's not Sam.

TWENTY-SEVEN

TODAY, 11.06

Maria answers at the third ring.

'Fucking hell, Malone, I'm trying to get some sleep.' She clears her throat; a deep, husky crackling, normally the trademark of the heavy smoker, that betrays her age. 'What is it now? This better be fucking important, man.'

'Maria …' I think about reiterating what I've already told her, but then I remember that a body's not yet been found; and although I think she believes me, I also think that a more simple – and appealing – explanation is that I have somehow imagined the whole thing. In other words, I'm losing the plot. 'Maria,' I go, 'I'm sorry, babe … I wouldn't bother you if it wasn't important, but something's come up.'

Pause.

'I need to show you something. It's important.'

She sighs.

'I know. What was in that envelope?'

I grunt non-committedly.

'Okay. Where you want to meet … the Moët?'

'No … let's go to the beach. You're planning to go there anyway?'

Another reason I've decided to go to the beach is because I figure it's the safest place, at least for now. If they're coming for me, they'll be waiting at my villa, and it wouldn't be that hard to abduct me from a bar or café. So to hide in plain sight on the beach makes more sense.

Firstly, although I wouldn't rule anything out from either group of psychopathic nutters, they would have to have some bottle to drag me from the beach, where there's a fairly heavy police presence, mainly to deter the black fellas from peddling crap to the tourists. I have seen drunks dragged from the beach before, but this is the prerogative of the Policía Municipal and not men dressed in black suits.

And secondly, if I were in their shoes, the beach would probably be the last place I'd be looking. Always anticipate what the enemy will expect you to do, amigo, and do the opposite.

***

But before I hit the beach, there's something else I need to check.

I'm in luck.

I find Mercedes arranging chairs and tables one-handed outside the Moët, holding her phone with the other and, by a happy coincidence for once today, it's her I want to talk to.

She was working last night; that I can remember too.

Let me tell you a bit about the Moët, as it features quite a lot in my life and so it's appropriate that I should share this with you.

The Moët is a pretentiously named but convivial little bar where the trendy people go. Note I say trendy, not beautiful. The beautiful people go to Puerto Banús and sip overpriced cocktails in the shadows of some of the largest privately owned yachts in the world, even if they know they're never going to get a ticket to board.

And they only do this because other people they envy do this, and not because they want to. Sure, I keep my yacht there, but mine is a mere dinghy compared to some of the Russian-owned ships.

Puerto Banús is Alderley Edge-on-Sea. If you don't know Alderley Edge, google it. It's one of the most expensive and sought-after places to live in the UK outside central London, according to Wikipedia.

Puerto Banús is overrated, overpriced, tacky and populated by fake people who hire Ferraris for two hundred bucks just to drive around the block for an hour. In fact, the only good thing about it is the Saturday market. Other than that, I don't have much time for the place.

And this relates to the Moët how, exactly?

Okay, coming back to the Moët ... the place has a curious mix of clientele; the later the hour, the younger the punters. There's a resident DJ at weekends, and I don't think I've ever heard last orders called. The service is terrible, but this is mainly because the staff know everyone, so every order taken or drink delivered is accompanied by a ten-minute conversation.

I take a seat, wait for Mercedes to finish her phone conversation, light a cigarette and admire her arse, resplendent in tight black jeans.

She turns, smiles at me as she clocks my eye line, and finishes her conversation.

'We're not open yet, Richie,' she laughs. 'Didn't you have enough last night?'

'It's not a drink I want, Mercedes.' I process this information. I must have been drunk, or appeared to be drunk. How best to elicit the information I require without giving too much away? So I go, 'By the way, your arse looks terrific in those jeans.'

Good call.

'You say that to all the pretty girls, señor Malone … like the one you were with last night.' She takes a seat opposite me, crosses her long, shapely legs, steals one of my cigarettes and lights it.

Mercedes is reputed to be one of the co-owners of the Moët, and she's a fine thing. Maybe nudging thirty, tanned Mediterranean skin, dark hair with sparkling mischievous blue eyes, and taller than your typical *chica caliente*. And although I constantly flirt with her, I've never been there; trust me, amigo.

So, she's a lucky member of that small, elite club then: women spurned by Richie Malone.

Ah, it's not that I wouldn't, amigo, I promise you. But there are certain women that you do not, as a matter of principle, have sex with. Maria is certainly one; any waitress in a bar you frequently patronise is another, and cabin crew on routes you fly regularly are also strictly off-limits. I once made the mistake of chatting up a good-looking Ryanair trolley dolly during a turbulent flight from Málaga to Leeds. When she gave this nervous flyer a little more than handholding in the service area, I got her number and promised her dinner in Málaga on my return.

Of course, I forgot, so the next time I fly to Manchester, she's on the flight and – let's just say – I figure she asked the pilot to find some turbulence and fly through it for as long as possible.

'Yeah … no, talking of which … Mercedes, *cariño*, do you … like, by any chance, know the young lady I was with last night?'

'No. Never seen her before. She looked Eastern European. Russian prostitute?'

'Mercedes … would I?'

She laughs. 'The state you were in, I doubt if you'd have been capable of doing it anyway.'

'So … I was drunk?'

'Never seen you so drunk. You asked me for champagne at about two, and I refused to serve you. Told you you'd had enough and you should go home.' Her brow furrows in concentration. 'Strange … one minute you were fine, then suddenly you were drunk. It was like someone flicked a switch.'

I don't get it. I very, very rarely get drunk and certainly not in the Moët, particularly with a girl with whom I now remember I had serious business to discuss.

'What about the girl? Was she drunk too?'

'Wow. You don't remember, Richie? She kept falling asleep on your shoulder, you charmer. Which was kind of strange cos she didn't drink that much. Maybe a couple of cocktails and a glass of wine. That was my area, and I remember thinking it odd. Come to think of it, there was something odd about the girl too.'

'Mercedes, think carefully … did you notice anyone … I don't know … new last night? Maybe a couple of Irish guys?'

'There *were* a couple of guys I'd not seen before. They were sitting behind you, close to the toilet as if they didn't want to be noticed. They were speaking English – yeah, with a similar accent to yours. They weren't here long.'

'Could you describe them if you had to?'

'What … are you in the fucking cops now, Malone?'

'Yeah … no, just stuff for my book.' I know I'm sounding suspicious, and I must be careful not to overplay my hand. Mercedes's on-slash-off boyfriend is Russian, and it would not surprise me to find a black suit or two in his wardrobe. 'No … I mean, could you describe them … if you had to?'

'Sure.' She stubs out her cigarette, pats my leg. 'Listen, this has been nice talking to you, *guapo*, but I've got shit to do.'

'Of course, I understand.' Then I go all Colombo. 'Just one more thing: what time did I leave here? And did the two hombres speaking English leave before or after me?'

'That's two more things. I'd say you left around … maybe two thirty? You had difficulty walking and were almost carrying the girl. Yeah … I remember, it was two thirty cos I called you a taxi.'

So that's how we got home.

'What about the two guys? Can you remember?'

'Sure. They left just before you. I remember calling the cab, then looking across and they'd gone. Left fifty euro for two drinks.'

I air-kiss her and leave.

The mystery unravels, but at least it explains my memory loss.

The possibility that the dead girl and I had been drugged has now become a probability.

TWENTY-EIGHT

TODAY, 11.17

I grab a couple of sunbeds and pay the ubiquitous Gora twelve euro.

As usual, he's on me like Clouseau's Chinese manservant, Cato, before my arse even hits the plastic.

Gora's from Somalia, where he studies economics, and he works the sunbeds for Pepe during the summer. Always dressed in immaculately pressed white shorts and a sleeveless white shirt, at around six foot seven he cuts a dashing figure, particularly with his braided captain's cap, of which he is inordinately proud. I can't help wondering if it may have been procured from the skipper of a cargo ship, hijacked in the Indian Ocean by some of his Somalian bros.

Unlike his Spanish predecessor, who was as much use as a one-handed clock, Gora has evolved an elaborate hieroglyphical system to record the sunbeds that are rented and those that are free; the boy will go far, and his assiduousness is totally wasted on Pepe.

Usually I'll pass maybe half an hour chewing the fat with Gora, but this morning, his enthusiasm, cheerful disposition and his infectious, dazzling white smile contrasting with the ebony of his skin do little to lift my spirits, so he scribbles me a receipt and off he fucks.

I change into my Speedos—

What? You actually wear Speedos?

Of course – what else would you expect Richie Malone to wear? Anyway, stop interrupting.

As I was saying, I put on my … swimwear, spread my towel and lie down where I have a good view of anyone coming onto the beach. I figure furthest from the sea, nearest to Chiringuito Pepe's Bar and to the right of the kiosk selling drinks, ice cream, inflatable toys and other shit to silence the kids, is the best vantage point.

As always, I lie on my front.

But I can't relax.

I try to let the tension of the last few hours wash over me, but I just can't let go.

It's like a Sunday night at boarding school, but a trillion times worse. You know, I still carry the burden of the Sunday Night Guilt Complex from my schoolboy years? The depressing finale to the weekend, slipping into chapel, hoping upon hope that my housemaster won't single me out to account for and face retribution for one of the host of illegal activities I'd got up to over the weekend. Only at boarding school, the worst that would happen was six of the best or a couple of weeks on a 'gating card', which meant total restriction to school boundaries and the curtailment of my extra-curricular activities.

No booze, no sex, no rock and roll.

But that was very far removed from the retribution I'm lined up for on this particular Sunday.

I light a cigarette, scan the horizon for incoming and review the situation.

I wonder if the Russians – I'm convinced it was them who were tailing me, particularly as I can't see Dempsey's mob dressed in black suits – would actually walk onto the beach dressed like that? It would be like the classic Madge scene from Benidorm. And how will I spot Dempsey's hoods? I need to narrow it down; and this, amigo, is the secret to good surveillance. Eliminate the impossibles: old women and kids; discard but keep an eye on the improbables: young lovers, obvious homosexuals, families and men over the age of sixty; and pay particular attention to everyone else … above all, anyone whose eyes betray the same thing I am doing – scanning, observing and filtering.

So far there's nothing suspicious. Of course, it's not inconceivable that they might arrive by sea – in fact, that's what I would do if I wanted to abduct someone from the beach – so I pay heed to all watercraft … yes, even pedalos, that come into my proximity.

There's still no sign of Maria, and for the first time it occurs to me how badly she could get caught up in all of this. Suppose either Dempsey's or Nikolaev's men – or even both, come to think of it – had been watching my villa this morning, they'd have seen Maria arrive and leave with me. So, another way of getting my compliance would be to lift Maria, who would be an easier target than me, and use her to draw me in.

I sigh and stub my cigarette out in the sand. This just gets worse and worse.

What to do?

I review my options. I could simply get dressed, hail a cab and get the fuck out of Dodge. But this would be the first thing they'd anticipate; therefore, they'd be watching the airport.

I don't suppose you have your passport on you anyway?

Of course, amigo. I always carry at least two passports – one of them British, in case things go totally to shit – my driving licence, and sufficient currency in sterling and euro to last me for a month so I don't have to use plastic.

If I could reach the bus station unobserved, I could get to Tarifa where I could catch a ferry to Tangiers and then a flight to the UK, but the probability is that they'll be watching the bus station too. Ditto the train station.

So … running away isn't such a good option.

And anyway, they'd only have to nab Maria and I'd come running back like the proverbial lamb to the slaughter. Stupidly, I got her into this, and I can't very well hang her out to dry.

My mind starts to explore other options, and I've just concluded that there aren't any – other than to go to the police and hand myself in for a crime that hasn't yet been committed, or perhaps even commit a fresh crime for which I'll get arrested – when I spot Maria on the boardwalk. She's wearing a bright, sky blue and yellow floral-patterned dress and a broad-brimmed sun hat, which is typically Maria – the sort of thing that wouldn't look out of place at a wedding or a garden party and is totally over the top for the beach. She'd be as easy to tail as a Spanish Easter procession.

She flops down on the sunbed beside me, pulls the dress over her head, and for an instant my mind reverts to normal function as I find myself hoping that she'll remove her bikini top. As you may recall, amigo, she's got an amazing pair of breasts for someone of her age.

Yes, I think you mentioned that.

She doesn't.

'Well?' she goes, following the arc of my eyes. 'Fucking hell, Malone … or should I call you *Malote* – *Malote* hombre, huh?' She laughs. 'Bad, bad man.'

I ignore this.

'Maria, were you followed here?' I know it's a pointless question as the words leave my mouth. She wouldn't register if there were a tank regiment behind her.

'How the fuck should I know?' She takes a sip from a bottle of water. 'You going to show me what was in that envelope?'

I sit up, pull the envelope from the newspaper and scan the beach. There's no one within thirty metres of us, and there are only maybe fifty people between us and the marina a hundred metres to our left. There are two couples on the other side, then the stretch of beach between them and the next *chiringuito* is deserted.

I sit next to Maria. If my attention's going to be distracted, I want to have the Paseo Maritimo in my eye line.

I hand her the newspaper. 'You'd better read this first.'

She takes the *Sur* and reads.

I fidget and light a cigarette, constantly looking around. I know I look more suspicious than a Scouser in Harrods, but my nerves are truly on edge. Fuck, I can't recall when I've ever felt this twitchy. But then I can't recall when I knew for sure that two of the most violent men on the planet both had a good reason for wanting to beat the proverbial shit out of me.

Or worse.

Maria hands me the paper back.

'Fucking hell, Malone. You in one hell of a shitstorm.'

'That would appear to be an accurate summary of the situation. Now, take a look at the photographs.' I hand her the envelope. 'But I warn you, even you will find them …' I search for the appropriate word, but she replies before I can find it.

'Remember what I do for a living? There's not much I've not seen before.'

She removes the photos and trawls through them slowly and deliberately.

I'm secretly gratified that the colour has drained from her olive skin, and for a moment I wonder whether she'll throw up as well.

She takes a deep breath, her colour returning slowly.

'Fucking hell, Malone.'

'You didn't believe me, did you? Go on, admit it …
I knew you didn't believe me.'

She doesn't reply but turns to hand me back the photos.

'Take a look at the back of the last one,' I tell her.

She reads the inscription, then passes the photos back.

'So …' she goes, 'let's see if I've got this straight. You don't know Nikolaev?'

'Correct. Never met him. I have no problem with the Russian mafia and, up until today, he's had no problem with me.'

'But you do know Dempsey?'

'Correct again.'

'And you wrote a book in which you claim that he's a homosexual gay and that he had man-to-man sex with you … you who is his enemy?'

'Ah … not with me, but with the author of the book. But other than that, I think that pretty much sums it up. Although it wasn't so much of a claim as a narrative line.'

'Does that make a difference?'

'You've got a point. Probably not.'

'And he's just been in a prison, where his cellmates would have known about this claim … or what you call it?'

'Narrative line. And yes … the book received quite a lot of publicity. It made it into the Amazon bestseller list and was even shortlisted for a couple of minor literary awards.'

'But you wrote it under another name.'

'Again correct. I wrote it under what's called, in the trade, a pseudonym … or nom de plume, if you want to be more precise. The name on the cover was Cecil C. Wingfield. And things would have stayed that way if Mandy hadn't opened her big fucking mouth.'

'So, now …' she continues.

I scan the beach and the Paseo Maritimo, and there's still no suspicious activity, other than a gaggle of black fellas gathering up their crap and dashing onto the beach to hide behind the toilet block as a cop car does a drive-by.

'Now Dempsey's out, and he wants the action back that Nikolaev took over?'

'Yes. I think you've got a pretty good handle on this, Maria.' I'm finding her slow process of summarising my predicament slightly irritating, but then I remember that she's here at my request. 'And, if you ask me, Dempsey's behind the murder of Nikolaev's daughter. He set the whole thing up to look as if I did it. That way, he kills two birds with one stone – pardon the pun. I'm framed for a murder I didn't commit. He has the evidence, and he can use it as he chooses. If he goes to the cops, I'll be blamed for disposing of the body in addition to her murder. And when Nikolaev sees those photos – which I'm pretty sure will be Dempsey's next move, minus the one with the inscription … otherwise why wouldn't he simply have left the girl in my bed and let events take their course? – Nikolaev will … well, it just doesn't bear thinking about.'

Neither of us says anything for a bit as Maria mulls over the facts and I mull over the possible outcomes. I'm searching for some positives.

Then I find one.

'Oh … one piece of good news,' I go, 'I've got my memory back – at least partially.'

TWENTY-NINE

ONE WEEK AGO

I'm sat having an early beer in the Punto Faro when my phone rings.

The Punto Faro is a beachside bar that occupies two corners of the marina and where the service is so bad, it almost rivals the Moët.

The clientele are mainly affluent locals, but there's been a recent influx of Russian punters as their business interests spread east along the Golden Mile, seeping menacingly into Marbella. And in shady corners of the Punto Faro, deals between aspirational locals and their eastern paymasters are noisily celebrated.

In the interest of setting the scene, amigo, the reason I like the Punto Faro is because it's a great place to sip a beer and watch the sun sink into the Mediterranean, to savour the heat of the day slipping away while rereading a day's writing. I have one very basic rule when it comes to writing – never to consume alcohol when I write, but always when I review; reason being, it puts a different slant on things, and something that may have been considered to be brilliant when written soberly frequently translates into utter rubbish after a couple of beers, and very rarely the other way around.

So, my phone's ringing, and I clock that's it a withheld number and don't answer it.

And then a shadow falls across my table, and I look up to see this angel smiling at me. She's tall ... very tall, maybe five ten; aged, I'd say... maybe early twenties? A pale-skinned, green-eyed beauty with straight jet-black hair cut in a bob. Her elegant nose and full lips accentuate high feline cheekbones that suggest she's Russian or Eastern European.

'Hi,' I go.

'Hi back,' she replies.

There's an awkward silence, and I begin to wonder if she's looking at me at all or maybe it's someone behind me she's connecting with, so I look round but there's no one there.

'You're Richie Malone, aren't you?'

Okay. This is starting to get interesting, but remember, amigo, I'm still smarting from my last Eastern European experience with the Ukrainian. So, to say I'm wary is something of an understatement.

'That depends,' I reply. 'Who wants to know?'

'My name is Natasha Nikolaeva.' She holds out a hand uncertainly, in a way that suggests that she doesn't really understand the etiquette of a handshake but feels that the gesture may, in some way, put me at ease.

Her hand is long and thin. Two fingers are adorned with rings as crammed with diamonds as a Ratners' shop window, and an arsenal of silver-charmed bracelets dangle from her slender wrist. It's a gesture that implies humility, and I take her hand and press it softly. If it had been attached to the Ukrainian, I'd have squeezed it until I heard the sound of crunching bone.

She perches on a stool, and instantly there's a waitress at her side. Did I tell you? That's another thing I like about the Punto Faro – the waitresses, despite being slower than Spanish bank clerks, are all exceptionally easy on the eye.

She orders a cocktail and I ask for another beer.

'What can I do for you, Ms Nikolaeva?'

'Please, call me Natasha. You *are* Richie Malone then, I take it?'

I'm tempted to deny that I've even ever heard of a Richie Malone. But as usual, my curiosity and the pleasure of finding myself unexpectedly seated opposite a beautiful young woman get the better of me.

'Sure, I be he. So, what can I do for you ... Natasha?' I repeat.

'Well, it's a bit of a long story, but I was wondering if you could help me?'

'To do ...?'

'I write, like you. I've recently had a book published.'

The penny's finally dropped – that's where I'd heard of her.

'*My Father and Other Animals*. You may know it?'

'I do. But I've not read it, I'm afraid.' I could add that I rarely, as a matter of principle, read novels written by women, for reasons I defined earlier.

I'd imagine because you're jealous?

201

No, amigo, you'd imagine wrong. It's because a disproportionate amount of poorly written prose gets published simply because women have penned it, and I don't want to fan the flames of this inferno of injustice.

But I don't. Instead I go, 'And so, how exactly can I help you?'

'Well, someone I believe you know quite well suggested that I should speak with you ... ask you for some advice.'

I'm beginning to not like how this is shaping up.

'And who might that be?'

'Mandy Kershaw. She wrote *Sex, Death and Naked Vacuuming*. You know it? It was an overnight classic. Real cutting-edge feminist stuff. To be honest, though, it's not my sort of book. Too much ... how do you English say ... bleeding heart, chip on the shoulder, Northern England little people's misery lit?'

Jesus. I'm gobsmacked. But, to be fair, it's a pretty good summary.

Our drinks arrive and I take the interlude this presents to ponder why that fucking bitch has to keep meddling with my life?

She continues, 'I believe that you and Mandy were once—'

'That was a long time ago,' I interrupt. It still hurts, but certainly not in a way I'm going to communicate to a total stranger, no matter how gorgeous. 'We're not in touch any more, it ... it ended badly.'

She disregards this.

'Anyway, she suggested that I should talk to you. She

was really helpful, you know, and even told me where I could find you.'

The mention of Mandy has coloured both my mood and my appreciation of Natasha as an object of sublime beauty. If she's been in contact with Mandy, she's tainted; no good will come of this.

'I'm sorry, I don't really think I can help you.' I throw twenty euro on the table and begin to pack my laptop into its hard case. 'Nice to have met you, Natasha.' And I mean it. And then I say one of those oft-regretted things that should have remained inside my head but somehow managed to escape from my mouth. 'By the way,' I go, 'you are an incredibly beautiful young woman.'

And before I can regret this, she smiles and actually blushes.

'Thank you,' she goes.

So I add: 'I hope your boyfriend appreciates his good fortune.'

'I don't have a boyfriend,' she replies with a broad and – or do I imagine this? – slightly seductive smile. Then she adds: 'and you're really attractive yourself … for an older guy.'

The sword of Damocles has been removed, temptation avoided with those four humbling words.

She's not done yet.

'Why don't you listen to what I have to say? Finish your drink. Give me five minutes … I have a proposition that I believe will interest you. If you're not convinced by then – go. But I believe you'll have missed a huge opportunity.'

I park my arse again.

'I'm all ears,' I go. I drain my beer and somehow manage to catch a waitress's eye and ask for another. 'Shoot.' Anyway, I've got nothing better to do.

'Okay. I know you write pornographic novels under a pseudonym.'

Fuck.

Fucking Mandy and her … her big fucking mouth, her fucking interference. Fuck her. I'm beginning to borderline hate the woman now.

'I know what it is, but don't worry; it's a secret that's safe with me.' She smiles. 'Actually, I read a couple in the interest of research. They're good. *Catch Sixty-Nine* … *Dungeon Diaries* …'

So here I'm thinking another Eastern European, another attempt at extortion … history repeating itself. You can't blame me for that, amigo?

'Believe me, I have no interest in exposing you. But I do have an interest in collaborating with you.'

'Collaborating? In what way?'

'Okay. I've written a pornographic MS. It's good, very sellable I've been told. But I don't want to publish under my name. It wouldn't be appropriate. So, what I'm suggesting is that you publish it under *your* pseudonym, and we split the proceeds. You take the plaudits … or, at least, your alter ego does, and you don't even have to touch a keyboard.'

Okay, this has a certain appeal, I'll admit. Her book was pretty well received; it hit the top twenty bestsellers and was even long-listed for the Costa Award. The girl can clearly write, but can she write porn? But then my own porn-writing days are certainly numbered, and decent (here I use the word loosely), original material is harder to come by. Plus the fact is that it's started to bore the proverbial shit out of me and, truth be told, I could do with the money.

'It's not my alter ego, by the way. "She" is a woman, I'm a man.'

She ignores this, pulls a folder from her Salvatore Ferragamo shoulder bag and hands it to me.

'Read it,' she goes. 'See what you think.'

I take the MS from its buff folder and examine it. One-sided, double-spaced, three hundred and forty pages ... so that equates to approximately the obligatory eighty thousand words. Seventy-six chapters, none of which run beyond ten pages without a page break, and plenty of dialogue. If you could weigh up a book by how the author presents its content, this is already bestseller material. Don't judge a book by its cover – but judge it by the craft of its construction. I'm nearly in. But, the sixty-four-thousand-dollar question has to be asked.

'What makes you think you can write porn?'

'What makes you think I can't? Read it. Be the judge.'

It's an appealing proposition, and I'm almost ready to fall for it.

'Here's the deal,' she goes. 'You read it by Saturday night, and I'll take you for dinner. Somewhere decent ... The Orange Tree, you know the place?'

'I do.'

'You like it, and we'll work out the figures. You don't
… we have dinner, maybe a nightcap, then you ride off
into the sunset, Richie Malone.' She smiles seductively.
Now I have fallen for it. I'm hooked.

'Sure,' I reply. 'Saturday.'

I gather up the MS, replace it in the folder and put
it in my holdall.

I look up.

She's already gone.

THIRTY

FOUR DAYS AGO

It's Wednesday afternoon and all is well in the world of Richie Malone.

It's another glorious late September day and I've had a productive morning, albeit reluctantly wading through the over-zealous edits that are threatening to choke the life out of *Viagra Falls*. Although, truth be told, I've not got much enthusiasm for this particular work of filth but, like I said, I could do with the money, and this will fly off the proverbial shelves like shit off the archetypal shovel – which is, in fact, a fairly accurate analogy.

I've just eaten a light lunch of gazpacho *andaluz* and an acceptable Waldorf salad prepared by Isabella, my housekeeper.

You have a housekeeper?

Of course, amigo. You surely don't expect an hombre with my hectic schedule to cook and clean? Anyway, Isabella's a gem. She comes in every weekday morning, and weekends if I'm entertaining, and she'll even dress up in the stereotypical maid's outfit for dinner parties.

She loves ironing and cleaning as much as I enjoy beer and sex. She's coy but endurably pretty – possibly even beautiful – if one were to remove her bifocals and let her hair down …

God, that's such a cliché.

Granted; but it's actually true in Isabella's case.

Despite her best efforts to look as plain as possible, she's a fine young thing with a gloriously curvaceous body, and – God help me – I've been sorely tempted on those rare occasions I've trusted myself to be alone with her, particularly when she's cleaning windows. You know what the cute thing is? She acts as if she has absolutely no idea how attractive she is; and that, amigo, is what turns a good-looking woman into an absolute stunner.

But reluctantly I've had to place her within that subset of women who you do not, as a matter of principle, have sex with.

Anyway, I'm finishing lunch on the pool terrace and pondering what justifiable deviation I can come up with to avoid returning to *Viagra Falls*, when I remember the MS.

I'd not looked at it since Natasha gave it to me, so I go and dig it out of my safe.

You see, amigo, I do learn. Since Mandy raided my house, I've been a bit more circumspect about confidential materials, particularly stuff that doesn't actually belong to me.

Or so I thought.

So I park my arse and begin to read.

It's called *Seven Days*, and the narrative's about this 'broad-minded' couple, Simon and Andrea … no, let's be accurate here, they're more than broad-minded; they're positively debauched. Anyway, it's set in Switzerland, and most of the action takes place in or around their chalet in the ski resort of St Moritz.

What happens, after a fairly depraved bit of sexual preamble with the neighbours – to set the tone of the narrative – is that this middle-aged American guy (David) has just discovered that Simon and Andrea recently shared a threesome with Natalia, his bought-off-the-Internet Russian wife.

So he goes round in high dudgeon to have it out with the culprits, there's a struggle and he ends up dead at the bottom of their spiral staircase.

His death was innocent enough – he'd slipped on some excrement that had seeped across the floor from a blocked toilet, and fallen – but someone had not only videoed both bouts of aforementioned sexual antics, but also the demise of the unfortunate Yank and the couple's disposal of the body in a state of blind panic.

And then the extortion begins.

The yet-to-be-identified blackmailer demands that the couple engage in seven acts of sexual depravity with person or persons unknown to them, within the period of one week and in their chalet.

Failure to engage with their 'victims' and correctly perform the prescribed feats of sexual perversion will result in the video being passed into the hands of the Swiss police.

An hour later, I'm a third of the way through, and two things strike me.

First, it's well-written – bloody well-written. I'll be the first to admit that her style, unobtrusive narrative voice and pace are far superior to mine. *Seven Days* has, without a hint of doubt, the tag 'bestseller' nailed to it. This book will make *Fifty Shades* look like a Girl Guides summer camp diary; the girl will do for pornographic fiction what John Travolta did for disco.

And then I remember that my pseudonym could be sitting – and indeed, effortlessly – beneath the title, and that's when the second thing, which has been hovering on the periphery of my consciousness for some time, hits me like an Ashley Mallett.

This narrative is strikingly familiar.

And that's because I wrote it.

THIRTY-ONE

TODAY, 11.20

'So, you have to explain to me, Malone,' goes Maria. 'Maybe I'm thick on the uptake but how would this girl ... this Natasha, get hold of your book?'

Yes, that's what I'd like to know too.

'It's *slow* on the uptake, Maria; and when Mandy downloaded the entire contents of my laptop, she'd have found it on her pen drive. It was just a project ... something I'd roughed out years ago and written the first ... I don't know, maybe fifty pages? I can't remember ... I can't even remember the title, either. Then I got bogged down with the plot and started writing something else. To be honest, I'd completely forgotten about it; that's probably why I didn't recognise it for so long.'

'Jesus, man – you actually write fucking porn.' Maria, for all her pretence at liberalism, is visibly shocked.

'It's more like soft porn,' I lie, realising that even with this dilution of my genre, we're only splitting hairs. 'It's just a bit of fun, and it pays well.'

'So that's how you got your ... your wealth?' She almost spits the word.

'I'd appreciate if you'd keep this to yourself, Maria, please?'

'Sure thing, Malone. You think I'm going to shout it about that my friend is a "pervert"? *Malote* ... bad, bad man.'

'I think the term pervert is a little too strong,' I reply, in an attempt to muster some sort of defence. 'Perverts are generally grubby old men who photograph under the skirts of young girls and sodomise schoolboys; think Jimmy Savile here.'

'Jimmy who?'

'Never mind. The stuff I write is' – I'm searching for a label that will elevate my craft to some level of acceptability – 'more sensual and visceral.'

'It's still porn,' she correctly observes. 'Anyway, why did she bring it to you if you wrote it?'

'Yes, it's taken me a while to work that out too, particularly as all this had somehow been scrubbed from my memory until recently. She told me, last night at dinner ... I remember. Mandy had contacted her, told her she just loved *My Father* ... and how big a fan she is, blah-de-blah. Of course, this totally blew Natasha away, and so they arranged to meet in London.' I light a cigarette and scan the beach; still nothing suspicious. 'So, when they meet up, Mandy asks her what she's currently working on, and she says: nothing – she's stuck on even getting a proposal together; you know, that Difficult Second Book Syndrome.'

I, of course, never had that problem, as the one thing about writing porn is that it's as formulaic as football: you just need to change the characters – heck, you don't even need to bother with that; just place them in different environments or situations and hang some sort of framework on it so that you have sufficient backdrop to indulge other people's fantasies. And this is one reason why *Seven Days* is so brilliant. The narrative is engaging enough to stand alone without overcooking the filth; the light brushstrokes which Natasha paints it with far surpass the smear, spread and smooth of my roller.

'Anyway,' I continue, 'Mandy says she'd started on this MS years ago, had a fully worked-out proposal for it, but now that she's become the new Virginia Woolf-slash-Germaine-bloody-Greer, a novel that was highly pornographic would – according to her agent – create considerable "brand confusion". So, she says to Natasha, why don't you take a look at it? You could run with the narrative, tone it down a bit. And then she suggests that her ex (me) might be interested in doing a bit of a collaboration with her, particularly as she happens to know that he's a bit short on original material at the moment. Makes out that we're still the best of buddies, and that this is a win-win situation for all of us.'

'So, what's Mandy get out of it?'

'Let me remind you of whom we're talking about here – a totally unprincipled, scheming bitch who uses everyone and everything at her disposal as a resource to exact revenge for her perceptions of injustice. The woman's crazy, Maria. Just look what she did to her ex-husband – she virtually ruined him for no good reason, and now he thinks she's actually going to remarry him, the daft sap.'

'So why is she after you? What have you done?'

'Good question – you'd have to ask her that. But Sam reckons this is all about my apparent indifference to her batting for the other side. And that she took my superficial lack of effort to win her back to mean that I just wanted out of the relationship by a back door that she'd left open. Then I started doing the Internet stuff, and when I met Sam – at the moment she'd decided to take me back – she felt jilted; and a jilted Mandy makes the Taliban look like choirboys.'

'So, this Natasha … did she write the book or not?'

'Oh yeah, I'd have to be honest; she did much more than a paint-by-numbers job. This is one work of fiction written by a woman that definitely *does* deserve recognition. She's done a bloody good job – so good, that as I said, I didn't even recognise it for the first hundred pages. Oh, it's her book, all right.'

'So why would Mandy give her this, when she must have known it would end up as a bestseller and you'd make money from it?'

'Okay, my theory is that Mandy didn't care about the money? All she wanted – or maybe needed to do – was to connect Natasha and me because Dempsey asked her to. Maybe it was even a condition for giving her the green light to write his memoirs … I don't know. But by murdering Natasha, framing me but holding the evidence back from the authorities, Dempsey's got his revenge on Alexei Nikolaev – who will extract vengeance from me – and Mandy's also got what she wanted – payback from me. The perfect triangle of retribution.'

'Jesus.' She does that thing with her nose which represents cognitive deliberation and is borderline sexy. 'So, doesn't that make Mandy a ... how you say ... accomplice?'

'Nah. She's way too smart for that. The only connection between Mandy and Dempsey will be that she's writing his memoirs. That's justification for the link between them, and no one will look any further.'

'Do you think she knew what Dempsey was planning to do?'

'Again, you'd have to ask her that one, *cariño*. Does it even matter?'

So it's at this point that I look up and see these three hombres step onto the beach from the Paseo Maritimo. They look ridiculously conspicuous in their black suits and ties, white shirts and Ray-Bans, and there's not a pair of eyes on the beach that's not trained on them.

Two of them are massive, shaven-headed and muscle-bound. The third is smaller, going bald at the front but with greasy black hair tied back in a ponytail, and I surmise that by dint of spending less time in the gym, he's the brains of the outfit.

I have to make two decisions, and I do not have the luxury of time to work through the pros and cons. The first is more straightforward than the second.

'Maria,' I go, 'see those three hombres?'

She nods.

'I'm going to be abducted in a minute, and I'm going to ask you to do something that may implicate you in this. Just say no, and I'll respect your decision. I promise I won't try to dissuade you.'

She reads my mind.

'You want me to take the photos?'

'Yep … please. I need more time, and I need to arrange some insurance. If Nikolaev gets hold of these, it's game over.'

'Sure. I have no problem with that, Malone.'

I'd have been surprised if she did. The other thing Maria has, in addition to delightful breasts, is the backbone to hold them up.

'I need you to go to my villa and put them in the safe.' I grab a pen from my man bag and scribble the combination number on the newspaper. 'Make sure you're not followed. If there's even the hint of suspicion that you're being watched, destroy them … burn them.'

They're less than a hundred metres away now, but they've not spotted me yet. I reckon I have thirty seconds, a minute at most. There's a bustle of activity as the black fellas dash for the sanctity of the toilets when a cop car cruises past. But this time it stops, two cops get out – one male, the other female – and suddenly they're on the beach advancing towards the Africans who now shoulder their sacks of knock-off merchandise and leg it like they're in the final of the four hundred metres. Truth be told, I've not seen this before, but it couldn't happen at a better time.

The suits clock them, but Baldspot-Ponytail's not to

be deterred, so they advance steadily further down the beach towards me.

Time's running out: unless I can create a diversion, I'm going to be lifted.

I know now exactly what I must do.

THIRTY-TWO

TODAY, 11.27

So it's at this point that three things happen.

First, I tell Maria to get the hell out of here before Baldspot-Ponytail and his amigos clock us. She needs no further encouragement, grabs the newspaper concealing the envelope with the photos, stuffs it into her beach bag, and she's gone.

The goons are fifty metres away when they spot me. But like true professionals, they don't let on and continue to saunter in my direction as if it's the most normal thing in the world to stroll onto a beach on a Sunday morning dressed as undertakers who sell drugs in their spare time.

But human nature being as it is, I note that most people have now lost interest and have gone back to reading, listening to music, drinking beer, surreptitiously scratching sweaty body parts, and other habitual beach-time diversions, so nobody even notices what happens next.

And that's when I call Gora over. True to form, he lollops enthusiastically towards me like a Labrador after food, and I can't help feeling terrible about what I'm about to do. But I've weighed up the options and, despicable as this may be, it is my least bad plan.

The proximity of the two cops is the key to this. They've given up their half-hearted pursuit of the black fellas and are still only twenty metres away, so I figure it would be virtually impossible for them to miss what I am about to do.

Of course, with hindsight, I should have known better than to rely on Spanish cops being of any actual use without the intervention of a substantial amount of euro.

'Gora,' I go, 'could you bring me over one of those wee plastic tables, amigo?'

He obliges, fetches one and sets the thing between us. I need the table because Gora is considerably taller than I am, and I really need to get this right; but I figure it's bound to work because he hasn't a baldy about what's about to happen.

The first part almost works out better than I could have hoped for. In a flash I'm standing on the table, with my hands – for balance and purchase – placed on Gora's shoulders. Nanoseconds later, and despite not having had this kind of engagement for a considerable length of time, I deliver the sweetest of headbutts to the bridge of his nose, and he goes down like a shot cow, totally unconscious.

I'm torn between concern for the unfortunate Gora and admiring my handiwork, when I realise two things: firstly, that the cops are completely oblivious to the incident, as the male cop is now gazing longingly into the eyes of the female cop, who has no interest in him whatever. And secondly, Baldspot-Ponytail has worked out exactly what I'm attempting to do; and here I am, still on the table like the Fat Controller, when the three hombres surround me.

Rarely has a plan failed so spectacularly, particularly as I realise that yelling for help is unlikely to improve the situation as the cops are now headed back towards their car.

'Mister Malone,' says Baldspot-Ponytail, 'my boss wants to have some words with you.'

So off the table I get, noticing that Gora is slowly regaining consciousness and is making strange gurgling noises, the redness of his blood contrasting the blackness of his skin before turning the sand a mottled red.

'You can do this the hard way, or you can come with us the difficult way,' he adds in an accent I'm guessing situates him somewhere west of the Volga.

Clearly, he's not impressed with my felling of Gora.

'How about I do it the easy way?' I suggest. 'I assume there is one?'

In my pomp, even armed only in my Speedos, I'd have fancied my chances of taking out at least two of them – I'd target the more intelligent-looking of the two slapheads first, then take out Baldspot-Ponytail. But, as Rwoopardo pointed out, I'm not in my prime, and resistance is only going to make things worse. And if I hadn't laid him out cold – a plan that totally backfired – I could perhaps have counted on Gora for a modicum of assistance, but now I'll be lucky if he'll even hire me a sunbed again.

'The easy way is for you to get dressed and come with us. Look, we don't want trouble. Mr Nikolaev is a reasonable man. He only wants to ask you questions, not to extract your teeth.'

'I didn't realise that he's a dentist,' I go. The two slapheads, on Baldspot-Ponytail's cue, start to chuckle at this, and soon we're all having a good old laugh at my attempt at humour.

'And I didn't realise that you are a comedian, Mr Malone,' he replies, 'in addition to being such a famous writer,' he adds, making no attempt to conceal the sarcasm.

I start to gather up my clothes.

'Okay if I get changed in the toilet?'

'Be my guest.' He unbuttons his jacket to reveal a pistol tucked into his waistband. 'But don't try anything stupid.'

Gora is getting to his feet like Bambi, and there's still a considerable amount of blood pouring from his nose. For an instant this attracts the goons' attention and I'm sorely tempted to make a lunge for Baldspot-Ponytail's pistol, but then I realise that holding them at gunpoint would only make a bad situation worse.

For now, the best thing I can do is to comply.

And then, with Gora muttering and giving me filthies as I walk towards Pepe's toilet, a ghost of an idea occurs to me, and I begin to construct the semblance of a plan.

THIRTY-THREE

TODAY – I HAVE NO IDEA OF THE TIME

I regain consciousness to find that I'm tied to a chair in a darkened room.

Shafts of dust-speckled sunlight are permeating what I initially take to be shutters, but as the fog clears from my brain, I can see they are in fact wooden batons nailed crudely across the window to prevent entry or – I suspect, more accurately – exit.

Further inspection of my environment reveals two things: I am – once again – incarcerated in some sort of barn; the rough earthen floor, the smell of decay and the lingering odour from the recent presence of animals bombard my senses.

And my second observation is that I am alone.

There's a cloth tied over my nose and mouth from which I detect the unmistakable sickly-sweet smell of chloroform.

And then I start to remember.

***

We'd walked back to the car park where I'd parked the Porsche and where they'd left their limo.

The lot is deserted, and I pretty much know what's going to happen next – I'm either going to be knocked out or drugged, and I'm a little surprised when Baldspot-Ponytail produces a bottle which is actually labelled 'chloroform' and begins to pour the liquid onto his handkerchief.

'I thought that stuff went out of fashion back in Jack the Ripper's time,' I go.

'Who is this Jack the Ripper, Mr Malone? Is he one of your imaginary characters?'

'Never mind,' I reply, and then a more salient thought occurs to me. 'I suppose you know how much of that stuff to use? Because if you overdose me on it, Mr Nikolaev is going to have to wait a considerable length of time before I'm in any condition to answer anything. Maybe even forever.'

Then I try a little bullshit. 'And by the way … my lawyer knows that you've abducted me, as an associate has sent photographs of the three of you marching me off the beach.'

'No one has been abducted, Mr Malone. You walked off the beach with us at your own volition, and there is no evidence to the contrary.'

Fair point.

So he looks at the bottle, and then he looks at me, as if trying to weigh up how much of the stuff he should pour onto the rag. Clearly, he hasn't got a baldy and then realises the flaw in the plan; if he delivers me to

Nikolaev either seriously incapacitated or dead, he's going to be out of a job – at the very least.

'Okay,' he goes, 'so … you know how much of this to use?'

I nod.

Then he actually hands me the handkerchief and the bottle.

Now let me tell you something here, amigo. Back in the day when I taught creative writing, I would fail – and I'm talking 'fail' here, and not some namby-pamby 'refer' which meant it could be amended and handed in again – a student's assignment if he dared to use the word 'surreal'. But I'm now going to break one of my fundamental rules and use it here, because this situation is so farcically bizarre as to actually be surreal.

'Let me see if I've got this right?' I go. 'You want me to take personal responsibility for self-administration of a potentially lethal dose of anaesthetic so that you can – I'm guessing here – bundle me into the boot of your car and …'

'How about we just knock him out, Vlad?' says the less intelligent of the two slapheads.

'How about you just shut the fuck up, Boris? And don't use my name, you moron.'

So that tells me that Baldspot-Ponytail – aka Vlad – is clearly not so cool under pressure, and once again I'm tempted to try my arm, particularly as I've been gifted a bottle of chloroform which, as you'd imagine, can do serious damage to the eyes.

But once again my instincts tell me that I will need to

confront Nikolaev at some point, and sooner is almost certainly better than later, when I figure Dempsey will have played his ace card and delivered the photos.

So what I do is make pretence of pouring the liquid onto the already saturated handkerchief, then hand the bottle and the rag back to Vlad.

And you know how much is a safe dose, I suppose?

In fact, I do. In the course of researching a previous work of filth, I learned that 100 ml is enough to put an adult to 'sleep'. Handkerchief exposure obviously isn't as well controlled as contact during a medical procedure, and the potential for over-exposure is thus increased. But if the hanky is removed after unconsciousness occurs, and if there is no subsequent exposure to additional chloroform, it's not likely that this amount would be fatal to most people.

But they don't know this; nor do they know that it takes around five minutes to render the victim unconscious, so I figure that as long as my hands aren't tied, I'll be able to remove the hanky once they dump me in the boot of the car.

And so this is exactly what happens: I tie the handkerchief over my own mouth and nose, so I look like Jesse James without a bank to rob, then I feign instant unconsciousness and slump dramatically to the floor of the car park.

I'm then manhandled into the boot of the Merc and the lid is slammed, casting my world into blackness. I immediately remove the handkerchief – which by now is making me feel both nauseous and lightheaded, as the gormless Vlad has saturated the thing with enough chloroform to stun an elephant.

And then I play my master card. Although the goons have taken my iPhone 6, they didn't bother to carry out more than a superficial body search, so I still have my iPhone SE secreted in my underpants: an old boarding school trick we used to conceal cigarettes. So I take it out, go into Google Maps, which displays my current location, and send a link to Maria via 'Share Location'.

And then I text Maria, instructing her to call Robocop – who acerbically left a business card, just in case the dead girl should turn up again – if she hasn't heard from me within three hours.

We've been travelling at considerable speed for around ten minutes, and it's then I note that we've just passed Calahonda, which surprises me as I'd expected that Mr Big would have his HQ somewhere in the region of Puerto Banús; and this just goes to show that you can't believe everything you read in the papers.

So it's when we turn off the A-7 a few minutes later at Fuengirola and head inland towards Mijas that I remember – according to the paper – the Russians were also raided at Mijas in Operation Oligarch, and so this is where we must be headed.

Now I don't know if you've ever been bundled into the boot of a car on a hot day, amigo, but I can tell you it's not a pleasant experience. A combination of heat and inhalation of chloroform has brought me to the threshold of unconsciousness, and I know what I must do before this happens.

Half an hour has elapsed; we've passed through Mijas and are climbing into the hills on the A-368. The car brakes and turns off to the left, and now we're moving rapidly down what I imagine to be a farm track, as I'm thrown around in the boot like a sock in a tumble dryer.

The limo slows and comes to a stop, so this is my cue to return my phone to my underpants and replace the hanky over my mouth and nose.

And this, amigo, is the last thing I remember until I come round in the barn.

THIRTY-FOUR

TODAY – AGAIN ... I HAVE NO IDEA OF THE TIME

So, I've just come round and recalled these events when I'm aware of a commotion outside.

The door opens and four hombres come in, one carrying a chair, two others carrying a sturdy-looking table, and the fourth has an anglepoise lamp in one hand and something resembling a toolkit in the other.

Vlad puts the chair close to the window, Boris and the other slaphead place the table in front of it, and the fourth man, who I now recognise as Feliks – Mercedes' part-time boyfriend – puts the toolkit and lamp on the table, plugs the wire into an adjacent socket and turns it on.

Vlad then adds to the drama by directing the light into my face, and all four take up their positions behind the chair, like footballers facing a free kick.

Feliks is the tallest and most athletically built of the four; he's dressed in a black T-shirt and cut-off denim shorts, and looks distinctly uncomfortable. I get the feeling that this is not his idea of how best to pass a

Sunday morning, and that he is not here entirely by choice.

'Hey, Feliks – good to see a friendly face,' I mumble through the handkerchief, and he looks away, which proves my theory.

No one speaks.

'So, what are we waiting for?' I ask, all bravado. 'All we need now is Mr Big.'

'Mr Nikolaev will be here in a moment,' Vlad replies. 'And if I may give one piece of advice, Mr Malone, it would be not to refer to him as "Mr Big".'

'I'll take that on advisement, Vlad, but thank you for your concern.' Just then, the door opens and in he comes. Now, as you know, amigo, I'd never met Nikolaev before, nor even seen photos of him, so he's not quite what I'm expecting. Maybe I don't know what I'm expecting? Perhaps a pumped-up version of Vladimir Putin stripped to the waist, riding a brown bear and pointing at me with customary Muscovite charm. And maybe it was just the lingering effects of the chloroform that projects these images into my mind, but the Nikolaev that enters the room is as far removed from my expectations as the England football team are from ever winning the World Cup again. Think Danny DeVito and you'd not be far wrong.

He's probably slightly taller, maybe nudging five four, but with the same wild wings of hair straddling his bald pate, the horn-rimmed glasses that magnify his eyes so they look as if they're swimming in a fishbowl, and the menacingly pouting smile.

He's smartly dressed in chinos, expensive-looking brothel creepers and a black Boss T-shirt, a huge Rolex strapped to his right wrist.

But there's something about him, I'll have to admit – something that demands instant respect.

Some men – and indeed women … Thatcher, who I met on one occasion, was a particularly good example – have an aura, a charisma about them, so that no matter how ridiculous their appearance, you instantly know that you really do need to take them seriously.

Hitler was another.

The mood changes the instant he enters the room.

Vlad is no longer in charge.

Nikolaev lowers his spherical frame towards the chair, and Vlad obsequiously shuffles it forward.

Nikolaev stares at me and says nothing.

I return his stare, then he leans forward, places his elbows on the table, steeples his hands and rests his chin on his forefingers. He clicks his fingers and Vlad is there again, handing him something. At first, I think it's a knife, then I realise it's a cigar. Boris steps forward, flicks a lighter, and there he is, puffing away on a massive Cuban.

Instantly the room smells better.

This little charade, of course, has all been carefully choreographed to scare the proverbial shit out of me, and truth be told, it pretty much works.

'Mr Malone,' he goes, in a voice that could belong to Danny DeVito with a Russian accent, 'I am sorry for the manner of your conveyance here.'

'Think nothing of it,' I go. 'It's not every day I get chauffeur-driven in the boot of a limo.'

We all have a bit of a chuckle at this.

'Untie him, Boris,' he goes, 'and remove that *thing* from his face.'

Boris obliges, and I shake my wrists to get the blood moving.

'Mr Nikolaev, I presume,' I say. 'I've read a lot about you.' I cross my legs and try to make myself look comfortable. 'What can I do for you?'

He puffs on the cigar, which has by now all but eliminated the lingering smell of chloroform.

'I understand, Mr Malone, that you were with my daughter last night.'

'That's correct. She asked me for editorial comment on a manuscript she'd written. I read it last week, and we had dinner last night in The Orange Tree. I can highly recommend it; the steak's excellent.'

'And after dinner?'

If I've learned one thing about lying, amigo, it's this: when you have to lie, keep your narrative as close to the truth as you can.

This is for two reasons – first, so that it's believable, and second, so that you can remember it.

'Okay ... we had a drink or two, then we went back to my villa. We spent the night together.'

And then he actually laughs?

So, I realise that either I'm still unconscious from the chloroform, or I've somehow been transported through time and space to some parallel reality, as I haven't got a

231

fucking baldy why he should find it amusing that I have had sex with his twenty-year-old daughter.

'Perhaps, in your fantasy, you did, Mr Malone.'

I uncross my legs and sit up. Stunned by this latest twist of events, I can no longer feign comfort. I haven't imagined this, amigo, or have I? Am I going mad? I know what I woke to this morning; the memory of mopping up the girl's blood will stay with me forever. And anyway, there are the photos to prove it … aren't there?

'Natasha left the Moët Bar a few moments before you, Mr Malone. One of my staff drove her home. I do not know who you spent the night with, but it most certainly was not Natasha.' He puffs on the cigar. 'Which is just as well for you.'

And with that, the door opens, and in walks Natasha, who is – in every sense of the word – very much alive.

THIRTY-FIVE

TODAY

So as my brain is digesting the news that Natasha is not dead, and is therefore not the girl I work up next to – who most certainly was dead – she flounces across the room and slaps me as hard as she can across the face; not once, but twice.

It bloody well hurts.

I can see a third slap coming, mightier than the others, but then she has a change of mind and pulls her arm back and forms a fist, and there's no mistaking exactly where that fist is headed, until her father intervenes.

'Natasha,' he commands. His voice is soft but authoritative.

The fist, which I can see is in fact shaking, freezes midway between her shoulder and my face, and I'm left wondering two things: first, whether I would have ducked the blow or taken it on the chin, like a man who has nothing to fear from being punched by a girl.

And the second thing I'm wondering is what the fuck have I done to deserve this? The girl's dander is clearly up and she is seriously pissed off with me, and I have absolutely no idea why.

But I think I'm about to find out, and I can't for the life of me see the explanation improving my prospects of getting out of here in one piece.

And then I note eye contact between Nikolaev and his daughter and the slightest of nods as he flicks cigar ash on the floor, and before I can react, her fist has slammed into my temple and, for the second time this morning, my world turns black.

THIRTY-SIX

LAST NIGHT

The Orange Tree, if you don't know it, is unequivocally the best restaurant in Marbella.

Aside from being a little enclave for expat Brits and itinerant Irish where I have yet to hear Spanish spoken, it has a spectacularly simple menu, and one that thankfully never changes. And Aileen, the Irish maître d', knows exactly what I'm going to order before my bum even hits the seat, so I don't have to bother looking at the menu.

I try to avoid eating here with women I intend to bed because Aileen has a thing for me, and although she makes Richie McCaw look like Miss World, it pays more dividends to keep that candle burning than it would to snuff it out.

But as I don't intend to bed Ms Nikolaeva, and I am here at her invitation and at her expense, I feel that I can waive the rule on this occasion.

Besides, the booking is in her name, and I introduce her to Aileen as a 'business associate', which is pretty much correct.

So how does she manage to escape your clutches … Ms Nikolaeva? After all, she's within your 'age range', isn't she?

Okay, amigo, this is for two reasons. First, because this *is* a business relationship, and I do happen to share the view that it's improper to mix business with pleasure – at least when it comes to bedroom time.

And the second?

And the second is that I have made a pact with myself that I will do my utmost to be faithful to Sam. Amigo, I did much soul-searching after the Ukrainian Incident, and, if anything, it's made me realise that this was just a blip. I really am in love with her, and the thought of losing her because of some idle flirtation is unimaginable. And as any residual love I may have harboured for Mandy is evaporating faster than …

A bit more than a flirtation, wasn't it? She saw the photos.

Yeah, well, that's all in the past now.

And, attractive as Ms Nikolaeva is, regretfully her embroidered Louis Vuitton black silk muslin glitter dress is going to remain swathed around her delectable body until she removes it in the seclusion of her own bedroom.

'So, what do you think?' she asks as we clink glasses and I sip the Veuve Clicquot Yellow Label Champán con crianza I ordered at her expense.

'What do I think?' Christ, she really is a looker. I prolong the moment of suspense and gaze provocatively into her deep green eyes. 'I think it's utterly brilliant.' I smile my George Clooney smile which rarely fails to melt ice. Of course, I'm not going to tell her that it was me who laid the foundations for this magnificent edifice of filth. 'For my money, it's a bestseller. Probably make the Waterstones monthly top ten ... maybe even higher. And that's not a bad place to kick off from.'

'Seriously?' she says, and sips her drink. She's clearly both surprised and thrilled, and consequently looks at me in a way that tells me that I have a better-than-average chance of sleeping with her if I want to. Of course, I have no intention of following up this non-verbal solicitation, but it at least negates her previous 'attractive for an older guy' comment.

And so we chat through the practicalities of publication. It is so well-written, I tell her, that I imagine it would only require a light edit, and consequently the timing is perfect, as it could be in the shops for Super Thursday.

What's Super Thursday?

Super Thursday, amigo, is the second Thursday in October and the day when publishers release many of the big titles expected to greet eager readers and their elderly relatives on 25 December. It's pretty much the publishing industry's equivalent of Black Friday.

We don't bother with a starter. Aileen always offers her favoured guests a small bowl of soup and the homemade bread of the day, so we have this then dive into the main course.

So, I finish my last mouthful of prime South Devon fillet steak with brandy and green peppercorn sauce, put my cutlery down and turn to business.

'So, Natasha, how do you see this working out for each of us?'

'How about eighty–twenty, as I've done all the work?'

'That's extremely generous of you, but I couldn't possibly accept it.' This is, of course, amigo, a bluff to throw her off guard. 'As you say, you've done most of the writing so … I was thinking more like, I don't know … maybe fifty–fifty?'

She laughs.

'No, Malone. I get eighty per cent, and you get twenty. You have had to do absolutely nothing for this. It's a pretty good deal for you. Take it or leave it.'

'Let me tell you something, Natasha.' I lean forward, my arms on the table, and I flash the George Clooney once again; only this time it melts no ice, and I know I'm up against a serious player here. She may only be twenty, but she's clearly chiselled from granite. 'You want this deal because you need to buy into my brand to publish this book. And you want this for three reasons: first, because my brand will guarantee publication and a high volume of sales. Second, because my publishing house will take care of everything, once I have signed this off. And third, because you don't want – and you would, in any case, have difficulty – to publish *Seven Days* under your own name. And should you try to publish it under a pseudonym – brilliantly written as it is – I can promise you it will end up on any number of slush piles. And this is because the sad thing about the publishing industry is that thousands of well-written

MSs end up there every day because neither agents nor publishers want to take a punt on a nobody without having a very good reason to do so. So, my final offer is that I take forty per cent and you get sixty. And that, my dear, is an offer embossed with gilt-edged generosity. Take it or leave it.'

I leave her to reflect on this.

I would in fact settle for thirty per cent because this will sell like the proverbial hotcakes; although, truth be told, Super Thursday may be slightly irrelevant, as *Seven Days* is hardly the sort of literary present that Great-Auntie Noreen should be unwrapping between the turkey and the Queen's Speech.

But I'm also thinking that there's almost certainly a movie deal nailed onto this, so I chuck this in for a sweetener.

'Tell you what,' I go. She's still mulling it over as Aileen clears the table and asks if we'd like to see the dessert menu. She shoots me a filthy, as she's clearly convinced that the only business I'm conducting with Natasha is negotiating access to what lies beneath her Louis Vuitton number. '*Seven Days* will almost certainly attract a movie deal. This is where the real money is to be made, provided we keep it 'in-house'. Just look at *Gone Girl* – Gillian Flynn did pretty well out of the book, but she hit the actual jackpot by insisting on writing the screenplay ... and that's what we will do. I'll write it, as I've written screenplays before' – which is actually true, amigo ... I've written two, and they both bombed – 'and you can have editorial veto. Now,

I really can't say fairer than that, can I?'

Aileen serves coffee, a Tia Maria for Natasha and a cognac for me.

'Okay,' she goes eventually, as I knew she would. She flashes a delightfully provocative smile, 'Okay, so we've got a deal – I get sixty per cent from all publication and film rights, and you get forty.'

'Agreed.'

The handshake is more natural this time.

We raise glasses and clink.

By my calculation, I have just made somewhere in the region of fifteen to twenty million dollars, and all for doing virtually nothing. I'm seated opposite an incredibly beautiful young woman who wants to sleep with me, but I have the willpower to reluctantly blow her out.

I'm not sure that life can get much better, amigo?

THIRTY-SEVEN

TODAY

Once again I come round in a darkened room, with my head throbbing from Natasha's left hook.

I instantly know it's the same murky barn from the lingering smell of cigar smoke, and for a minute I get a sense of déjà vu – until I realise that I'm on my own, and this time I've not been tied up.

The table and chair are still here, as is the anglepoise, which has been turned off, but the toolbox has gone, and I feel a strange sense of relief at this because I had my suspicions that its contents had not been obtained for the express purpose of actually fixing things?

So why have you been left alone? And where have they gone?

That's what I'm wondering, amigo. I was kind of unfinished business following my KO, so I get the sense that something ... maybe something quite dramatic must have happened to interrupt my 'interview'? I'm guessing here, but I figure if this hadn't occurred, the probable progression was for one of the goons to douse me with cold water to bring me round, and for Nikolaev to continue with whatever it was he had in mind when he ordered my abduction, probably with the aid of his thugs and the contents of the toolbox.

So my mind drifts back to last night, which is where it had been as I was coming round, and three things occur to me.

The first is that I have absolutely no idea what has happened to engender Natasha's seismic mood swing. Last thing I remember with any clarity is that we're sitting in the Moët enjoying a drink and she has one hand on my knee, and I'm feeling my resolve weaken, but keep it I just about do … and that's where I remember the second thing – there's something incredibly familiar about her.

It's like I've met her before?

You know when this happens? You see a face in a crowd or a bar that you're sure you recognise, and you spend hours racking your brain before you eventually concede that you're not going to get to the bottom of this because you've probably not met her before, and there are just certain physical or maybe behavioural similarities that you can't connect to an actual person that you know.

And this is the case here because I can visualise her face now, and I'm still trying to work out why it looks so familiar?

But I can't, and that's when the third thing strikes me – Natasha's Louis Vuitton number was black, and the dress she's wearing in Maria's photos is white. This means that either Natasha had a white dress stowed in her Chanel purse that she magically changed into – or the girl in Maria's photos is not Natasha.

And that prompts one further question—

Two, actually – if you ask me.

Well, amigo, I wasn't asking you, but as you clearly want to intercede, please enlighten me?

What was Maria doing there, and why did she take photos of you and the girl?

Correctomundo.

THIRTY-EIGHT

TODAY

And with this thought, the door opens and in comes the author of my physical discomfort, who is also – presumably – now my erstwhile business partner.

Now, I can honestly say that, even with extreme levels of provocation, I have never hit a girl … never even come close. But I'm thinking that her left hook was practised to the extent that there could just be a first time, should she show signs of further hostile action.

The efficacy of the headbutt I delivered to the hapless Gora has given me assurance that I've not entirely lost my touch, and this will be my chosen method of self-defence, should the need arise.

So I stay seated, but ready myself to stand and create the power-base from which I will fell her, when I sense that her disposition has changed and, thankfully, physical force will not be necessary.

She parks her bum on the edge of the table, crosses her slender legs – this morning clad in Gucci Genius Jeans – and folds her arms across her ample chest. And then she smiles at me, and once again I'm wondering if I've slipped back into that parallel reality, and if it wasn't for my aching head I'd be convinced that I'd imagined the punch.

'Why the …?' I go.

'Why the heck did I punch you?' She's still smiling, but I'm not yet entirely convinced of the sincerity of her smile. 'I'm sorry, Malone. It turns out I was wrong. I apologise.'

'Wrong about what?'

'Wrong about it being you who drugged me.'

'I'm still none the wiser' I reply. 'You see, one minute we're having a drink, celebrating our deal, then …' I hesitate. I don't want to go down the road of waking up next to the dead girl.

But I don't have to.

'Then you wake up next to a girl who looks a lot like me and who's had her throat cut?'

There's silence for a moment as I digest this.

'How the fuck do you know about that?'

'I know about that because while you were having your small sleep, some photos were delivered.'

'Delivered? What photos?' I don't know why I ask this because I know very well that these will not be holiday snaps. 'And who the hell delivered them?'

I'm really not liking the way this is going, as the appearance of the photos can only be attributable to one of two people: Dempsey – and I'm thinking he's the obvious candidate – or … I really hate this thought to even cross my mind once again this morning, but cross it, it does – I gave Maria the photos I'd received, and, for whatever motives, this could just possibly be her.

'Don't know. Feliks, one of my father's men, got an anonymous call telling him to look for an envelope in the mailbox by the entrance.'

'Fuck,' I go.

'Does it actually matter who delivered it?'

'It does to me.'

Because now I know who delivered it. There's only one person, other than those in this hacienda, who knows where I am.

And that person doesn't know that Natasha Nikolaeva was not the corpse I woke up next to this morning.

But what really matters, and what I urgently need to find out, is why she delivered it.

THIRTY-NINE

TODAY, 13.04

So now we're sitting in the living room of Nikolaev's Puerto Banús gaff, and both the environment and the atmosphere couldn't be more different.

This time, I'd been politely requested to put myself into the boot of the limo without the aid of chloroform and, as I consider this to be a perfectly reasonable request, I obliged.

I know we're in Puerto Banús because I'm able to follow our journey using Google Maps on my secreted phone; plus, all I can see beyond the massive infinity pool is sea.

Let me tell you about the living room first.

I've never seen anything like it. It's huge. Ikea could set up a store in here and still have room for a meatball factory. Two external walls consist entirely of glass, which is the same configuration as in my villa; only there's about an acre more glass.

Then there's the furniture, which is Parker Knoll-meets-Roche Bobois and appears to have been chosen by someone who was either drunk or colour-blind.

And as for the decor, everything is boy-made-good bling. My eye catches a massive glass coffee table supported by two black squatting nudes and it takes me a minute to realise that they are actually made of ebony.

Then there's this colossal, weird ceramic white bulldog wearing sunglasses in one corner and – I kid you not – a life-sized elephant with an inflatable doll on its back in another.

Here is a triumph of bad taste in interior design such as I've never seen before – even in Ireland – and that's quite a challenge. Rococo rubs shoulders with over-the-top baroque, while the overall ambiance hums art deco fused with Wild West music hall. It goes without saying that the television is the size of a screen you'd find at a rock concert, and the floor is tiled with black and white squares so you get the impression that you're walking across a very large chess board.

Nikolaev is sitting in an oversized armchair that has the effect of making him look even smaller than he is, puffing on another massive cigar.

Natasha is standing by the fireplace, her elbow resting on the black marble mantelpiece, and as she's a good foot taller than Nikolaev – and bears absolutely no resemblance to him – I'm left wondering how on earth he managed to sire this beauty? And then, there's still something about her … something familiar that I can't quite put my finger on?

I'm seated on one end of a settee that a 747 could land on and, aside from the Nikolaevs, the only other person in the room is Vlad.

No one says anything for an age, so I break the silence.

'Well this is all very nice and cosy, Nikolaev, but do you think you could possibly tell me what's going on?'

Now I'm no expert in body language, but I've been in enough powder keg situations to sense when things can suddenly kick off, and there's a palpable air of tension in this ridiculously tasteless room. I look at Natasha and she's scowling at her father, and Vlad doesn't look too comfortable either.

'It would appear, Mr Malone,' says Nikolaev eventually, 'that there is someone who has hostile intentions towards you.'

'No shit?' I reply.

It would be easier to make a list of people who *don't* have hostile intentions towards me, but I keep this to myself.

Nikolaev is unmoved by this.

'It would also appear,' he says, 'that this … someone, who has hostile intentions towards you, also is intent on harming my family.'

'Yeah … well I figure you don't need to look too far to work out who that is. From what I've heard, you've upset a certain Mr Dempsey, and I have personal experience of how he reacts when he's upset. And it's not a pleasant experience, I can tell you.'

'And what, may I ask, did you do to incur his anger?'

I figure I've nothing to lose and I tell them, and Natasha actually laughs? At least it lowers the tension to defcon two.

'Fucking hell, Malone,' she goes. 'Why the heck did you write it?'

'I've asked myself that same question a few times today,' I reply. 'It seemed a good idea at the time; both my agent and my publisher loved it. And, to be fair, it was solidly written and sold pretty well. I just didn't know that he was going to do time when I wrote it. He used to be pretty much untouchable, back in the day.' I didn't know that my sociopathic bitch of an ex was going to shop me either, but I keep quiet about this.

And then a thought occurs to me.

'Can I see the photos?' I ask Nikolaev, who thinks about this for a moment, then clicks his fingers at Vlad who leaves the room and returns with the manila envelope. He looks at Nikolaev, who nods in my direction, and then hands them to me.

I already know who's delivered the photos, but if she's been clever she will have left the one with the inscription on the back with the others, because this threat links them to Dempsey. Although, for the life of me I don't know why her 'intervention' appears to have the intent of stirring things up between the Russians and the Irish. But if – and I'm pretty sure that it was – Dempsey had been responsible for delivery of the photos, the one with the inscription would have been removed because his intention would be to frame me for the murder of the girl in my bed. Who was, as far as he was aware, Natasha Nikolaeva.

I go through the photos slowly and methodically, trying to blank out the grossness of the content. Christ, the girl really is the spit of Natasha and I'm wondering how this is possible, but that's not really the issue right now.

The issue right now is this: whoever murdered the girl clearly also took the photos, and whoever did this may not be the person I had assumed it to be. And this doesn't bear thinking about.

But think about it I must, because there, on the back of the last photo, is the inscription.

FORTY

TODAY, 13.57

Sometimes, amigo, one has to make a pact with the devil in order to stay in the game, and this is precisely what I have just done.

There's a certain irony about an Irishman joining forces with a Russian to fight another Irishman, but the deal Natasha floats and her father agrees to makes sound strategic sense, and I'm beginning to suspect that this is the prime reason that I was abducted.

I'm also beginning to comprehend where the brains are behind the Russian operation, and I'm not sure whether this is a good thing; but for now, it's not that important.

So, I'm back home alone at my villa – apart, that is, from the battalion of Russian gangsters secreted in concealment points in and around my property – and I'm waiting for Dempsey's men to lift me.

The Russians are supposedly here for insurance … in case things don't go to plan. Although, truth be told, I don't trust Nikolaev as far as I could chuck him, and it wouldn't surprise me if this turned into the shootout at the O.K. Corral, with my villa doubling as Tombstone, Arizona.

Of course, there's no telling how long this stakeout will take, but I'm guessing it'll be sooner rather than later because Feliks – whose main usefulness to Nikolaev's organisation appears to be that he's some sort of resident stool pigeon – knows one of Dempsey's men and has phoned him to tell him where I am. Of course, this information is given in exchange for the promise of a large amount of euro, to make the tip-off more convincing.

So just exactly what is this master plan?

Ah, you're still there, amigo? I thought you'd bailed by now.

Still here … but only just. One minute you're in Nikolaev's place, and now you're back home – I'm sure we'd all like to know how you achieved that quantum leap.

Oh, that. Okay, but I can't go into detail right now, as there is something I need to find out, and also something I need to do while I still have the opportunity.

And so I ask the Alexa gismo to turn on Talk Radio Europe, a local station that broadcasts in English and will have an on-the-hour news bulletin coming up.

And sure enough, it does, and the first news item is what I was hoping not to hear.

A man walking his dog discovered the body of a woman this morning on a piece of derelict land on the outskirts on San Pedro. The woman, who, the National Police have identified as Olga Antonova, a twenty-two-year-old Russian sex worker, is believed to have had her throat cut and to have been dead for several hours before her body was discovered. Police believe that a bread knife found in close proximity to the body could be the murder weapon. In a brief statement, Chief Inspector Mateo López refused to speculate that the knife might have been placed there deliberately by a third party wishing to identify the murderer. Señor López said: "We are currently exploring all lines of enquiry. We will know more when the autopsy results are received, but so far evidence suggests that the murder was committed elsewhere, and the body was dumped in San Pedro some time later. We are also awaiting the forensic report on the bread knife, but we have been able to obtain clear fingerprints from the knife and we hope that this will shortly lead to an arrest. In the meantime, if any members of the public have any information …"

Blah-de-fucking-blah.

And so, for the third time today, I'm going to have to phone a friend.

FORTY-ONE

TODAY, 14.05

Sam picks up on the second ring.

'Malone?' she says, all surprised, which is probably fair enough as I don't think I've ever rung her twice in one day. 'Okay ... you're either bored, in hospital or ...'

'Sam – I need your help. I am about to be in some serious fucking shit.'

And so, I tell her everything.

When I'm finished, she says nothing for an age and I wonder if she's even heard any of it, and then I hear her sigh.

'You do realise that you brought all this on yourself, don't you?'

There you go – girlfriend experience.

'That's not really the point right now, is it?' The hardness in her voice that was the hallmark of our previous conversation has gone, and I can tell that she is seriously concerned.

Silence.

'Sam?'

'Malone?'

'I love you, Sam.' And then I don't know what prompts this, because it just pops into my head and I come right out and say it: 'Marry me, will you? If I get through this alive.'

'Malone,' she replies, 'go fuck yourself.'

'Can I take that as a maybe?'

She laughs.

'I'll think about it.'

'Thank you.'

Then she gets all serious again, which is probably for the best because I've now got tears in my eyes, and this really is not a good time to get all emotional.

'So, your plan is to actually get abducted by Dempsey?'

'*Sí*,' I go, 'two abductions in one day, but then Mr Nikolaev is my guardian angel, so nothing—'

'Who?' she goes.

'Yeah, the Russian guy ... Alexei Nikolaev? "Mr Big", except as he's a dead ringer for Danny DeVito, you wouldn't want to call him that.'

I realise I've not mentioned him by name before, so I'm mildly surprised at the consternation in her voice.

'You know him?'

There's a pause.

'Was there a girl there, at his villa? Aged about twenty?'

'Sure ... a tall, good-looking girl. Doesn't look anything like him, luckily for her.'

I'm not sure where this is going, so I keep the book deal arrangement and – naturally – the fact that it was all I could do to keep my hands off her last night, strictly to myself.

'Why?'

Another pause.

'No reason in particular,' she finally says.

The proverbial penny's finally dropped, but before I can pursue this, the line goes dead.

FORTY-TWO

TODAY, 14.22

It occurs to me that physically cutting someone's phone line is a bit last century.

But then I'm forgetting that my overriding memory of Dempsey is that he's something of the clichéd old-school sort of sociopath, and so he's probably done this for two reasons.

The first is to announce his arrival and to generate a frisson of tension, and the second is to tell me that he – or his men – can see me from where they are, somewhere on the other side of my oleander hedge that borders the western boundary of my property, and that he knows I'm using the landline to talk to someone.

Of course, it's unlikely that he'll be getting his hands dirty with the chore of abducting me; this task will have been delegated to his foot soldiers, a psychopathic bunch of goons who progressed into organised crime when shooting and blowing up the Brits was no longer required.

And I can actually see one of his hoods putting a ladder up against the post while another holds it, then climb the thing and cut the wire.

Vlad has given me a two-way radio, which crackles before he utters something indistinguishable, but I don't need him to tell me that it's about to kick off.

And what I'm really hoping is that the Russians play by the rules and don't open the scoring by taking out the Irish contingent.

Of course, in some ways this might not be such a bad thing, unless I get caught in the crossfire; but as I have only counted four of Dempsey's men and Dempsey is certainly not amongst them, this would be a skirmish at best and would serve no purpose other than to spell out to Dempsey that it was a trap and I have been used as bait, and therefore was complicit in the plan.

So I'm hoping good sense will prevail, and while I'm waiting to see if it will or not, there's something else I need to do.

I take out my mobile and call Maria.

Her phone goes straight to voicemail, so I leave a message: 'Maria, it's me. I know you delivered those photos to Nikolaev, and I have absolutely no idea why you did it. Jesus … I thought you were my friend, Maria? Why the fuck did you do it? Okay … I suppose you must have your reasons, but I'd sure as fuck like to hear them. Am I to take it that our friendship has been a sham all along? Anyway, I have some news for you.' I pause and check what's going on outside. Nothing yet … there's an almost eerie lack of activity as both sides ready themselves for action. 'You're probably surprised that I'm making this call, because you'll be expecting Nikolaev to have topped me for being – at the very least – an accessory to his daughter's death. But that's not happened, and the reason that it's not happened, Maria, is that the girl I woke up next to was not Nikolaev's daughter but some unfortunate Russian hooker who just happened to look a lot like her. And if you don't believe me, check the Talk Radio Europe website. I've not got to the bottom of how the girl got substituted for Natasha, but get to the bottom of it I will … and you're pretty close to the top of my list of suspects.'

I ring off, tuck my iPhone SE into my underpants and look up to see four guys carrying assault rifles walk across my lawn towards the entrance as casually as if they were Jehovah's fucking Witnesses carrying bibles.

FORTY-THREE

TODAY, 14.23

The last thing I remember before the carnage begins is a small but not unpleasant vibration in my groin as a text pings.

I pull out my phone because I reckon it's either Sam or Maria, so it's important; although of course it could just be O-fucking-2 telling me that my bill is available to view online.

It's Sam:

On way to airport. Will b at Malaga at 5.30. Try not to do athng stupid til I get there. BTW I will but only if u swear to keep it in your pants. Luv u S Xx

I smile, as I don't think it's my iPhone she's referring to, and a kind of glow like I've never experienced before lights me up and for a second transcends the reality that there are four heavily armed men who are almost at my front door.

Hang on a minute … there aren't any flights to Málaga

from any airport in the North of England on Sunday afternoons. I've just checked.

Jesus. Spare me.

Let me tell you, smart-ass, that for a very reasonable twelve grand you can charter a Learjet from Leeds; and before you suggest that I'm not worth it, this angel has just agreed to marry me, and it would totally scupper her plans if I died.

So anyway, the goons are about to knock on the door, ring the bell or storm right in. But I'll never know which because before this happens, Vlad is out of the bush, moving like a Russian Jason Statham on steroids, and I hear four pops and see a small puff of smoke from a suppressor following each one, as Dempsey's men go down like dominoes.

Three of them are dispatched by a single shot in the back of the head, with clinical accuracy worthy of mention. The fourth manages to turn, face his executioner and raise his rifle, but before he can get a shot off, Vlad plugs him between the eyes.

I have to say that I've not seen anything quite so efficient for a very long time, and if I were still in the mercenary business, I would move heaven and earth to recruit this guy.

Then, just as I'm thinking this, I see a puff of smoke, and I barely have time to register that he has fired another shot when my front window shatters. I feel a blast of wind brush my face, something sharp as a needle grazes my temple and it's 'Goodnight, Sooty' for the third time today.

FORTY-FOUR

TODAY, 15.30

So I come round, and my head feels like I've been in a good old-fashioned rugby game where real men throw punches and not handbags at each other.

I'm lying on a metal-framed cot, and when I try to get up, I realise my left wrist is handcuffed to the bed. There's a bandage around my head from which blood is steadily dripping.

I'm guessing I'd struggle to pass one of Maria's HIAs, and the thought occurs to me that maybe I'm in a hospital; but are patients actually handcuffed to beds in Spanish hospitals? Perhaps they are.

I look around the room, but there's not much to give me a clue as to my location. The bed is against the wall, in the centre of the room. There are a couple of pictures, one of the Pope and one of Christ on the cross, but this is de rigueur everywhere in Spain. There are a few uncomfortable-looking chairs dotted about and a small bedside table, and that's pretty much it apart from a large French window on the left-hand side of the room, beyond which I can see a small terrace.

And then I note that there's a drip in my right arm and I'm wired up to one of those machines that monitors your vital signs – I think they're called – and in the movies, if you mess with them alarms go off everywhere and nurses burst in to see what the fuck you're up to. And this is precisely what I do, and, to my surprise, it achieves the desired outcome.

But unfortunately, in addition to three nurses, one of which I would certainly rattle, in strides the ubiquitous Robocop. And although I'm sufficiently mentally agile to work out that where there are handcuffs, the police cannot be far away, I'm still not sure whether or not I trust this fucker.

Robocop says nothing but pulls up one of the chairs, turns it round and straddles it, all the while giving me one of his trademark withering looks.

The nurses adjust the knobs and buttons that I had fucked about with, the pretty one smiles at me, and then I remember that I have recently had a marriage proposal accepted on the condition that this sort of behaviour is curtailed.

So, you are going to stop flirting?

Amigo, I certainly have that intention.

When they've finished with the machine, the good-looking one removes the bandage, examines my head and dabs some solution on the wound which stings like fuck. It's all I can do not to scream, then the pain eases and she starts to dress the wound.

'*Tuviste mucha suerte*, señor Malone,' she says, and before I can reply, Robocop jumps in.

'She says you were extremely fortunate. But what she didn't tell you is that three millimetres higher and we would not be having this conversation.'

'I know what she fucking well said ... I speak Spanish, you cretin.' I realise that this is probably not the most diplomatic way to begin what will obviously become another inquisition with Robocop, but I'm seriously pissed off that I've been chained to the bed. 'And perhaps you can tell me, Constable, why the fuck I'm shackled to this bed like a common criminal?'

'It's Inspector Jefe. May I remind you that I am a Chief Inspector, and that my name is Mateo López, señor Malone,' he continues, 'as it was this morning, when we first met. And the reason you are chained to the bed like a common criminal is because you are a common criminal. When the medical team determine that you are fit to travel, you will be transported to La Comisaría de Policía in Málaga, where you will be formally charged with the murders of five people. You will then be locked up pending trial, and then, when you are undoubtedly found guilty, you will be incarcerated for a period of time which will almost certainly coincide with the end of your life.'

This is not good news.

'Five people?' I reply feebly. 'Who are these five people? And would you mind telling me how, when and where I'm supposed to have murdered them?'

And it's then that the memory of Vlad dispatching Dempsey's goons filters back, and I'm beginning to see where this is going.

Two of the nurses have left, satisfied that now I'm under Robocop's jurisdiction, I'm not going to fuck about with the monitor again, and the good-looking one mutters something to Robocop which I can't quite make out.

'He can rest as much as he likes once he's in custody,' he replies in Spanish, in what I would call a fairly misogynistic manner, and so off she trots, leaving us alone.

'Señor Malone,' he goes, 'we received an anonymous call informing us that there had been shooting at your property. We arrived to find the bodies of four unarmed men close to the entrance of your villa, and you were lying on your living room floor with this minor head wound, holding the handgun that was used to commit the murders.'

I actually manage to laugh at this?

And the reason I'm immediately suspicious is because no one lives close enough to have heard the sound of supressed gunfire. My nearest neighbour – you may remember me telling you that it was Javier Bardem – happens to be away shooting on location somewhere in Africa.

'Let me tell you something, Inspector López,' I go, 'I imagine that even you will have managed to detect that three of the dead men were killed by a single bullet to the back of the head.'

'Correct.'

'So, unless they walked up my garden path backwards carrying assault rifles, I fail to see – as would a jury, let me tell you – how I could possibly have shot them.'

Well, López, that makes it forty–love, I'm thinking.

'No one was carrying an assault rifle: another figment of your imagination, like the dead girl in your bed ... although perhaps that was not a figment after all, but we'll come to that in a minute. That will be a matter for a jury to decide, whether or not you shot them in the back. But this much we do know: you were in possession of the gun that was used to kill them. The ballistics report has confirmed that the gun in your hand was the murder weapon.'

Hang on a minute ... he wouldn't have had the ballistics report back already?

Well ... that's my initial thought. But then I remember researching this for a work of filth, and in fact, if the Crime Scene Unit is well staffed, it only takes between fifteen to thirty minutes to prepare a report. But if it's not, it can take up to two days, so there's no actual way to tell if he's bullshitting me.

So, I point it out to him that I don't buy this, and he couldn't possibly have had the report so quickly.

He shrugs. If he's bluffing, he's seriously good.

'You, or your legal representative, will naturally receive a copy of the report in due course.'

But I don't think he's looking quite so cocky now, and there's another reason I know for certain that this will be laughed out of court.

Which is?

All in good time, amigo ... remember, I'm a writer, so show – don't tell.

So, I go for game, set and match.

'And then,' I say, 'just for good measure, I use the same gun to shoot myself in the head, I suppose? Because if the four men I had just shot were unarmed, I must have done, mustn't I?'

'We have yet to find the bullet that grazed your head, señor Malone, but yes, what you suggest is quite probably what happened. You certainly would not be the first person to shoot themselves to divert suspicion.'

Now, once again, amigo, at the risk of sounding like a smart-ass myself, I happen to know that even an incompetent CSI team would have found that bullet within minutes. Therefore, my suspicion of Robocop reaches defcon four, as I'm beginning to think he has very good reasons to want the bullet not to be found. Or perhaps he's already found it and pocketed it himself.

'Jesus ... If I'd being trying to divert suspicion from myself, I may well have shot myself in the foot ... or the hand ... or even shot my knee. But not in the head, you idiot, three millimetres away from killing myself.'

'As I've already said, señor Malone, that will be for a jury to decide. In any case, there is the matter of the other victim.'

So entangled in López's web of utter bullshit had I been, I'd forgotten about this.

'And, for the record ... he is?'

'He is a she, señor Malone. This morning a girl was found on some wasteland in San Pedro. Her name is Olga Antonova, and she was a twenty-two-year-old Russian prostitute. Her throat had been slashed by your bread knife ... or, at least, a bread knife on which we found your fingerprints. Which are the same fingerprints as those we found on the gun that was in your hand at your villa. But we know you killed the girl at your home and transported the body some time later to San Pedro. We know this because luminol was used to detect the girl's blood in your bedroom, your bathroom and in your car. And not just traces of blood ... a very large amount of blood.

Fuck, I'm thinking. Fucking fuck.

FORTY-FIVE

TODAY, 16.22

La Comisaría de Policía in Málaga is as drab a building on the inside as it is on the outside.

I'm sitting in a windowless room with white featureless walls and a huge mirror – which is doubtless a two-way adaptation behind which a bank of psychiatrists stand, tut, observe and analyse visual clues dropped by the new sociopath in town.

Across the desk from me sits López, and the fucker has what I can only describe as a smug look on his face.

Although the room is uncomfortably warm, he's wearing a three-piece suit and a tie, and his slicked-back blond hair and pencil moustache just add to the pretentiousness of the fucker.

If I had to age him, I'd say around forty, but he clearly keeps himself fit, and the lines on his face are from trying to look like the complete bastard he is, rather than from age.

I take out my cigarettes and I'm about to light up when he goes: 'Smoking is prohibited anywhere in the building, señor Malone.'

I light up anyway, just to piss him off, and say, 'Well, in that case you can add this to my list of crimes. Because if I'm looking at five life sentences, I hardly think it matters.'

He shrugs, drums his fingers on the table, and I think by now he's worked out how much this affectation irritates me.

He says nothing for a while and there's silence, until there's a knock on the door. He answers it and a uniformed cop hands him some papers, and he sits down again and studies them.

Then he hands one to me. I can see it's a transcript of something. I read it, and, once again, antifreeze hits my veins, as I know that this – irrespective of the fact that it is complete fabrication – will be enough for them to lock me up and throw away the proverbial key.

FORTY-SIX

And then, before I can say anything, there's another knock at the door.

There's a fairly animated conversation between López and another plain-clothed cop, only this time he doesn't look anywhere near as smug when he sits down.

'It looks like it's your lucky day, señor Malone.'

'I fail to see how being charged with five murders – which I certainly didn't commit – and facing conviction based on a totally trumped-up piece of fake evidence can be described as lucky?'

This is greeted with another of his trademark shrugs, table-tapping and a further pause.

'Because,' he replies, 'someone who has a lot of influence and a considerable amount of money has managed to arrange bail for you.'

So there is a God.

'There are some papers for you to sign, and then you are free to go; at least for now. You will surrender your passport to the Policía Nacional in Marbella in the morning.'

Just then, the thought occurs to me that I might not actually want to be bailed?

Who could be behind this?

It's got to be either Nikolaev, for whatever reason, or Dempsey, for a list of reasons that keeps on growing.

But I have to get out of here because I desperately need to speak to the one person who holds the key to all of this.

FORTY-SEVEN

TODAY, 16.40

So, we're in Natasha's Bentley Continental, and there's a bit of a silence because I'm still trying to take in everything that's just happened and to work out whether I can in fact trust her or not, and she's probably thinking the same about me.

First, I sign some sort of declaration, then this lawyer who works for Nikolaev and is on first name terms with the cops – which suggests he has almost certainly done this before – countersigns, and then Natasha produces this leather briefcase and proceeds to count out one point five million euro in bank notes. She gets a receipt, and off we trot.

I'm not even introduced to the lawyer, who stays behind to talk with López who is still looking seriously pissed off.

I've got two sheets of paper in my hand: one is a copy of the ballistics report, and the other is a copy of the transcription of emails that were supposed to have been exchanged between Olga Antonova and myself.

And the only person I know capable of doing this is Mandy; but, for the life of me, I can't see her involvement going this deep.

'What are those papers?' she asks eventually.

I tell her.

'And what do the emails say?'

'You really want to know? Want me to read them to you?'

She does.

'Okay … but two things first: one, is that they are pretty graphic in content, and two, is that I most certainly did not write them.'

'Okay, Malone – how about you just read them?'

I take a deep breath and start:

Friday 21 September, 2018. 19.50 Mia: Re: You received message from customer from Euro Girls Escort directory

Is very nice to read this email. Yes, I would love to, same time?

Friday 21 September, 2018. 19.51 Richie Malone:

Hi. 8 pm Saturday would be great. Do you want my address? Where are you coming from? I could pick you up if you like? I have a nice car. Richie.

Friday 21 September, 2018. 19.51 Mia: Re: You received message from customer from

Euro Girls Escort directory

Baby I'm located in Ricardo Soriano 39, i guess you can pick me up, why not? Lol

Saturday 22 September, 2018. 09.58 Mia: Re: You received message from customer from Euro Girls Escort directory

Good morning baby. I see you tonight at 20.00. I have just one question, do you want one hour or more? It's easier for me to arrange my agenda, if you know what I mean. Wish u a very good day baby

Saturday 22 September, 2018. 09.59 Richie Malone:

Hi. Could we make it earlier on Saturday – maybe 6? I have a dinner date later. I would like to start with just one hour thank you. And could you confirm what services you provide please? For example, I really like oral without condom – I am a very clean person and am considered to be quite good-looking. I also really love licking pussy. Thanks, Richie.

Saturday 22 September, 2018. 10.02 Mia: Re: You received message from customer from Euro Girls Escort directory

Sure baby! That's ok and yes oral is without as you want so, licking pussy Is of course in and Anal is 30€ extra if you like it so let's say 180€ for one hour with anal for the test. tong kissing Is included, body

2 body and of course all kind of Positions. Let's say
a bit of everything darling

Saturday 22 September, 2018. 10.03 Richie Malone:

That sounds pretty good to me but I don't want anal. You certainly sound as if you know what you're doing and I look forward to learning from you. Shall we say 18.00 on Saturday at my villa? I don't mind picking you up if it helps? R

Saturday 22 September, 2018.10.03 Mia: Re: You received message from customer from Euro Girls Escort directory

Thanks baby, yes, I do know what I'm doing lol. And yes baby, please pick me up. Ricardo Soriano 39 but we conform tis afternoon anyhow, for in case anything can happen to any of us

There's silence, apart from the purring of the Bentley's four-litre V8.

'Who's Mia?' she asks. 'I thought the girl was called Olga something?'

'Search me. López claims to have taken them from the phone of the dead girl, Olga Antonova. I can only assume that "Mia" is … was her working name.'

She actually laughs?

'So, you really love licking pussy.'

'Natasha,' I reply, 'this is not an appropriate conversation to be having with you … for so many

277

reasons. And, may I remind you ... I most certainly did not write those emails.'

'Then who did, Malone? Just how did these get into the girl's phone? If you didn't write them, who then?'

FORTY-EIGHT

TODAY, 16.55

So we're sitting in Nikolaev's ridiculously vulgar living room once again.

It's pretty much déjà vu, only this time Vlad's not here, and I have a sneaking suspicion that I'm not going to see him again; at least not in the company of Nikolaev and while there's air in his lungs.

I might as well go straight for the jugular, so I ask Nikolaev, 'Anyway, where's Vlad?'

He visibly winces, and it takes him a moment to get the words out.

'It would appear that Vladimir, Mr Malone, has put his own interests above those of mine and those of my organisation.' He pauses and lights another of his trademark fuck-off-huge cigars. 'This disloyalty does not sit well with the Bratva, so when we find him – which we will – I will permit him sufficient time to explain his actions.'

Before what, I'm wondering? But I pretty much know the answer already.

'So … let me see if I've got this right, Nikolaev …

the shooting of four of Dempsey's men at my villa, and a pathetic attempt to frame me for it, was not sanctioned by you?'

'Correct. Why would I do that, Mr Malone? We had an accord. It would appear that Vladimir had … how do you English say … sold his soul … to a certain Columbian cartel who are currently seeking a larger market share on the Costa del Sol. And it would also appear that he, and not Dempsey, was responsible for feeding information about my organisation, my activities and my resources to the Spanish police. And I have friends – powerful men, Mr Malone – in the Policía Nacional who suspect that one of their number is also working for the Columbians. The net is closing in, and it will not take me long to catch the one who is behind this.'

'Now, I wonder who that could be?' In my mind, I already know the answer. I light a cigarette and ponder which of a very long list of questions I should ask next.

'So why did you get me out of jail? I mean … first you abduct me, then you set me up as bait to lure Dempsey in, and then you get me bailed? I just don't quite get it?'

'Let me be honest with you, Mr Malone. I have known for some time that when Mr Dempsey was released, he would try to oust me by kidnapping and threatening to harm my daughter. He is an extremely evil man.'

Pot … kettle … black, I'm thinking, but keep this to myself.

He gets up and skips across to a solid oak writing bureau, takes out a folder and hands it to me. It contains several photos of Natasha: sunbathing topless by a pool, getting out of her car, leaving Club Pangea and undressing in what I imagine to be her bedroom. And, on a sheet of paper, the simple handwritten message:

Ask yourself what is more important: your business – what was my business – or your daughter. Think about it.

He continues: 'But I had not realised that he would be prepared to go as far as to commit murder. And so, I had Natasha' – and here she actually scowls at him – 'subtly escorted by my men, for her own protection.' He smiles at her but she's not dropping the glower. He goes on: 'And it was just as well that I did. So, I naturally assumed that it was you who had drugged her for nefarious reasons, such as your reputation would suggest, and that you would be followed home by the Irish, where she would be kidnapped ...'

'My reputation? What do you know about my reputation? Anyway ... I'm hardly likely to drug myself, am I?'

'Your reputation, Mr Malone, precedes you. You are well known throughout this region as an unprincipled womaniser, which is why I had particular concern over your liaison with my daughter.' He laughs; Natasha doesn't. 'Oh, I know quite a lot about you, particularly as you frequently use girls from my escort agency. Let me remind you: Eurogirlsescort.com?'

'So much for confidentiality,' I go. 'And that's "used to", Nikolaev – I'm a reformed character now, I'll have you know.'

This time it's Natasha who's giving me evils, and I just know I've seen that look somewhere before, which fans the flames of my theory.

'So, tell me ... your guys failed to notice that two of Dempsey's men were also in the Moët, and that one of them spiked our drinks – my drink, as well as Natasha's?'

'Yes. That is correct. But then again, Mr Malone, you failed to notice this yourself ... is that not also correct?'

Fair point.

'So, let me guess ... you just happened to have a girl who was the spit of Natasha on hand to pull off the subs' bench if it looked as if your daughter might get into trouble?'

'The spit? What is the spit, Mr Malone?'

'Dead ringer ... doppelgänger ... lookalike.'

'That is correct. Mia ...'

'Olga. Her name was Olga, Nikolaev.'

'Yes ... Olga bore a remarkable resemblance to Natasha. She worked for my agency, and she was rewarded extremely well to stand in for Natasha, which – let me tell you – she did willingly. Five thousand euro for an evening's work.'

'Five thousand euro to be fucking murdered? Jesus ... and I suppose she was willing to be drugged as well?'

'I deeply regret Olga's murder, and let me assure you that when I find out who was responsible, it will not be pleasant for them. It will be most unpleasant.' And, as if to emphasise this, he stubs out his cigar with a vehemence that sends a shiver down my spine. 'And no, she had not agreed to be drugged, but it was necessary because even you, in your condition, would have noticed that she was not the same girl by her speech and mannerisms.'

'I very much doubt it, Nikolaev, as I failed to notice that the girl I was with went to the toilet wearing a black dress and returned in a white one.'

And then something else strikes me.

'You wanted her to get kidnapped, didn't you? Otherwise your hoods would have "escorted" us back to my villa and intercepted whoever it was – we're assuming it's Dempsey's goons here – before they could abduct … no, as it turned out … before they could murder the girl in cold blood as we slept, drugged up to the fucking eyeballs, in my bed, while Princess Natasha sleeps it off in the comfort and safety of her own fucking boudoir.'

For a second Nikolaev looks as if he's going to explode, and I wonder if I've overstepped the mark. If I push him too far, it would be simple for him to 'assist' me in breaking one of the conditions of my bail so that I would end up back in clink; and I've worked out by now that I'm probably safer closer to him than under López's jurisdiction.

But it's Natasha who intercedes. 'There's no need for

that, Malone. We are all devastated by what happened to Olga. It was a bad plan, and if Father had listened to me, we would have done it my way.'

'Which was?'

'Which was to bide our time and find out who was behind this, instead of rushing in and—'

And just then a text pings on my phone.

It's from Maria.

'I need to take this,' I say, and open the message.

Malone I'm in trouble. Find me. But come alone.

And before I can speculate whether this is a trap that Maria is implicated in, a trap set by Vlad and López, or a trap that Dempsey has set – because a trap it indubitably is – my phone pings again as another message comes through.

It's a Spanish number I don't recognise, but I open it, as I figure that it's somehow connected to the text I just received.

I figure correct.

I have your girlfriend Malone. Drive to the location I will send you. You have exactly one hour. Come alone. If you are not here by 18.00 I will kill her. And if she dies her daughter and granddaughter will also die.

FORTY-NINE

TODAY, 17.03

A couple of months ago, Maria and I had this conversation that somehow stuck with me, but I didn't realise its significance until now.

We were dining, late one summer evening, in a restaurant in Orange Square ... can't remember which one, it's not important. But it must have been July, maybe early August, because it was hot, bloody hot, the place was swamped with tourists, the drains stank and the service was truly dreadful.

She began by asking me why I hated myself?

Hate yourself? Now that's rich, I've never come across anyone more in love with himself then you.

Well, as it turns out, that's just where you'd be wrong, amigo.

Anyway ... what's this got to do with the narrative, or have you lost the plot yet again?

Be patient. You'll find out why this is significant in a moment.

So, anyway, I reply that actually it's not myself I hate, but her.

And the reason for this is quite simple: I have never felt guilt nor regret about my philandering and egotistical behaviour until recently, when I've been with her. And I can't quite put a finger on exactly why, because she's never criticised, nagged, nor been in any way judgemental about my antics; in fact, truth be told, she's always found them to be a source of entertainment. So why do I feel like this now?

I couldn't think of the reason at the time, but a couple of minutes after receiving the second text, I know exactly why it's her I hate, and not myself. Bizarre as it may sound, it's because I love her ... not in a sexual way, but I care deeply about her; and this whole mess – as Sam pointed out – is totally my fault, and if anything happened to her or her family I'm not sure that I could live with it.

And there was something else she said in the course of that conversation that I hadn't processed until now.

She told me that I should try to learn to love myself.

Love myself? Make up your mind, I replied. First you tell me I hate myself and now you say I should love myself? Besides which, I had absolutely no idea how to process this.

Now this I really don't believe ... anyway, where's it leading? Clock's ticking ...

I'll tell you exactly where it's leading, amigo. It's leading to my redemption – my road to Damascus – although I didn't know it at the time.

I hate her because she made me care ... okay, I don't really hate her, but you know what I mean.

I think that maybe now I finally understand this, and therefore maybe I'm beginning to love myself?

And it's not because I'm good-looking, fantastic in bed, witty, charismatic and wonderful company ... not because I can look into the eyes of a beautiful woman and know that – more than likely – if I want to, I can sleep with her ... all of which, of course, is true. But this isn't the stuff I love about myself; it's the stuff that makes me *in* love with myself, and that's completely different and something I never understood before.

No, I love myself because I care deeply about three people: Sam, who I am in love with; Maria, who makes up my life; and Olga, who probably would still be alive if I hadn't written that fucking book.

Because I know – and don't ask me how – nothing that Maria has done in all of this has been done without compulsion.

FIFTY

TODAY, 17.05

The first thing I do when I've worked this out is to realise that along with caring comes a duty of responsibility, and it's my responsibility, and no one else's, to sort this mess out.

I ring Sam.

Her plane's approaching Málaga and I fill her in on what's happened and tell her I'll forward the location I've just received. It's near a town called Casares, somewhere in the hills behind Estepona, so I figure it'll take around an hour and a half to get there from Málaga.

Hang on – she's on a plane, so how can she use her mobile?

It's a private jet, amigo, where customer satisfaction is top priority; it's not Ryanair. And if she should have the sudden desire to piss on her seat, there wouldn't be a problem with that either.

So anyway, I tell her that she will be met at the airport by three of Nikolaev's men who will drive her to the periphery of this location, where they should remain inconspicuous and observe what's happening.

And when the time comes, on the basis of what their observation tells them, they will know exactly what to do.

I also tell her that she must not – under any circumstances – call the police, because until we've worked out who is kicking with which foot, their involvement is only likely to make a bad situation much worse.

'You do realise that I'm supposed to defend criminals, Malone, and not team up with them?'

'Sam, we can worry about the ethics when we've got Maria and her family back and found out which one of these fuckers killed the Russian girl. And if you still feel like defending them, that's your call.'

And the thought crosses my mind that if she hadn't got that scumbag Dempsey out of prison, none of this would have happened – until I remember that it was I who was the catalyst for his actions.

But I'm regretting saying this, even as I say it, because there's a harshness in my voice spawned by the severity of the situation, and I owe her a huge debt already, irrespective of the outcome; a debt that I doubt I'll ever fully repay. But if I get Maria and her family and, of course, myself out of this alive, I will spend the rest of my life trying.

So I ask Nikolaev for two things, a car and a gun, and a few minutes later I'm seated in Natasha's Continental with a Glock G20 in the glove compartment.

I'm beginning to develop a closet admiration for Nikolaev, because the Glock G20 – if you don't know it – is the handgun I would have chosen myself. And not only that, he even offers to come with me; but this, I tell him, is something I must do alone.

If things go wrong, he says, just call and I can get an assault helicopter there in minutes.

Good to know, I reply.

I key the address into the Bentley's satnav.

Hang on, shouldn't you take a less conspicuous vehicle ... you know, something like a Kia, that's not going to draw attention to yourself?

Critical as the situation is, amigo, I have my standards. In any case, I want to draw attention to myself for reasons that you will appreciate shortly, if you would only shut the hell up and listen to the narrative.

I hit the AP-7 and the satnav tells me I'm thirty-six kilometres away which will take me forty minutes.

I light a cigarette – ignoring Natasha's instructions not to smoke in her car – and try to relax and figure out exactly what's going on, and how I'm going to play this.

***

So, by my thinking – and you've probably worked this out as well, amigo – there are three groups of villains in this piece.

Nikolaev is the first, but unless he's playing an incredibly complex double bluff, I cannot see how I can point the finger of suspicion at him.

After all, he's just bailed me, given me a car, a Glock, offered to come with me and to send in an Apache in if it all goes to shit. And that's hardly how someone would play it if his or her intention was to kill you.

Of course, I could be wrong, but as he is one of the few people I seem not to have pissed off on the Costa del Sol, he has no particular reason – other than suspicion that I was intending to bed his daughter, all of which has been cleared up now – to harbour hostility towards me.

Then there's Dempsey.

As I've already given you the highlights of our relationship, I don't think I need to go into further detail. Suffice it to say I'm expecting that he will be mine host when I arrive at Casares, and I'm not anticipating a particularly warm welcome.

And I figure that it's he who has abducted Maria, for the simple reason that he wants to draw me in … it's probably what I would do in his situation: textbook ex-terrorist stuff.

And then there's the Columbian connection, which I'm assuming is headed by the duplicitous Vlad and that pernicious dickhead, López.

Now, I'll freely admit that I still could be wrong about López, but to charge me for the murders of Dempsey's men was, at best, sloppy police work and, at worst, a corrupt plot to get me out of the way and to ratchet up the tension between Dempsey and Nikolaev. And this is what I'm now convinced it is.

And for reasons that I will disclose shortly, amigo, it will take Sam about three nanoseconds to get these charges dropped.

So does this worry me? Not in the slightest.

I'm thinking that this nasty little turf war that has just kicked off and is about to escalate is simply a plan hatched by the Columbians to clear the marketplace by getting the opposition to cancel out each other.

Sweet.

Except that unfortunately I've got caught right in the middle of it, and – worse still – so has Maria and her family.

I couldn't give a tuppenny fuck who controls organised crime on the Costa del Sol as long as it doesn't affect me or my own. But unfortunately, right now it does.

And I have a feeling that whoever kidnapped Maria's daughter, Sofía, and her granddaughter, Daniela, is not the same person who is holding Maria. This is for two reasons – first, why go to the trouble of kidnapping three people from two different places, when one would be sufficient to draw me in? And second, there was something in that text … what was it? Yeah:

And if she dies, her daughter and granddaughter will also die.

If I were threatening to murder three people, I wouldn't phrase it like that.

Why, does it make any difference?

It does actually, amigo – to me, anyway.

You see, the way I read it is that if Maria is murdered, then as a consequence her daughter and granddaughter will be murdered, and that is because they will hold little currency in a trade-off by whoever is holding them; and I don't think that this is the same person.

So, this is the way I read it – and I'm prepared to be totally wrong here – I believe that Sofía and Daniela were abducted to coerce Maria into involving and implicating me. Remember that phone call she made when I visited her gaff early this morning? She was the one who got López involved. I was suspicious of this at the time, and I'm convinced of it now.

And remember that it was Maria who delivered the photos to Dempsey? There's no doubt about this, because she was the only person who knew exactly where I was. And if we take Nikolaev out of the frame, that just leaves *los dos paranoicos* representing the Columbian team: Vlad and López.

FIFTY-ONE

TODAY, 17.40

So I'm bouncing down this dirt track in the Bentley and I'm questioning if the satnav knows where the hell it's sending me, when I come to this massive walled estate in the middle of nowhere, shaded by cypress trees.

You're probably wondering how I'm feeling, and, truth be told, I'm pretty nervous. But there's a certain part of me that just can't wait to get this party started. I've always been clear-headed when about to enter what we used to refer to as the operational theatre, because to overthink possible negative outcomes serves as little purpose as a health warning on a Spanish fag packet.

But one other thing occurs to me as I slow the Bentley to a crawl and position it so it's facing the sea and away from the estate.

I grab my phone and call Nikolaev. There are a few other cars parked outside the gates and they are all – like most Spanish cars – white and nondescript; and this, amigo, is why I wanted to take the Bentley. I needed something that would be instantly recognisable from a distance, and from the air.

Nikolaev answers.

'I'm here,' I say. 'Nikolaev, do you honestly have an Apache helicopter?' I'm pretty sure I know the answer to this, because if there's one thing I've learned about him, it's that he's not a Billy Bullshitter.

'Of course,' he replies. 'It is my new toy – I've not used it yet. It's not a new one, of course, but it came with a full service history, and only minor damage to the fuselage. I have it standing by right now. Do you need me to send it in?' I can almost hear the excitement in his voice, and this proves he's not bullshitting.

'No,' I reply, 'give it an hour. I think I may have the semblance of a plan. But if you've not heard from me by 18.40, send it in. Tell the pilot to approach from the sea. If the Bentley's outside the estate wall, facing down the slope, give them the green light them to engage. If it's gone, pull back.'

'What about collateral damage?'

'If I'm still here in an hour, my plan won't have worked so I'll have to take my chances. But at least I'll know you're coming.'

'18.40?' he repeats.

'18.40 exactly,' I tell him.

We synchronise watches and I ring off.

FIFTY-TWO

TODAY, 17.42

I kill the engine and decide to leave the keys in the ignition and the gun in the glove compartment.

The first thing they'll do is frisk me, and in any case I won't need the gun until I get back to the car with Maria – if I get that far.

So out I get and stroll towards the gates, and as I do, they swing open and two guys come out dressed entirely in black, wearing military Aviator sunglasses and carrying assault rifles. They're both in good shape, tall, athletically built, and look the part.

And this confuses me for an instant because they also look as if they could be South Americans, until one speaks.

'You Malone?' he asks in a West Belfast accent.

'I be he,' I reply.

He motions me with the gun, and I approach him.

'Frisk him, Charlie,' and Charlie obliges. Of course, they find nothing other than my phone, my cigarettes and lighter, all of which they keep.

'C'mon inside.'

And I follow them through the gates into a yard where several other ordinary-looking vehicles are parked.

Inside the gates is a huge – what I would call … hacienda? A well-tended garden is bordered by a circular, cloistered pathway leading to a colonial-style villa.

On both sides of the villa are several outhouses, and I can tell by the whinnying of horses that one is a stable. There's a large garage which houses two black Mercedes limos, and next to this, in a carport, sits a Hummer with Irish plates.

'Nice gaff,' I say. 'Looks like your boss picked up a wee bit of sophistication while he was inside. Just hope he didn't take his Pet Shop Boys CDs with him.'

'I'd keep your gob shut about prison if I were you,' says Charlie. 'You're in enough shite already without makin' wisecracks about that.'

So we walk up the pathway in silence.

There's almost an aura of serenity about the estate, and under different circumstances it would make an ideal writing retreat, but I fear that Dempsey has read enough of what I've written so he's unlikely to encourage me to write more.

Charlie's walking about a metre in front of me, and the other guy, who I'd noticed walks with a slight limp, is about the same distance behind.

I figure that I could probably take out the guy behind me, as an assault rifle is not the most effective weapon at close quarters, but unless I can be certain of disabling both of them, this is unlikely to advance my cause.

We enter the house by a side door and I'm marched down a long wooden-floored corridor, galleried with typical Spanish colonial art.

At the end of the corridor, a door swings open and I'm directed into a long room with a high ceiling, wooden beams and a massive fireplace. There's a wooden table surrounded by a dozen or so uncomfortable-looking chairs, so I'm guessing this is the dining room.

And there, at the head of the table, sits Tom Dempsey.

FIFTY-THREE

TODAY, 17.46

The room's dark, as ceiling-high, half-shuttered windows limit the ingress of sunlight, so it takes me a while to register that Maria is sitting opposite him.

There are four other guys also dressed in black standing behind Dempsey, and they're wearing shoulder holsters containing what I guess are probably Glocks. So that makes at least six, I figure.

I happen to know that Dempsey, like Nikolaev, knows his weapons, and the Glock in various guises was the handgun of choice for the upper ranks of the IRA for many years.

Nobody speaks.

It's nearly thirty years since my last meeting with Dempsey and he hasn't aged well. There's fragility about his saggy frame, his hair is wispy and unkempt and his face is thin and ashen. I don't suppose his time in prison helped, and I have no doubt that he will remind me of that soon enough.

I look at Maria. She tries to smile at me, but I can see she's not taking this well.

But she's not tied up and I can see no evidence to suggest that she's been mistreated, so I take this as a positive.

'Babe … you okay? I ask.

'Malone, how many fucking times do I have to tell you not to "babe" me? Good to see you, *guapo*,' she replies, and that tells me all I need to know.

'Sit down,' Dempsey commands. His voice sounds the same as it did all those years ago, but I'm thinking it's fortified by the anger I can see clearly etched on his face.

I comply.

'Anyone got a smoke?' I ask cheerily, trying to lift the sombre mood. 'Your goons confiscated mine.'

'Shut the fuck up.'

Again, I comply.

He's staring at me with an intensity of venom that I hadn't imagined possible.

For an age there's silence, then he speaks.

'*Whiskey in a Big Gay Jar*. Have you any idea … any fuckin' idea what I had to put up with because of that fuckin' book?'

There's no correct answer to this, so I say nothing.

He clicks his fingers and one of his men goes to a sideboard, opens a drawer, takes something out and hands it to Dempsey.

It's a copy of the book, feathered with dozens of paper bookmarks, and he opens it at one.

'"Chapter Six … He kissed me with tenderness unimaginable for a man whose life was immersed in such extremes of violence. I felt revulsion and nausea as memories of the abuse I was forced to endure as a small child came flooding back. But I understood that unless my response was utterly convincing, I would pay with for this deceit with my life.

'"So I placed my hand between his legs and felt his small penis stiffen."'

And Maria crosses herself for the second time today.

'Jesus Christ, Malone ... you fucking write that fucking filth?'

I shrug. Normally I would jump to the book's defence by claiming that the sale of over five thousand copies in the first week put it on the Amazon bestseller list, but I fear that this isn't going to help things.

So I go, 'Look ... I can understand where you're coming from, Dempsey ... Tom – may I call you Tom?'

He doesn't reply but continues to glower at me, and I'm thinking that maybe him and López took evening classes at the same charm school.

'Tom, then ...' I continue, 'I can understand how you feel about this, and I would really, genuinely like to apologise for any offence caused. I mean it. Seriously. But I mean ... it was only fiction.'

So he goes to another of his bookmarks and starts to read.

'"Chapter Nine ... He kissed the tip of my penis softly and put it into my mouth. I closed my eyes and tried to imagine that somehow, mystically, he had been transformed into Tori Black. But it didn't help ... nothing would help. No porno star fantasy would stir my limp dick, and my manhood popped out of his mouth like a piece of soggy orange peel.

"'I'm more of a giver than a taker,' I told him, unzipping his jeans and cupping his small balls in the palm of my hand.'"

'Fucking hell, Malone …' goes Maria. 'You really are a homosexual gay … why don't you admit it?'

Out of the corner of my eye, I catch one of Dempsey's men place a hand over his mouth and turn his head to supress a smirk.

The others look uncomfortable, and I can tell I'm not the only one in the room who hopes he's not going to read any more.

Thankfully he doesn't.

'Just tell me, Malone … give me one reason …' he says, 'one reason why I shouldn't cut you up piece by piece while you're still breathing and feed you to my pigs? I'll start with your tongue cos that's where most of your shite comes from.'

There's only one way to survive here, I figure, and that's to do what I did at our last meeting: feign confidence.

But before I can reply, he continues: 'I have so many reasons to kill you and to make you die badly, that I've lost fuckin' count.'

He pauses. This isn't a good time to interrupt, so I have the manners to let him continue.

'First, you write that fuckin' book. Not only do you break your word about never sayin' a word about what happened back then … you actually write that load of

… fictitious fuckin' obscenity.'

Again, he pauses. Still not a good time for me to speak.

'Next there's the damage you did to my knee. It still fuckin' aches in winter.'

'Come on, it was a fair fight. I stuck to the rules of engagement and beat you fair and square. And bear in mind the odds. You were armed with a gun and a knife … well, a knife, anyway, as well as three armed men, against one guy who's had the shit kicked out of him for twelve hours,' I reply. 'Oh … but yes, of course, he was heavily armed with a nail.'

Dempsey ignores the taunt, which is only what I'd expect. I told you he was old school, amigo.

'And then, this morning, you and Nikolaev shoot four of my men. Four of my best fuckin' men, who were only there, I might add, to bring you here; not to kill you. In fact, they had clear instructions not to touch unless you were stupid enough to attack them.'

Another pause.

'And added to all of this, you were workin' undercover for the fuckin' Brits back in the day. But that's the least of your crimes cos that doesn't matter any more. You know Charlie here?'

'No.'

'Well Charlie was also one of you SRU cunts once upon a fuckin' time. But I can be forgiving, Malone. I'm a reasonable man and I can be forgiving about most things … but to ridicule me … to depict me as a fuckin' arse slabberer … and for what? Money? I kept my word,

Malone, I let you live, and this is how you repay me? With filth and lies? So, give me one good reason why I should let you live. To use the last words you said to me: "I'd say that's just about nailed it."'

There's silence in the room; you could cut the tension with the proverbial knife, and I figure it's best to let his words resonate before replying.

Maria looks at me questioningly, and for a moment I'm not sure whose side she's on?

'He's got a point, Malone,' she goes.

'Thanks, Maria. Thanks a lot.'

Dempsey clicks his fingers, issues an instruction to one of his guys, and my cigarettes and lighter are flung onto the table in front of me.

'Thanks.' I light one. 'Okay ... okay, I'll admit that you have a point, Tom. But I can in fact give you not one, but three good reasons why it would be folly to kill me. Folly, in fact, to lay a finger on me ... or Maria, for that matter,' I add.

He actually laughs, and I can tell he's enjoying this.

'This I can't wait to hear.'

'But first, let's clear something up: I had nothing to do with the murder of your men ... nothing. Nikolaev's men were only there as backup in case things got out of hand with your guys. They were only supposed to observe – nothing more. But one of them – Vlad ... Vladimir, I don't know his second name ...'

'Vladimir Popov? Nasty lookin' wee fucker going bald at the front, with a greasy ponytail?'

'Perfect description. You know him?'

'Aye … evil wee bastard; son of a priest.'

I'm thinking for a sociopathic freak such as Dempsey to refer to an adversary as an 'evil wee bastard' must define a whole new meaning for the word 'malevolence'.

He continues: 'He's known as Vlad the Bad, or sometimes Vlad the Mad, depending on who you're talkin' to. So he was there?'

'He shot your men. One shot to the back of the head for the first three, and one between the eyes for the last guy, who managed to turn and face him. Then he shot at me, but luckily he missed and only grazed my head.'

'Luck had nothin' to do with it, Malone. If he's wanted to kill you, you wouldn't be sitting here now. He might be a cunt, but he's the deadliest cunt with a handgun I've yet to meet. So what happened to the rest of Nikolaev's men? They just stood there and watched?'

'Don't know. I was rather preoccupied as you might imagine, so I didn't get a chance to note that. I assume they thought that there'd been a change of plan and Nikolaev had ordered Vlad to take them out. That'd be my guess, but who knows?'

He raises his eyebrows and sighs but says nothing, so I continue.

'So then, this guy López, who's supposed to be a cop – but I don't buy that – turns up while I'm out cold. He removes the rifles your guys were carrying, and plants – or it may have been Vlad who did it, before he fucked off – the murder weapon in my hand so it looks like it's me who killed them. Only I happened to suspect that

305

a certain person sitting close to me' – and here I give Maria as withering a look as I can – 'had disabled the security cameras earlier.'

'I'm sorry, Malone. But you would have done the same fucking thing if your family had been taken and you were threatened that they would be killed if you didn't do what they tell you.'

'Well, we'll never know, Maria, as I have no family. But probably, yes, I would,' and this floods a tsunami of relief over me.

'So anyway,' I continue, 'after this pernicious little bastard and his mates had called in earlier to inspect the dead girl – who I assume was murdered by you to scare Nikolaev off, only it didn't work because a) it wasn't his daughter you killed, but a Russian hooker called Olga Antonova who looked a lot like her, and, b) someone had removed the body from my bed and dumped it in San Pedro—'

'What the fuck are you talking about, Malone? I never killed any girl, prostitute or not.'

There's another silence as we both try to process this.

'And I suppose you never threatened Nikolaev? Sent him photos of his daughter sufficient to convince him you meant business and how easy it would be for you to get to her? And a message, something along the lines of "What's more important: business – or your daughter?" '

'No.'

'What about your two goons who were in the Moët last night?'

'Aye … two of my men were there to lift you. That

306

was the plan. But when they saw the state you were in, I told them to leave it until you were sober.'

'So who did kill the girl, then?'

There's this ... what you might call ... pregnant silence? Then Maria confirms what we're both thinking.

'It was Vlad and López. They sent the pictures and the message. And they killed the girl believing she was Nikolaev's daughter. Or they as good as killed her. They made me disable your cameras, cancel the security system and give them access to your villa. Then they forced me to take photos of you and the girl in the Moët—'

'The wrong girl,' I interrupt. 'Olga's dress was white; Natasha's was black.'

'I didn't know that she wasn't Nikolaev's daughter. Not that it matters.'

'Tell Olga's parents that.'

'You know what I mean, Malone. I did not know a girl was going to be murdered; and anyway, what was I the fuck to do about it? She looked like the same girl.' I can see how close to tears she is, and Maria in tears is something I've not witnessed before. 'And they said if I say a word, then Sofía and Daniela will die. So better for us you have a fucking good plan.'

FIFTY-FOUR

TODAY, 17.54

I'm aware that the clock is ticking, and this isn't moving us any further along the path of resolution.

'So,' goes Dempsey. 'Let's just say you're both telling the truth – unlikely for you, Malone, but let's just go with it; what do they stand to gain from killin' Nikolaev's daughter?'

'Obvious,' I reply. 'They know you're out of jail and want your action back from Nikolaev. But these dudes, who I'm assuming head up the Columbian cartel, want to pull the rug from under both of you by starting a turf war. They kill the girl, blame it on you, watch the dominoes fall, then move in and take over when you've neutralised each other. Simple.'

I light another cigarette.

'So let's go back to my three reasons why revenge is a dish best served with a modicum of good sense. Reason number one ... and let's get the personal shit out of the way first: I'll issue a public apology and a retraction for the book. Look ... you can even have the royalties if you want.'

'I don't want your money. No amount of fuckin' money could compensate for what I had to go through.'

'I can't tell you how sorry I am, Tom. But in my defence, how was I to know you were going to end up in Mountjoy? Anyway, I'll go public and fess up. And as the bitch who shopped me is writing your official biography, any reputational damage I caused will soon be forgotten.'

'I'll think about it. But you'd better come up with something better than that.'

'Sure. Reason number two: you've already lost four men today. And these guys won't stop until they've nullified you. So, ask yourself a question, Tom … do you want to be fighting a war on two fronts? And once the lesser players – the Turkish, the Chinese … heck, even the Liths and the Albanians – smell blood, you'll soon be fighting a war on more fronts than songs by the Village People.'

'That isn't fucking funny, Malone. Don't push your luck.'

Maria shoots me a filthy.

'Sorry. Inappropriate comment … it just slipped out,' I go. 'Okay, so what I'm suggesting is to do a deal with Nikolaev. Sit down with him and work out a compromise. Then I'll help you take Vlad and López right out of the picture.'

He thinks about this, and then laughs softly.

'I need *your* help? I hardly think so.'

'Oh, I think you do. You see, I can make sure that both these hombres disappear for a very long time.'

'Okay ... I'm interested. Tell me how?'

'All in good time, and only when we have an agreement.'

'And the third reason?'

I stub out my cigarette, light another one and say nothing. And I'm back in South Armagh all those years ago, in Dempsey's bear pit, and at the precise moment when I knew I was in control and exactly what was going to happen next.

'The third reason' – I look at my watch – 'is that in precisely thirty-eight minutes, if Maria and I are still here and you have not reached an agreement with Mr Nikolaev, he will send in an Apache helicopter and turn this magnificent old estate into firewood, and anyone who's still in it will be left with more holes than the plot of *The Big Sleep*.'

FIFTY-FIVE

TODAY, 18.02

So we're in the library now, Maria and I.

Dempsey has my phone and is talking to Nikolaev, and wants us out of the way, probably because he's afraid that if I somehow get out of this alive, I'll write about it – which is precisely what I am doing right now.

But I'm not sure how confident I am of these two agreeing to anything, particularly if his response to my supplication for a treaty is anything to go by.

No sooner have I finished talking than he instructs two of his guys to fetch something, and a couple of minutes later back they come carrying this wooden crate containing an FIM-92 Stinger, which – if you don't know – is a portable Air-Defence System and operates as an infrared homing surface-to-air missile. For the layman, it's better known as a SAM: the sort of thing that brought down Malaysia Airlines Flight 17.

Wasn't that a BUK missile system, fired from an armoured vehicle?

Oh, you're still there, amigo? Okay, so you have access to Wikipedia.

And I said 'the sort of thing', not the *actual* thing.

Still here, yes. Actually, I want to see if this narrative has more holes than The Big Sleep. *I imagine it will have, as I can only remember one.*

Well you remember wrong, amigo.

So anyway, first, Dempsey has a big grin on his mottled face and says, 'How's that for a snooker?' And then he adds, 'Plenty more where that came from.'

This looks as if it's going to turn into a cock-measuring competition, and I'm thinking that the best thing to do is to get Maria and myself the fuck out of Dodge.

Trouble is, the door's locked, and it's not the sort of door you'd buy from B&Q, so nothing short of a grenade or an assault rifle is going to get us through it.

And the windows are on the same level and of a similar size to those in the dining room, so even if I could smash them, nothing larger than a cat would be able to get through.

So in the absence of a plan, I park my arse on one of the leather-coated King Charles antique chairs and look around the room for anything that may at some point come in useful, and eventually my eye falls on something.

So how do you know it's the library?

I know it's the library, amigo, because three of the walls have floor-to-ceiling shelves that are literally groaning with books. There's even one of those library stepladder things on wheels, and so I'm thinking that either I don't know Dempsey very well, as – other than the keen interest he has developed in my book – I wouldn't label him as a bookworm, or perhaps the more likely explanation is that it's actually not his gaff?

There's a huge fireplace that dominates one wall and a random collection of tables, desks and more uncomfortable-looking armchairs dotted around the room, and there's also the pervasive typical musty book smell that goes with libraries that are rarely used.

Maria sits facing me.

'Well?'

'Well what?' I reply.

'If I don't get out of here, Sofía and Daniela are going to die.'

'We will get out of here, Maria. Trust me,' I reply with a confidence I don't feel. 'They'll be fine.' I light a cigarette, and this gives me an idea. 'If the worst comes to the worst, I have a plan to get us out.'

And I have, but it's also a plan that could get us killed.

Do share?

All in good time, amigo.

I'm thinking I'll give it twenty-five minutes and, if we're still here, then it will be time for action. In the meantime, I want some answers.

'When did they lift Sofía and Daniela?'

'Yesterday morning,' she replies. 'Sofía called me at around ten and she said they were going to the supermarket and asked if I come to lunch tomorrow. Then this guy called me around midday, when I was at work, and said they had taken Sofía and Daniela, and if I do not do exactly what he tells me then I will never see them again. He didn't give me his name nor nothing but said he was part of some powerful … I don't know …. some carton?'

'Cartel?' I interrupt.

'Cartel … *sí*. That is what he said. At first, I didn't believe him, so he told me to go the window, and then he rang off.' Again, she's on the verge of tears and, truth be told, I'm lost as to how to react because this is new territory. 'So,' she continues, 'I went to the window and my phone rang again. I answered it and it was Daniela. She said, "*Abuela*, please … *Abuela* … do what they tell you or they kill us." And then this cop car drove by slowly and I saw Sofía and Daniela in the back. A cop was driving and a guy in plain clothes in the passenger seat was staring up at me and smiling.'

'López?'

'Maybe López, I don't know. I was on the sixth floor. My eyesight is not so good as it used to be, so I cannot fucking swear to it.'

There's silence for a moment.

'He told me what I had to do. I was to work my shift like as normal, then go to my home. Then I was to go to your villa at nine. Then I had to turn off the security system and the same with the cameras. And then I was to go to the Moët after midnight, where I had to talk to you and to the girl. Then I was told to take some photos of you both and to buy you a drink—'

'So it was you who drugged us … Jesus.'

Silence.

'I had to, Malone. I had no choice.'

'Out of curiosity, what did you use?'

She shrugs.

'Scopolamine.'

'Jesus fucking Christ ... do you know how deadly that is? You could have fucking killed me.'

Excuse me ... hello ... what exactly is scopolamine?

Scopolamine, amigo, colloquially known as 'the devil's breath', is an odourless and tasteless Columbian drug that eliminates free will and can wipe the memory of its victims. It's the deadliest drug in Columbia, and that says quite a lot. Scopolamine turns people into complete zombies and blocks memories from forming. So even after the drug wears off, victims have little or no recollection as to what happened.

Then a thought occurs to me, a thought so horrific that I don't even feel the butt of my cigarette burn my fingers.

'It was me who killed the girl ... the hooker ... Olga, wasn't it?'

There's a long pause, and then she answers.

'You cut her throat ... yes, they told me that. But I know that she was dead before they got her to your villa. They didn't know – no one knew that this wasn't Natasha, nor that this girl – this Olga – had been sedated by Nikolaev's men before they ... what they say in the movies ... made the switch. Together the mixture of the sedative and the scopolamine was completely too much for her and she suffered a massive heart attack. I wanted to call 112 ... maybe she might have lived.

I doubt it … but they wouldn't fucking allow it. They said it didn't matter because you were going to fucking kill her anyway.'

'And they were there, in the Moët … Vlad and López?'

'No. I helped the girl into the taxi. She was convulsing. Having a heart attack. I called López and asked what the fuck I was to do.'

'Why the hell didn't you call 112 anyway?'

'Because, Malone, when bad men with no principles who care nothing for life have your family, you do exactly what you are fucking told.'

Silence. Of course, she's right.

'She almost certainly would have died anyway. She was too far gone, poor thing. She did not know nothing about it.'

'So … I don't get it. Why did I have to slice her throat open if she was already dead? And why did I use a bread knife?'

'Because they wanted to draw attention away from the real cause of death. But a pathologist would have picked it up like in a flash. This is why they wanted her to bleed out and why you were given instructions before they told you to sleep: to mop up the blood in the morning … to be sure to leave nothing. You were also told to put the body in your car, drive to San Pedro and dump her body and the bread knife the next morning after you had cleaned up. Then to ring me.'

'But why do I remember some parts but not others? I remember waking up next to her then clearing up, and

I remember everything from the time I called you. But I'm damned if I can remember anything about putting her body in my car and dumping it in San Pedro?'

'That's the way the drug works. Usually it blanks everything out – depending on the strength of the dose – for maybe eight to twelve hours. But for some reason that particular memory stayed with you while others did not. In any case, I didn't put all of the fucking stuff into your drink. Just enough so they would know that I had done it, and that is probably why you have left some memory. And maybe it was because it was so horrific. I don't know. I'm a traumatologist, Malone, not a fucking psychiatrist.'

And then I'm thinking that maybe I've been a victim of this drug before?

And my mind goes back to the Ukrainian Incident, because the pattern is remarkably similar.

'Wait ... what time did I call you this morning? Look at your phone – that'll tell you.'

'I haven't got my fucking phone. He made me text you, the gay homosexual Irish guy, and then he took it back.' She wrinkles her nose in thought. 'I don't know exactly. It was around seven ... maybe seven fifteen; fucking early, anyway.'

Okay.

So I was woken up by her blood around six ... yeah, five forty-five. I remember now. I cleaned up and then I can't remember what I did. Yeah, no ... I remember: I read my journal because I figured it had some bearing on this. So then there's an hour missing, and that's when I must have loaded her into the car and driven to San Pedro.

Is this really important?

It is to me, amigo. If my time had been accountable so that I couldn't have driven to San Pedro, then it would call into question Maria's version of my involvement.

Then another thought hits me.

'And why the bread knife?'

'A serrated edge is going to sever the carotid arteries more easily. That I *do* know. She would bleed out faster, and they thought that the faster she did, the better the chance of removing the evidence that she had been drugged. But they were wrong. Besides, when the real police find traces of her blood, they will find out soon enough.'

I'm stunned – utterly floored.

For a moment I think I'm going to throw up, so I go to the mantelpiece, place both hands on the cold marble and take deep breaths until the nausea passes.

But you didn't kill her. You don't even remember anything about either cutting her throat or dumping her corpse, so why do you feel so bad about it?

Let me ask you a question, amigo. Have you ever done something that you didn't remember doing – something reprehensible, but maybe not as reprehensible as cutting the throat of a dead girl – and then when you either remember, or someone tells you what you did … or maybe said, you ask yourself how and why the fuck did you do it and you feel utterly disgusted with yourself?

No.

Okay, so in that case you'll just have to accept that, as someone once said, 'For those who understand, no explanation is needed. For those who do not understand, no explanation is possible.' This is how I feel right now, and neither my military background, nor the fact that what I did was done under the influence of a drug that removes your willpower and the ability to withstand suggestion, makes me feel less bad. And the probability that unless my plan works perfectly, I will end up in prison, does little to mitigate this.

Anyway, back to the narrative.

'So, Vlad and López believe that you're the only person to tie them to the murder,' I ask, 'which is why they're not going to give Sofía and Daniela up without a fight?'

'Correct.'

There's a silence, then eventually I say, 'Maria ... you do realise that you – and probably also me – are going to go to prison for this? And possibly for a very long time?'

'I had to do what I had to fucking do, Malone. And if I was faced with the same situation tomorrow I would do it again.' There are tears in her eyes and suddenly she's sobbing uncontrollably. I go to her, put my arms around her and hold her tight. I feel mildly uncomfortable because this is as far from the Maria I know as Kim Jong-un is from winning the Nobel Peace Prize, but it's clear that the strain of the last twenty-four hours has brought her to this.

After an age she regains composure and gently pushes me away. 'I will look any judge in the eye and ask him what the fuck he would do if his family was taken the fuck away from him and that was the only way to get them back. And if he sends me to prison, he sends me to prison. Think I give a fuck compared to the losing of my family?'

There's no answer to this, but just then an idea occurs to me.

'Maria … you said you didn't put all of it … this scopolamine, into our drinks?'

'That's right. I'd read about it, like maybe ages ago. I know what that drug can fucking do. It's fucking evil, man. And you don't even have to swallow it. If you breathe it in it has the same effect.'

'So, you have some of it left, right?'

'Yeah. It's in the plastic vial they gave me.'

'And where is it?'

'At home. What … you want some more?' She laughs.

'Would there be enough left to induce similar effects on two people?'

'Should be. I only used about half of it.'

'And how long does it stay in your system?'

'The amount that you and the girl had? Between eighteen and twenty-four hours; certainly no longer.'

'So it will still be in my bloodstream?'

'*Ciertamente*, despite you trying to wash it out with alcohol. Maybe if you had exercised … or even had sex, it would have got out of your system by now, but a blood test should confirm this.'

Okay ... so now I *do* have the semblance of a plan.

But it will only have a chance of working if Dempsey and Nikolaev can reach an agreement, and this is totally out of my control.

FIFTY-SIX

TODAY, 18.18

So, I'm just about to put my escape plan into action when I hear footsteps approaching and a key turn in the door.

And how, might I ask, were you planning to escape from a locked room, with no possibility of getting through the windows? By magic?

My plan, amigo, was to escape through the chimney. And before you laugh, I had worked out that it could in fact be done. The aperture above the hearth was large enough to place the ladder inside. I could easily reach the point where the flue narrowed, and from there, with a little assistance, using my back and my legs, push myself upwards and climb out onto the roof. I had estimated that from the top of where the ladder would leave me to the exit point was only around four metres, and so, if I collected maybe fifteen to twenty thick, leather-bound volumes from the bookshelves and stacked them on the top step of the ladder, this would take me within easy reach of the top.

And what about Maria?

Amigo, where there are gangsters and where there are horses there are also ropes. I would climb down a drainpipe – okay, this part I would have to play by ear – see what I could find in the stable, return to the chimney and haul Maria up the flue, using a rope or by knotting together lead reins from the headcollars. Okay, I know it's not a fantastic plan and one fraught with pitfalls, but when faced with the prospect of being caught in the crossfire between an Apache gunship and an FIM-92 Stinger, it would have to do.

Anyway, thankfully I don't get the chance to put it to the test because the door swings open and in comes Charlie carrying the obligatory assault rifle.

'Boss wants to see yis.'

FIFTY-SEVEN

TODAY, 18.20

So we're back in the dining room, and Dempsey's mood hasn't improved.

I'm not that optimistic that there'll be a happy ending, and now that we're out of the library, our chances of escape before Nikolaev has the opportunity to play with his new acquisition are about the same as those of a Spaniard indicating on a roundabout.

I've just outlined my plan, and Dempsey says nothing. Then he throws me my phone.

'You are one lucky fucker, Malone. You had better fucking pray to the Almighty that this works. Call him.'

'Call who?' I ask, but I already know the answer.

'Who the fuck do you think? Call López and set up the meet. Your place, in an hour's time … no, give him longer – make it seven thirty. Tell him to bring the hostages. And by the way, she stays here,' he nods at Maria, 'until this is done.'

'No way,' I reply. 'I need her with me for reasons that I thought I had made perfectly clear. And I'm hardly likely to ride off into the sunset while her family are being held hostage and there's a bail order on my head. Either she comes with me, or I don't make this call.' Again, it's a big chip to play, but play it I do.

Silence.

'Okay. But let me make one thing quite clear, Malone. When this is over, if you're still alive you issue that retraction and public apology straight away. And don't go thinking that you and I are going to become buddies ... cos if you ever write anything about me again, I will have you fuckin' killed. Just be sure your shadow never falls over mine, or that's exactly what'll happen.'

'I think I can agree to your terms, Tom. So, you cut a deal with Nikolaev?'

'Not that it's any of your business, but yes, we've come to an agreement.' I sense his mood shift incrementally, then he asks, 'How's that lawyer friend of yours, by the way? The one who got me out? I need someone to tie this thing up legally.'

And I'm thinking, do scumbags like Dempsey and Nikolaev, who operate totally outside the law, actually believe that a legal contract as to who to sell drugs to, who each can launder money through, and who each can generally extort ... do they consider for one moment that any agreement – legally endorsed or not – will be in any way binding? I think this, but thankfully manage to keep this thought inside my head.

'Funny you should mention it, because she's on her way over here.' I'm not going into specifics here, as Sam turning up at his gaff with three of Nikolaev's heavily armed foot soldiers is probably not exactly what Dempsey meant by 'coming alone'. Besides which, I need to tell her there's been a change of plan.

He laughs.

'You really know how to piss women off, don't you? Both your ex and your girlfriend almost tripped over themselves in the stampede to shop you.'

I figure it's probably best to ignore this, although I'm tempted to tell him that Mandy Kershaw would be the last person on the planet I would instruct to write my memoirs. But this, in the course of time, he will undoubtedly find out for himself.

So I call López and I can tell he's surprised to hear from me, although not as surprised and pissed off as he was when Natasha got me bailed.

As there are no pleasantries to get out of the way, I hit him straightaway with my big play.

'I have something that you want, and you have something that I want, López.'

I give him the summary of what I have in mind but I don't tell him everything, and he goes silent for a moment.

'Is that the best you can do, señor Malone? Because if that's it, I'm afraid it's insufficient to tempt me to even think about a trade. I'm not even remotely concerned by what you claim … even if it happens to be true, which I very much doubt. You are going to prison for a very long time for the murder of five people, and I am tempted to add trying to bribe a senior police officer to the lengthening list of charges against you.'

'No,' I reply. 'Well, there *is* something else.'

So I tell him, and again there's this lengthy silence, but I know I've got him this time.

Eventually he asks, 'And how do you intend to prove this?'

'Because the mother and grandmother of the hostages you are holding is the senior traumatologist at the Hospital Costa del Sol, and a simple blood test will substantiate this. And then, of course, there's also the evidence that she is prepared to give against you when she testifies.'

Another lengthy silence.

'So, what exactly are you proposing?'

This time, it's me who hesitates before replying.

'We meet at my place in an hour's time: seven thirty precisely. You bring the hostages with you; Maria will be with me. You come alone … no heavies … no guns. Oh, and you bring that Russian scumbag mate of yours along with you. You fail to comply with any of this and there's no deal, and I'll just take my evidence to the British Consulate ... and the Irish Consulate … and anyone else who is incorruptible and will take as much pleasure as I will in busting your sorry Columbian ass. *Entiendes?*'

I don't bother waiting for him to reply before I ring off.

FIFTY-EIGHT

TODAY, 18.33

We're in the Bentley, and I'm flinging it down the same dirt track towards the road to Estepona when my phone rings.

It's Nikolaev.

'I understand that I'm expected to stand my helicopter down?'

I can almost feel the disappointment in his voice.

'Yeah, sorry,' I go. 'I'm sure there'll be another opportunity. It's probably a good idea for you to get some bodies over to my place, though, but make sure you keep them out of sight; not like the last lot. And also, make sure they're men you can genuinely trust, or this could go horribly wrong.'

I say this because I'd had the same conversation with Dempsey, and he had not only offered to grace my gaff with his presence but to bring along Charlie and five of his Kalashnikov-wielding buddies.

'So between you and Dempsey, that's around twelve, and that should be more than sufficient if things don't go to plan. I assume you'll be there yourself?'

'Of course, Mr Malone. I wouldn't miss this for the world. It should be most entertaining. And of course, I have some unfinished business with Vladimir.'

Killing Vlad is not part of my plan, but I keep this to myself for now.

I ring off and call Sam.

'Where are you?' I ask.

'Just gone past Puerto Banús. We're about half an hour away.'

'Okay, two things: first, turn the car around and head to my villa. There's been a change of plan. Get the more intelligent-looking of Nikolaev's goons to call their boss, and he'll explain what's happening and what they're to do. Secondly, call your "high-profile" Irish client because he wants you to legitimise some sort of rogues' charter between himself and Nikolaev.'

'Anything else?'

There's a pause.

No 'How are you bearing up, darling?' No 'Can't wait to see you … let's start looking at wedding dresses if you get through this.' And I have the strangest sensation … one I've never had before, that I actually love a woman more than she loves me? And this is as disconcerting as the disproportionate sense of relief that follows what she says next.

'Malone, don't get yourself bloody killed. You may be a twat, but you're the twat I want to grow old with.'

FIFTY-NINE

TODAY, 18.50

I double-park and stick my hazards on, Spanish style, outside Maria's apartment block, and she goes to fetch the two items we need.

So, for the first time since this morning – apart from when I'd either been knocked out or incarcerated – I'm alone and have some actual time to think.

First, I run through the fine detail of my plan.

It all hinges on one key moment where Maria and I need to work in unison. Get this right and we will be in control, but get it wrong and there will be a bloodbath, because there is no doubt that Vlad and López will no more come alone than I will, and the first people in the firing line will be us.

I consider it's unlikely that they would kill the hostages, but Maria would be the first target as she is a key witness, and I would be next because I hold the evidence. And this would happen so quickly that there would be nothing either Dempsey's or Nikolaev's militia would be able to do about it.

And then I get to thinking about López.

Before leaving Dempsey's gaff, I asked him what he knows about him. It's always best to understand your enemy and Dempsey clearly appreciates this, having gathered an impressive amount of intel remarkably quickly.

López, it turns out, is Columbian. No surprises here.

He'd risen to the rank of colonel in the Columbian police by the age of thirty, and, as is normal with this status, a large part of his income was derived from ensuring that rival cartels could operate independently and without curtailment of their activities by the authorities.

So one day he's requested by the Medellín Cartel to escort a shipment of eighty-five kilos of coke from Bogotá to the port of Santa Marta. The Medellín Cartel – if you don't know it – is pretty much top dog when it comes to organised crime throughout Central America and is a highly organised and most-feared Colombian drug cartel, obviously based in the city of Medellín.

You certainly do not mess with these people; but mess with them López did, foolishly deciding that what he was being paid to nursemaid the drug run wasn't enough.

And so he helped himself to three keys.

When they discover that some of their merchandise has gone missing, it doesn't take them long to link this to López and, as they say in the trade, put the X on his head.

But López learns of this through some low-level scumbag informers and decides that his days in the

Colombian police force are numbered. So he manages to get a flight to Madrid with half a million dollars in his suitcase from the disposal of the coke.

After a couple of years the heat has died down a little, López gets bored and drifts south to Málaga where he joins the Cuerpo Nacional de Policía, and again he rises swiftly through the ranks.

But enough is never enough for López, and in his role of senior enforcement officer with jurisdiction for organised crime, he soon discovers that there are easy pickings to be had by controlling the activities of the major players on the Costa del Sol and using the intel he receives from his informers to further his own interests.

And soon the cartel he establishes is right up there, alongside the Irish and the Russians, and the clever thing about it is that none of the other players have a baldy who's cleaning up.

Then Dempsey goes to jail, and Irish infighting opens the door for López to expand. But being a greedy fucker, his business model is based on total market domination, so this is when he decides that the best way to get rid of the opposition is to encourage them to do this for themselves.

So what about Vlad?

Vlad? Dempsey had known for about a year that Vlad had teamed up with López.

But why did Vlad 'defect'?

The usual motivations, amigo: greed, greed and even greater greed. What Nikolaev was paying him wasn't enough, and he knew that his boss was your archetypally avant-garde oligarch, so he would never be regarded as 'family' and reap the rewards that this would bring.

But this arrangement suited Dempsey because the intel that Vlad fed to López served to undermine Nikolaev, and this was not a bad thing as far as he was concerned.

But what Dempsey didn't know until today – when I told him – was the fact that López was in fact gamekeeper turned poacher, and that the clever little fucker was running his own cartel, which was why Dempsey was being undercut and why his market share had declined so dramatically.

Maria tapping on the window interrupts my thoughts and I unlock the passenger door.

'Got it?' I ask as she gets in and buckles up.

'Yep.'

I start the engine, stick it in drive, turn off the hazards and look in the rear-view mirror where I clock a cop car, blue lights flashing, sirens blaring, pull out to overtake me.

It slams to a halt in front of the Bentley. Two cops get out and walk towards us.

And I can tell by the fact that they're both pointing guns at us that I'm about to get more than a ticket for double-parking.

SIXTY

TODAY, 18.58

Okay, so this wasn't in the plot, I'm thinking, and curse myself for not anticipating that López would try to take us out before the meet.

Another schoolboy error?

Correctomundo.

To kill Maria and myself would be the solution that I would seriously consider if I were López.

With Maria dead, there is no one to testify against him and Vlad. And with me out of the way, the evidence stays buried.

But this is the time for action and not analysis, so I gun the Bentley's engine and point it straight at the two cops who are now blocking the street.

The cop on the left manages to get a shot off, which comes precariously close but shatters the wing mirror, before both of them have the good sense to dive the fuck out of the way.

If this police intervention is just a routine enquiry, that will be something I will have to worry about later … if there's a later to worry about.

I'm thinking we've just about cleared the immediate danger when the other cop fires a shot that penetrates the rear window and catches Maria on the shoulder. I hear the dull thud of the nine-millimetre shell from the Sig Sauer P226 impact with flesh and bone, and she squeals and slumps forward.

I haven't time to examine her injury as I fling the Bentley down the Avenida del Mercado and hurtle the wrong way down a one-way street, praying that there'll be nothing coming towards us and that with the sound and sight of a Bentley in full flight, pedestrians will have the sense to realise that the centre of the Calle Valencia is not a good place to be right now.

My luck holds, and I fling this missile of a car into the Ricardo Soriano, causing oncoming traffic to brake so violently as to give more than ample justification for the traditional Spanish response.

We're now heading towards Puerto Banús, and I haven't even got the baldy of a plan.

'You okay, Maria?'

'Oh yes, dear. Just fine, thank you. This fucking hurts, you know.'

'Yep,' I reply, 'getting shot does hurt. But you'll live.'

'I don't need you to tell me that, Malone. I know I'll fucking live. If you don't fucking kill us both with your driving.'

There's blood everywhere, crimson dripping onto the burgundy leather, so she rips material from her dress and dabs it on her shoulder to stem the flow.

'You need to see a traumatologist,' I say.

'Shut the fuck up, Malone.'

So I do.

I need time to figure out where to go and what to do. Clearly the meet at my place isn't going to take place, and it's also becoming evident that the prospect of doing a deal with López is as likely as Maria completing a sentence without the use of an obscenity.

I'm just about to call Sam when my phone rings.

It's López.

'Señor Malone, it would appear that you have broken a condition of your bail. I have been informed that you refused to stop when two of my officers approached you in Marbella.'

'They fucking shot at us, López.'

'They drew their weapons, señor Malone, because you are a dangerous criminal. May I remind you that you are charged with the murder of five people? My officers were instructed to check your documents and to enquire why you were driving a Russian-registered car. That is all.'

'Bullshit.'

Silence.

Then a thought enters my head, and I share it with López.

'You haven't really thought this through, López, have you?'

'What do you mean, thought it through?'

'Well, for someone who defrauded the Medellín Cartel and lived to tell the tale, I'd have expected you to be a bit … I don't know … brighter?'

There's a silence from which I can tell he wasn't expecting me to know this.

'Brighter? What is brighter?'

Maria's clearly in agony and seems to be slipping in and out of consciousness, and I'm wondering whether the wound is worse than both of us had thought.

'Yes … brighter, López. You see, if you kill two unarmed civilians – one of whom is Spanish – on the streets of Marbella in broad daylight, you're going to have a lot of explaining to do, because I hardly think that double-parking is considered to be a breach of bail condition. And in any case, even if it is, it's generally not considered good policing to murder suspects who unwittingly break the rules.'

'Thank you for your concern, but allow *me* to worry about that, señor Malone.'

'Let me tell you what we're going to do, López. We're going to stick to the original plan—'

'Impossible. This is what *you're* going to do, señor Malone.'

I can hear the anger in his voice, and this is when I know I've got him. Offing us was a big play, and it hasn't worked.

He continues. 'You are going to drive to La Comisaría de Policía in Málaga, where I will meet you, and you will surrender yourself. You will make a full signed confession for the murders for which you have been charged, and hand over to me what you consider as the evidence. Maria Espinosa will accompany you and will make a statement saying that she acted as an accomplice in the abduction and murder of Olga Antonova. If … and only if I am satisfied with this, I will give instructions for the release of the hostages. Justice will then take its course.'

I look at Maria. She's lost a lot of blood and looks frail and weak, but her spirit's still strong because she says, 'Tell him to go fuck himself, Malone.'

'Did you catch that, López? Because if you didn't, let me repeat it for you: go fuck yourself. *This* is what is going to happen: you and your sorry-assed Russian mate will be at my place with the hostages' – I look at my watch and calculate – 'at exactly seven forty-five, or I take the evidence to the proper authorities. And should you try to top me again, my lawyer now holds the evidence and she will make sure you rot in a cell forever if I disappear.'

I hang up, and that's when I remember the call I was about to make to Sam.

SIXTY-ONE

TODAY, 19.03

Truth be told, Sam's not best pleased when I tell her what I need her to do.

But I can't do this on my own, and clearly Maria is as incapable of supporting anything as an Italian road bridge; in fact, by now it's clear that she needs to get to a hospital, and get there fast.

'You do realise that I would be disbarred for this if it ever comes out?' she asks.

'It won't come out, Sam,' I reply. But in all honesty I'm not that confident that my plan is even going to work; particularly as there's now the added complication of having to substitute her for Maria.

So, the first thing I do after I get off the phone is to drive to the Hospital Costa del Sol. Although she's in a sorry state, Maria manages to phone ahead, and sure enough, one of her colleagues who could easily pass for 'Doc' Brown in *Back to The Future* rushes out of the entrance, tails of his white coat flapping like Batman's cape, and he's holding the largest syringe and needle I've seen. I assume it's for Maria, but it's not.

Ignoring Maria, who is now moaning like a Belgian diplomat, he puts this rubber band round my arm, swabs the inside of it and plunges the thing into me. Satisfied that he's got enough blood, he pulls it out, sticks a plaster on it and smiles.

'Thanks, Dracula,' I say, and I'm thankful that I'm sitting in the driver's seat, otherwise I'd probably have passed out.

He smiles and hands me a piece of paper. A phone number is written on it.

'Ring this number in an hour or so. I will have the result back by then.'

Seconds later, these two guys in scrubs – I don't know if they're porters or doctors – arrive wheeling what I think you call a gurney and manhandle Maria onto it. She's clutching her phone in one hand and her bag in the other, and one of them starts working on her arm – I deduce he must be a medic because hospital porters don't usually put drips into patients' arms, even in Spain – and off she's wheeled.

I look at my watch.

Forty minutes til showdown.

SIXTY-TWO

TODAY, 19.20

My gaff is literally down the road from the Hospital Costa del Sol, and five minutes later I'm flinging the Bentley at the gate when I remember that I don't have the remote jobby to open it.

So I leave it blocking the entrance and clamber over. This would normally trigger the alarm, but I happen to know that the thing's been turned off.

And I know this because I also know that Maria turned it off, and although I reactivated the security cameras, I left the alarm off in case I needed to gain access to my villa without waking every fucking dog on the Costa del Sol. Or, more importantly, raising the alarm at the Marbella cop shop.

There's another car parked further up the road, which is pretty unusual as no one else lives here other than Javier, and, as I've said, he's not around because he's what I think they call 'on location'?

And as it's a Mercedes and it's a limo, I'm guessing it must belong to Nikolaev. And sure enough, it does, because as I scramble over the gates, I'm greeted by

Boris and his fellow slaphead lolloping across the lawn like a couple of overfed Rottweilers; then they drop to prone positions and point assault rifles at me.

I stop, raise my arms and, thankfully, they recognise me.

'You, Malone?' asks Boris, displaying ominously poor short-term memory retention, and I have to remind myself that we're not dealing with potential doctorate candidates here.

'Sure, I be he, Boris,' I reply, and I can't help adding, 'as I was on the beach, and as I was in the boot of your car this morning.'

Of course, this totally goes over his bald pate, and I'm led into my living room through the window Vlad shattered when he shot me.

Sam's sitting on the settee precisely where I sat when we spoke on the phone this morning, and that conversation seems light years ago. She gets up, tiptoes over and hugs me, like, really hard.

There's another goon I don't recognise in the living room and he doesn't appear to be armed, but I'm betting that there's a Glock not too far from his reach.

He introduces himself as Anatoly and we shake hands. His grip is firm, and he's taller and considerably leaner than his two colleagues. There's something slightly unbalanced and menacing about him to the extent that he reminds me of a Russian Jimmy Nail, and both my training and instincts tell me that this hombre is one psychotic sonofabitch; and if this goes tits up, I would definitely want him on my side.

I can't help noting how fantastic Sam looks, and again, that strange, warm sensation floods over me. For a moment, the tension dissipates, and I pull her tight and kiss her mouth softly … run my lips down her neck … fiddle with that seductive little curl of her hair that first caught my eye.

'This'll soon be over,' I say, because of course it will … one way or another.

'I know,' she replies, and smiles.

'So, Mr Malone,' goes Anatoly, all businesslike, 'please be so kind as to go over your plan.'

I show him the plastic vial of scopolamine that Maria gave me before I left her at the hospital.

He looks at it … let's say, in a sort of disbelieving, quizzical way, and my conviction that the plan is going to work begins to evaporate.

'So you think that by simply blowing this … stuff into their faces, you will deprive them of willpower and they will do exactly what you tell them?'

'That's precisely what I'm thinking, Anatoly,' I reply. 'Do you know anything about this … "stuff"?'

He shakes his head.

Well, for a senior member of an organisation who specialises in illegal and highly dangerous-slash-toxic drugs, you're not very well informed, are you? This thought thankfully stays inside my head, and instead I tell him what I know about scopolamine.

'So, for example, should I decide to tell López to give his old mucker Vlad a blow job …'

'For God's sake, Malone – is there really any need

343

for that?' goes Sam.

'Yeah … no, actually there is? Because that's how the drug works. And I happen to know from personal experience, and not once, but twice. So it *will* work.'

'You gave someone a blow job?' asks Sam, and I can't tell if she's thinking this may have been a possibility or if she's just trying to lighten the moment.

'No … I did *not* give anyone a blowjob, Sam.' I light a cigarette. 'I'm just using this as an analogy to illustrate the … I don't know, the potency of the drug?'

'And since when did you start smoking?'

There you go, amigo, what did I say about 'girlfriend experience'?

Anatoly's pacing the living room now, and I know damned well that all he wants to do is to shoot the fuckers – particularly Vlad – and I wouldn't have a problem with this if it weren't for the fact that they are holding two hostages, and furthermore, these hostages are being held basically because of me.

I remind him of this and he just nods.

I hear another car pull up somewhere beyond my gaff, and I'm guessing it's probably Dempsey's mobsters because it sounds like a Hummer. And of course, being old school, it's totally impossible for Dempsey to be anything like subtle, even when the situation demands it.

So, that's a bit like you taking a Bentley when you went to his estate, then?

Oh … hello, amigo. You're still there? Yes, I suppose it is, but I did have a reason for taking the Bentley, and one that I *have* already explained.

Anatoly's not done with the scepticism just yet.

'And you think they are just going to stand there and let you blow this … stuff into their faces, just like in some Harry Potter movie?'

I'm tempted to tell Anatoly that from what little I know about Harry Potter, I wouldn't be entirely sure that he uses a highly toxic drug as a method of sorcery; but, of course, I could well be wrong. But I'm thinking that he's got a point and, truth be told, it *is* beginning to strike me as being a bit Hans Christian Andersen.

Sam voices what I'm thinking.

'He's right, Malone. What's your backup plan?'

I point to the Glock Nikolaev lent me, tucked into my waistband.

'Other than this, I don't really have a backup plan.'

She just shakes her head.

I shrug my shoulders.

'Okay … so does anybody have a better idea?' I ask, a tad defensively.

Apparently, nobody does.

SIXTY-THREE

TODAY, 19.30

At this point there's another car approaching, and I look up to see a second black limo drive past my entrance.

'Yours, I assume?' I ask Anatoly.

I'm beginning to think he's a man of few words because, once again, he just nods.

Boris and his mate have fucked off to hide in my foliage like it's a kid's fucking birthday party, and Anatoly – who is clearly as adept at finding things as he is economical with words – points my spare remote at the gate, which slides open and in comes Nikolaev, dwarfed by three of his mobsters.

'So that makes six?' I mutter to no one in particular.

Anatoly just nods and there's a bit of a rustle in the bushes as the Russians vie for position.

'I think we're going to need a bigger bush,' I go, trying to lighten things up, but nobody either understands this or finds it funny.

The gate has closed again, and it's at this precise moment that Dempsey and, I'm counting, four, maybe five of his men appear.

'Who the fuck are they?' asks Anatoly, and sure enough the Glock is out and pointed in the general direction of the Irish contingent.

'You don't know?' I go, which is a stupid question because clearly he hasn't a baldy. 'That's your boss's new business partner and some of his employees, so I wouldn't point that gun at them if I were you, by the way. And they're here for the same reason you are – and that's just to observe while the lady and I sort this mess out.' He just shrugs, tucks away the Glock and presses the remote so the gate opens, and in they come and start searching for somewhere to lie low.

Unfortunately, the first area they choose – which I'd have to say, I'd have chosen if I'd been in their shoes – is already occupied by the Russians, and a few frank words are exchanged.

It doesn't take a genius to work out that, although Dempsey and Nikolaev may have signed the rather pointless – at least in my opinion – agreement that Sam drafted and emailed, there is no love lost between them and this is a marriage of convenience in the literal sense.

There's enough tension building without this kicking off, I'm thinking, and thankfully off they fuck to look for cover elsewhere; and moments later my garden looks like the tranquil sanctuary it normally is, and not a potential battlefield concealing twelve or so heavily armed villains and the killing field that it was this morning thanks to Vlad.

And then the strangest thing happens.

Just as the gate starts to close, another car screeches to a halt behind mine, and before I have time to register who the driver is, this shape darts through the gate and is halfway towards the villa, when two things occur.

First – or maybe they both happen at the same time? – Anatoly's Glock is out again and pointed at the advancing figure.

And second, Sam is on her feet and running towards her daughter.

SIXTY-FOUR

TODAY, 19.38

So, while this is a genuinely heart-warming moment and confirms what I'd suspected, it couldn't have happened at a worse time.

I look at the two women and there's no possibility that they're not related. Natasha is taller and has jet-black hair – which may or may not be her natural colour – but the facial similarities, and even the likeness of their mannerisms, are striking.

To begin with, Natasha hasn't a baldy why this woman, who she's never seen – at least not since she was in the delivery suite – is hugging her like she's that irritating Portuguese footballer who's just scored from the penalty spot, and sobbing her actual heart out?

And then the proverbial penny drops and she realises why. 'Mother?'

Sam is literally lost for words, and now I know what this is all about and why she is really here, but now is not the time to dwell on this.

So while they're enjoying this moment of, shall we say, intimacy, let's just review the situation?

Please do.

Okay, amigo ... so, two cohorts of heavily armed psychopaths who don't trust each other are secreted in my garden, waiting for the arrival of two men. One of these men dispatched four members of one of the aforementioned gangs, and the other – who has been masquerading as a respectable senior police officer, while amassing considerable wealth from the proceeds of organised crime – has been playing both gangs against each other. Clear?

Crystal.

And right now, I'm waiting to neutralise these two hombres by drugging them in a very unscientific fashion, which may or may not work. And the purpose of this is to get them to make full confessions, which I will film, and then tell them to drive to the La Comisaría de Policía in Málaga, where they will hand over a copy of the disk that clearly shows one of them murdering four armed Russians before shooting me. And here they will make also formal statements confessing to this, the abduction of Maria's family, drugging me – or causing me to be drugged – and their involvement in the murder of Olga Antonova. And before they do all of this, they will hand over Maria's daughter and granddaughter to me, unharmed.

So, amigo ... *entiendes?*

No ... not entirely. I thought Maria had turned the security cameras off?

Correctomundo, amigo, she had. But when López turned up this morning and I began to question whether he was a real cop and whether I could trust Maria, I checked and found they *had* been turned off. So, I turned them back on again.

Anyway, back to the summary.

So, while I'm waiting for them to rock up, the woman who I thought had been murdered in my bed is reunited with her mother, who happens to be the woman I am going to marry – if we get out of this alive – who she has never met.

Claro, amigo?

Claro.

So, the stage is almost set, and we're just waiting for the two final members of the cast to make their entrance. Reluctantly, it's time for me to make an intervention.

But before I can do this, Anatoly has literally grabbed Natasha, prised her away from her mother and half dragged, half carried her towards the stairs. I have no idea what his plan is, but I just have to trust him because, right now, I don't have an alternative.

He's halfway to the stairs when he stops, fishes in his pocket and throws something to me.

It's the remote for the gate.

'You're going to need this,' he says with what I think is an attempt at a smile; and then they're gone, and we're left on our own.

I look at Sam and she's clearly terrified. But she's also more radiant and alive than I've ever seen her, even after I've given her a damned good seeing to.

'You need to focus, Sam. Take deep breaths, hon.'

So she does, and then there's this calmness that transcends her and I know she'll be fine.

'Give me the stuff.'

I take out the vial and pour half the scopolamine into her outstretched hand, and I'm about to tip the remainder into my left hand before pulling on a jacket to conceal the Glock.

But then a thought strikes me. I can't tell you why, amigo, but I just have the sudden perception that putting all your eggs in one proverbial basket is not such a good idea, and I put the vial back into my trouser pocket.

'Whatever you do,' I tell her, 'make sure you don't breathe it in. You never know what I might make you do,' I say, and try to smile.

Just then, another car draws up.

'They're here. Be brave, darling. We'll be fine. We'll be laughing about this over dinner in a couple of hours' time.'

I wish I could sound more convinced of this because I'm truly not sure how it's is going to go down, and Anatoly's cynicism hasn't helped.

I press the remote, the gate slides open and López walks up my drive like he's Warren fucking Beatty walking onto the anecdotal yacht.

SIXTY-FIVE

TODAY, 19.45

The first thing I note is that there's no Vlad, so this makes the Columbian team one cowboy short of a full posse.

'Where's Vlad?' I ask.

The window of my living room has obviously become the new door, and López struts in, parks his arse on the settee and makes himself at home.

'Vladimir,' he says, crossing his legs and flicking an imaginary speck of dust from his trousers, 'is the least of your problems, señor Malone.'

'Oh, I don't think so, Officer López. You see, my instructions were quite clear. I distinctly remember telling you that I expected yourself, your Russian sidekick and the two hostages to rock up at my villa.'

He fixes me with one of his trademark stares and says nothing.

This isn't going to plan.

So eventually he goes, 'Vladimir is in the car with the girl and her daughter. When I am satisfied that your evidence exists, I have it and your signed confession, and I am assured that I have everything else I require, I will give him instructions to release them.'

'So, I thought you wanted a signed confession from Maria?' I nod in Sam's direction.

'That's no trouble,' she goes, if I'm honest, a little too enthusiastically? 'I can easily do that.' Getting López close to Sam while she scribbles something meaningless on my writing desk was the cue to release the scopolamine, and I'm thinking this may be even better, because if Sam can neutralise López while he's bent over the desk, the first instruction I'm going to give him is to get Vlad and the hostages in.

But that's never going to happen because while my attention's diverted, he pulls his Cuerpo Nacional de Policía issue Sig Sauer, which he's now pointing at me.

'Do you really think I'm that stupid?' he asks.

'I'm sorry … I don't follow?'

The gun's now pointing at Sam.

'Señora Sloane, please tell me the current whereabouts of Maria Espinosa.'

Silence.

'Did you seriously believe that I'd fall for this? Put your hands above your head. Both of you. And do not unclench your fists, because I know exactly what is inside them.'

'Maria … bloody Maria, you bitch,' I mutter.

'Yes, Maria, señor Malone. She has been most helpful. She has kept me informed as to your movements and your plans. However, she has now served her purpose and when she comes out of surgery, an officer under my jurisdiction will obtain a statement from her, confessing how she assisted you with the murder of Olga Antonova. Then, and only then, will the hostages be released. Fortunately for her, the bullet missed the mark.'

'Ah, you should have sent Vlad, López, if you didn't have the bottle to do it yourself. A piece of advice, though: never send a boy to do a man's job.'

He ignores this, and marches us into the kitchen.

'Face the sink … both of you. One wrong move, and I will kill you without hesitation.'

So we're now in the kitchen, and this is seriously bad news because it's the one room in the villa that can't be seen from the garden, so any prospect of intervention from my guardian angels secreted in the shrubbery is as likely as another Brit winning Wimbledon.

'You first, Malone. Go to the sink, turn on the tap and wash off the scopolamine.'

I oblige.

'Now it's your turn, señora Sloane.'

I dry my hands with a tea towel and lob it to Sam, my mind desperately searching for some sort of plan because, thanks to Maria, unless I can come up with something, and come up with it fast, we're up shit creek without anything remotely resembling a paddle.

'Turn around,' he goes. 'Now, I want the disk that contains the evidence, the one you claim to have taken from the hard drive to which the cameras are connected.'

For a moment I think of telling him that there is no

disk ... there is no evidence, and that my claim to have rebooted the security cameras so that they recorded Vlad shooting Dempsey's men and myself was a total fabrication. But then I remember that Maria would almost certainly have passed on this particular nugget of information.

And we're just at the point where we desperately need a snooker, when the cue ball cuddles up to the baulk cushion and the black obscures the last red.

And the last red, ironically, is there standing behind López and pointing a gun at him.

SIXTY-SIX

TODAY, 19.52

Anatoly's Glock is trained on López, and I have absolutely no doubt that his finger is itching to pull the trigger.

I'm right, and I'm about to find out why.

'Put down the gun.'

López obliges.

'Now kick it over to me.' This he does.

'Turn around. Place both hands on your head.'

Anatoly frisks him with a thoroughness that tells me he's done this sort of thing before.

As I said, amigo, if things go tits up – and the jury's still out on this one – this is one psychotic fucker I want on my side; and I'm not entirely sure who's side he is on?

'Who are you?' López asks the question that I want answered too.

'Yeah, umm … so I take it you don't actually work for Nikolaev, then?'

The gun's pointed at me now.

'Shut up, Malone.' It's Sam.

'Yes, shut up, Mister Malone. You have served your purpose. Do not get involved in business that does not concern you.'

And I'm thinking: you're standing in my kitchen, pointing a gun at a man who had just been pointing a gun at my fiancé and me. And the man you are pointing a gun at kidnapped the family of someone who I had hitherto considered to be my best friend, before she conspired and collaborated with gangsters against me.

And not only that: before you disarmed him, he was hellbent on obtaining a false confession that would have seen me spend pretty much the rest of my life in prison.

And outside in my garden are two virtual fucking armies who wouldn't hesitate to take each other out.

And, let's not forget – four people have already been shot dead on my lawn this morning, after a dead girl appeared and then disappeared from my bed.

So tell me, please ... just how the *fuck* can this be business that does not concern me?

I'm thinking this, but thankfully this thought stays inside my head, so I just shrug, raise the palms of my hands towards him in what I hope he will recognise as a gesture of submission, and shut the fuck up.

Anatoly deftly pulls a fag out of a packet in his jacket pocket and lights up.

'Any chance I could have one of those?' I ask.

He just shoots me a filthy.

'You two,' – the gun's wavering between Sam and me – 'get your hands on your heads as well.'

Maybe you're not so smart after all, Anatoly, I'm thinking. Because if I'd been you, the first thing I'd have done would have been to frisk the pair of us, and, had he done so, I would not still be in possession of the Glock.

'You really thought no one would come after you?' This question is addressed to López.

López says nothing; just stares at him with the same level of contempt that he stares at everyone with.

Anatoly continues.

'The people who engaged my services have long memories, señor López. And tomorrow I am taking you back to Bogotá to address the consequences of your actions.' He stubs the cigarette out, fishes out another and lights it. 'You see, they wish to make an example of you. They will demonstrate to the world that no one steals from the Medellín Cartel and escapes justice.'

Suddenly I see where this is going, and I'm honestly not sure if this unexpected twist of events is a good or a bad thing? On the upside, it removes López and the prospect of my incarceration from the equation, but on the minus side, there's still Vlad, smouldering somewhere outside like unstable uranium and holding the hostages. And I'm almost borderline feeling sorry for López? And that's because he may be a total cunt, but if I were in his shoes right now, I'd be begging for one of those cyanide pills the Gestapo used to carry around in little silver cases.

I slowly raise my hand to attract attention, like a nine-year-old asking to be excused to take a shit.

He glowers at me, and I take this as an invitation to talk. 'Look, Anatoly … could I just ask you, like … a really big favour … please?'

He says nothing, but continues to glower at me.

'As you say, your business with López is between you, López and the Medellín Cartel, and the last thing I want to do is to get involved in any of that. But outside my property, Vlad is holding two people – one a small child, and the other, an innocent young woman – as hostages. Can you please help me get them back, before you remove this scumbag from my home?'

Now when I say I have no Equity card, I genuinely mean I can't act for shit, but this little speech comes over as … I don't know … sincere? And I think it maybe even touches him that I care so much about the family of someone who has basically fucking shafted me.

'And what do you suggest, Mister Malone? If your little Harry Potter plan had worked,' he goes, with what I would call something approaching contempt, 'all we would have to do would be to get López to command Vladimir to bring the hostages in.' He stubs out the cigarette, and adds, 'And then I could shoot him.'

'Ah, well, funny you should mention that.' I raise my hand again and slowly point to my trouser pocket. 'May I?'

He nods, and I pull out the vial containing enough scopolamine to stun, if not an elephant, certainly López.

And sometimes, it's not such a bad thing when my instincts are right.

SIXTY-SEVEN

TODAY, 20.02

As I've already mentioned, amigo, sometimes one has to make a pact with the devil in order to stay in the game, and it isn't long before I realise this is a path that I will once again have to tread if I'm going to get Sam, myself and Maria's family out of here.

'Give me the vial,' goes Anatoly.

I lob it to him, and off he goes to look for a glass. I tell him where to find one and also that's there's juice in the fridge, because I can see where this is going.

So back he comes, places the glass on the kitchen table, pours orange juice into it and throws in the remainder of the scopolamine.

'I'm parched, Anatoly,' I tell him. 'Any chance I can get us a drink, please?'

He thinks about this, then nods his head, so off I trot and come back with two glasses. So, as I'm pouring juice into the glasses, I'm thinking that there are now three identical glasses on the table which contain roughly the same amount of juice, but one of them contains sufficient scopolamine to deprive the victim of free will and to elicit total compliance for a good twenty-four hours. And it is really essential that I pay very close attention to which glass contains the scopolamine if my plan is to work.

What I need is a distraction, and … praise be, just as I'm thinking this, someone upstairs gifts me one.

And I'm not talking about God here … I'm talking about someone upstairs in the literal sense.

Natasha.

The sound of breaking glass alerts me to the fact that Natasha – who I assumed Anatoly had locked in one of the bedrooms – has had enough of confinement and has decided to do something about it. And the last thing Anatoly wants is for her to escape and inform her father that another of his key assets is something other than what he appears to be.

So off he sprints, and there's just the four of us left in the kitchen.

Time to produce the Glock.

Truth be told, López doesn't even flinch as I chamber a round and flick the safety off, so I figure that he'd actually prefer that I put a bullet into him than that he drinks that stuff, and meekly trots off to face the extreme rendition that will surely follow if the Medellín Cartel get hold of him.

So, he's … to say the least, a bit surprised by what I have to say.

'Okay, López,' I go, 'now I suggest that you listen to this very carefully indeed, because this is literally a once-in-a-lifetime opportunity I'm offering you, and we don't have time to debate it because Anatoly will be back down here in around ninety seconds,' this being the time I calculate it will take him to clamber across my roof and recapture Natasha. 'Here's the deal. But before I tell you, you need to ask yourself one question: which would you prefer … to be taken back to Bogotá and face the Medellín Cartel, or to instruct Vlad to release the hostages, to make a full confession and hand yourself over to the proper authorities?'

This, of course, is a total no-brainer, and he buys it.

SIXTY-EIGHT

TODAY, 20.08

Anatoly's back in the kitchen ushering in Natasha with the Glock, and she gallops across the room to Sam who wraps her in her arms and bursts into tears.

I've tucked my gun out of sight because it serves no purpose other than to complicate things, and it's important that Anatoly still believes he's in charge and that I'm totally on his side.

But I figure it's time for a bit of small talk over a drink before we get down to business. It's an old trick I learned from a mate in the Marines who was about as useless at magic as Tommy Cooper, but this was one he could generally get right and it proved helpful more than once when dealing with the Taliban.

'So, how long have you worked for Nikolaev?' I ask.

'Not that it is any concern of yours, but since this morning. He needed a replacement for Vladimir and, coincidentally, his helicopter pilot had an unfortunate accident.' He lights a cigarette. 'I happened to have the right credentials and gilt-edged references. And since you ask, I'd been tracking señor López for ten days and your, shall we say … situation provided me with the opportunity I was looking for. As I said, Mister Malone, I am grateful for your facilitation in this matter.'

'My pleasure.' My eyes track his fag packet. God, I only took it up again this morning and I'm addicted already. 'May I?' I ask.

He shrugs and throws me the packet and lighter. I light up and place the packet and the lighter on the table.

'Do you want a drink? I ask. 'I've got some excellent vodka. Żubrówka … you know it? It's called Bison Grass Vodka.'

'Polish vodka is shit. Only Russians can make vodka,' he says, making no attempt to conceal his contempt for all things Polish. 'But I will have some orange juice.'

So I fetch another glass, place it in front of him and pour, and it's at this precise moment that Sam pushes Natasha away, then grabs her by the shoulders and slaps her – I'd have to say with even more force than Natasha slapped me this morning – across the face.

Natasha does what I'd probably have done, and shrieks, and the three seconds during which this action takes place allows me to swap the glass destined for López's consumption for the one I had placed in front of Anatoly, without him noticing.

Anatoly actually laughs? 'Ladies … ladies, please,' he says. 'We already have quite enough drama.' Then he goes all serious. 'You' – he motions to Natasha with the Glock – 'you're trouble. Get over there … stand by the fridge and place your hands on your head.'

Natasha is glowering at her mother and wondering what the fuck is going on, which, I'd have to say, is exactly what I'd be doing in her position.

'And you' – he's pointing the gun at Sam now – 'you really are one violent bitch. But I like that in a woman, and if time permitted, I would have pleasure enjoying it more.' Not on my watch, I'm thinking. And I'm also thinking that he hasn't even scratched the surface yet when it comes to Sam and rough sex. Thank God I've managed to get her to tone it down a bit. 'Get over there' – he points to the other side of the kitchen – 'and get your hands on your head.' He looks at me, as if for, I don't know … some sort of support?

'Women!' he goes, and I crack a sardonic smile in tacit agreement.

SIXTY-NINE

TODAY, 20.13

'I'm not drinking that ... no way. You can shoot me,' says López.

Of course this is all an act, and I'm just hoping to fuck that's it's not going to backfire. 'Go on, then ... shoot me, get it over with.'

I'd put money on my hunch that Anatoly will only get paid if he delivers López alive to the Medellín Cartel, and to shoot him here in my villa would probably leave his employers almost as pissed off with him as they are with López.

You can't really make an example of someone by shooting them in a foreign country where the news won't even be reported, especially if Dempsey and Nikolaev get their way. I would imagine that López's death would be a play of many acts, all of which would be filmed and, as is de rigueur these days, posted on the Internet.

Of course, if Anatoly decides that shooting López is the way to go, it will not be a cloud totally without a silver lining because it will get me off the hook.

However, it will still leave Vlad holding the hostages, and so ultimately this will not advance my cause.

This is a very big chip to play because if it all goes to shit, Vlad will still have the same bargaining power as he holds right now. And I have no doubt that he will not even bother to shed one proverbial crocodile tear over the shooting of López.

'Drink it,' goes Anatoly, 'before I lose patience.'

'No. No fucking way. Go fuck yourself.'

And I'm thinking that maybe you're in danger of overacting here, López? Because although Anatoly comes across as the ultimate professional, every man has his limit, and, actually, you're making quite a good case to be shot.

It's time for an intervention.

'Look …' I go. 'Why don't we all just calm the fuck down and have a little drink? Are you sure you don't want some vodka in that, Anatoly?'

I've somehow, like a wasp to a sugary drink, got to attract him to the glass, and I can see him begin to weaken ever so slightly.

'I suppose shit Polish vodka is better than no vodka,' he goes, and so I trot off to the drinks cabinet and come back with an unopened bottle of Żubrówka.

He grabs the bottle from me and pours a generous measure into the glass in front of him. I have no idea how Żubrówka will mix with scopolamine.

'I am going to drink this now.' He stares at López. 'And if you have not drunk that by the time I have finished mine, I will shoot you. And I will shoot you in several places, which will cause you significant pain before I kill you. Your death will not be pleasant. So, if I were you, I would drink it.'

Then he passes the vodka bottle to López who unscrews the top and fills his glass to the brim without taking his eyes off Anatoly.

Remember, amigo, what we have here in my kitchen are two seriously evil hombres because – added to what I already know about López – the Medellín Cartel would not have contemplated hiring the services of Anatoly, had he not come with a blue chip CV both as a professional assassin and as a thoroughly unscrupulous piece of work.

The Columbian's hands are shaking, and I can't tell how much of this is an act and how much is genuine.

Anatoly raises his glass.

We all raise our glasses, with the notable exception of López who just stares angrily at it.

'*Salud*,' goes Anatoly. Sam and I respond, and once again, we're in a Tarantino movie.

Anatoly's glass is now half empty, and López hasn't touched his yet.

And I'm thinking, you're cutting this a bit fine – and for someone with absolutely zero personality or charisma, this is right up there with one of the best dramatic performances I've seen – when he grabs the glass, mutters, 'Fuck you … fuck you all,' drains it and slams it down on my kitchen table.

Anatoly calmly finishes his drink and puts the glass down.

'There,' he goes with a smile, 'that wasn't so difficult now, was it?'

Pause.

'Now … López,' says Anatoly. 'I want you to call Vladimir and instruct him to bring the hostages in. Tell him you have obtained what you need and that he is to come unarmed.'

So López takes out his phone and does just that.

Truth be told, this is all going a bit too well because unless I somehow managed to mix the glasses up, López is heading for a fucking Oscar for his role in this little charade.

There's this uneasy silence for a moment, and I know that I have to test it. The stuff is supposed to have an almost instantaneous effect, but what if it hasn't?

If it hasn't and I've got this wrong, I'm dead.

And right now, my heart is beating like a Neil fucking Peart drum solo.

SEVENTY

TODAY, 20.20

I think about telling him to hand over his gun but then decide it might be better to dip my toe in the proverbial water first.

'Anatoly,' I go, 'there's a flight for Bogotá that leaves Málaga at 09.20 tomorrow morning. You transfer at Madrid. I want you to book one seat on that flight.' He just stares at me. 'Right now. Economy class will do.'

And, excuse me, but how do you know this?

Oh, it's you again, amigo. I happen to know this because while I was waiting for Maria to fetch the scopolamine, I googled it. My original plan was to persuade López to take himself back to Bogotá to face the music. That was before I even knew that the Medellín Cartel had sent someone after him. But there's legal justice, and there's mob justice, and – being the good humanitarian that I've become – I'd prefer that López faces imprisonment rather than dismemberment.

So, I'm thinking, if the scopolamine hasn't kicked in yet or, heaven forbid, I somehow mishandled the transfer of the glasses and López actually drank it,

Anatoly will question whether to book one seat or two on the flight.

He doesn't.

He takes out his phone, fiddles with the thing for a couple of minutes and he just books it.

'Okay. It's done,' he goes.

'Excellent. Good boy.' I suppose he could be bluffing but I doubt it. So now it's time to dive right in.

'Give me the gun, Anatoly. Just hand it over … nice and slowly.'

The Sig Sauer he took from López is sitting on my kitchen table and his own gun is in his shoulder holster, so I figure if this goes tits up, I can draw my gun before he has the Sig Sauer in his possession. But not before he can draw his own gun, so this really is stress-testing the Space Shuttle; and, Houston, we could have a fucking problem.

For a moment he just stares at me as if he hasn't understood, then he picks up the gun slowly and passes it to me.

'Good,' I say. 'Now take your gun out of the holster and pass it to me.'

He obliges, and I can't help emitting a sigh of relief, because for the first time today I figure I hold most, but not yet all of the aces.

I give the Sig Sauer to Sam and the Glock to Natasha.

'Why are you giving me this, Malone?' Sam asks. 'I've never held a gun before, let alone shot one.'

'Here, let me show you,' goes Natasha, flicking off the safety and chambering a round, and for a moment

I get this weird notion that she's about to shoot her mother to repay her for the slap. Then she smiles. 'It's okay … Mother, I know why you did it,' and that's when Sam's face lights up. 'But it bloody hurt.'

'So this is what you're going to do, Anatoly,' I tell him. 'You're going to get into Vlad's car in a minute – because he's not going to be needing it – and you're going to drive to the Vincci Selección Posada del Patio in Málaga. I've stayed there many times. It's a nice hotel … heck, you might as well enjoy yourself – you've earned it. Stick it on your platinum Amex. Then you're going to drive to the airport tomorrow morning and catch the flight to Madrid that connects with the flight to Bogotá.' I pause, and he's following my words like a fucking Labrador follows food.

'Can you pass me your cigarettes, please?' He does, and I light up.

'And when you arrive in Bogotá, you're going to go straight to the person who sanctioned the … shall we say, abduction and repatriation of López? And you're going to explain to him – or possibly her – that before you could apprehend him, he was arrested for, hmmm … let's see: fraud, extortion, the murder, or certainly his part as an accomplice to the murder of five people, kidnap …' I turn to López, 'Am I missing anything, López?' He shakes his head. 'And so, señor López will not be available for a demonstration of what happens to people who steal from the Medellín Cartel for some considerable time.' I pause. 'Now, have you got all that?'

Anatoly just shakes his head.

I know I shouldn't, but I can't resist it.

'Anatoly,' I go, 'give López a blow job.' And this has the precise effect that I thought it would, as Anatoly walks across the kitchen, starts to unzip the Columbian's trousers and both women shriek my name.

SEVENTY-ONE

TODAY, 20.43

There's a knock on the kitchen door, and I'm guessing it's Vlad with Sofía and Daniela.

Daniela is only seven, so before I tell them to come in, I command Anatoly to zip up López's pants and go take a seat in the lounge.

Of course, I wasn't actually going to make him go through with this; I just wanted to see at first hand, rather than as a victim, how mind-bendingly powerful this scopolamine is.

So in comes Vlad, followed by Sofía and Daniela, and I can see they're unharmed. But there's real fear on their faces which turns to masks of horror when they see three guns, two of them held by women they've never set eyes on before and the other by me, pointed at their captor. And there's something else that's terrifying them, but I can't see it right now.

So Vlad does what I expected him to do and makes himself the meat in a hostage sandwich, and it's only then that I notice he's got a gun buried in the small of Sofía's back.

Except his plan's not going to work because he's taller than both of his victims and there are three guns pointing at him, so one of us will always be in a position to shoot him.

I'd be surprised if Natasha was any less adept with a handgun than she has proved herself to be at writing pornographic fiction, so that makes two of us who know what we're doing.

'Put down the gun and give them up, Vlad,' I go. 'It's over.'

Of course, this is still very far from over, and I know this.

'No way. Go fuck yourself, Malone.'

'There is not the remotest possibility that I would ever do that, even if I could,' I reply. 'Let's review the situation, shall we?'

López is still standing there in something approaching a state of shock, probably contemplating what he should be more grateful for: avoiding dismemberment by the Medellín Cartel or a blowjob from Anatoly. But then I remember how dangerous the fucker is and tell Natasha to frisk him. She does, and finds nothing.

'You just keep your hands on your head, López. I'll deal with you in a moment.' I light another cigarette and turn to Sam. 'Babes, could you be an angel and grab the disk with today's date on it from my desk? It should be … I think, in the second drawer on the left.'

'Babes? Fucking hell, Malone.'

She goes over and comes back with the disk.

'So … the situation, Vlad, as I see it, is this.' I wave

the disk at him. 'This disk contains footage recorded by my security cameras over the past twenty-four hours. Amongst other things, it shows you and your amigo López entering my premises last night, carrying both Olga Antonova and myself, as I was virtually unconscious and she was already dead, as the autopsy will prove. Let's fast forward to this morning, and it then shows you murdering four men carrying assault rifles on my lawn before shooting me' – and here, for dramatic effect because, truth be told, I'm actually beginning to enjoy myself for the first time since I woke up this morning, I point to the shattered window in my living room. 'And by the way, I'll be sending you the bill for that.'

I pause to let this sink in, and he places the gun against Daniela's temple. And in a funny sort of way, this is in fact not such a bad thing.

She screams.

'It's all right, Daniela … it's all right, darling. The nasty man who has kidnapped you is going to let you go, and this will all be over in a minute.'

I'm not sure if a seven-year-old who speaks very little English knows what 'kidnapped' means, but I have a reason for saying it, and saying it loud and clear.

I continue.

'And outside, as I suspect you're aware, because you will have no doubt clocked two black Mercedes limos and a Hummer with Irish plates on your arrival … outside are two groups of around six heavily armed and highly dangerous men. And the one thing they have in common is that they consider they have very good reasons for wanting to see you die.' I can see his face falling, so just when he's sure I'm going to hit him with my second bouncer of the over, I chuck in my slower ball.

'And all this, let's call it, climatic scene ... is being filmed for posterity, because the cameras are still switched on, and this little sequel will shortly be transferred to disk, and then both disks will be presented to the authorities.'

And this is in fact true, because, although I can and I usually do switch them off, the only rooms without cameras are the bedrooms and the bathrooms. So now I walk over to the security control centre in the entrance lobby and turn the cameras off. This is for our ears only.

'So ... this is what I'm going to offer you. And like the deal I offered López – which he accepted – this is totally non-negotiable and you have precisely five seconds to accept it. And should you decide not to accept it, Sam will call Mr Dempsey and I will call Mr Nikolaev, and we will invite both these gentlemen in for a glass of vodka and a little chat with you.'

He's visibly bricking it now and my perception about his vulnerability under pressure has proved to be spot on. López was clearly the brains of the Columbian operation.

And if any confirmation of this is required, it is delivered in the form of an outburst from López: 'You really are a fucking moron, Vlad. Why the fuck did you have to shoot those guys? None of this would have fucking happened if you could have … just for once, kept your fucking gun in your pocket.'

'Gentlemen … gentlemen, please, there are children and ladies present,' I say, and it's then that I know I've totally got them.

SEVENTY-TWO

TODAY, 20.56

I park the Bentley outside the Costa del Sol Hospital in a disabled space.

I know ... I know, I've changed, and everything that's happened since I woke up this morning has probably made me a less selfish person, but a Bentley still out-trumps an ambulance in my book. And anyway, the main car park is fucking miles away.

I'd better tell you at this point, amigo, that I'm here for two reasons.

Hang on, what happened to the hostages ... and López ... and Vlad?

I was coming to that ... but okay, here is exactly what happened.

As predicted, Vlad handed over the gun. It turned out to be a Ruger LC9s – which, incidentally, is a gun so girly that it may as well have been pink and have 'My Little Pony' inscribed on the barrel. And while Sam comforts Sofía and Daniela, who appear to have come through their ordeal pretty well, I tell Natasha to do three things.

First, I tell her to instruct her father to stand his men down and go home, as I will deal with López and Vlad. And on the condition that he does not attempt to interfere, I will keep any involvement he has had with this whole sorry episode away from the ears of the authorities when it's time to face the music. For example, I can see no justification for connecting him with the four hombres who Vlad shot.

Then I tell Sam to ring her 'high-profile' client and tell him the same thing. And I'm sure that Maria – when I catch up with her – will have no intention of pressing charges against him for kidnapping her.

Of course, neither of them are particularly happy about this, but part of being a successful gangster, I would imagine, is having the sense to realise that sometimes an element of compromise can in fact make you stronger?

And as neither of them has lost a modicum of their dignity over this, and they stand to see a significant increase in their turnover, honours are about even. I'd even go so far, if I were either of them, as to call it a good day at the proverbial office.

I then make a call to Mateo Rodríguez, a delightful fellow I once met at one of Javier's soirées and who is the director of the Centro Nacional de Inteligencia, or CNI.

Understandably, Mateo is less than delighted to be contacted on a Sunday evening by someone he can barely remember, until I tell him what Málaga's most senior police officer – and the person tasked with keeping the lid on organised crime – has been getting up to. Fortunately, he agrees that this is indeed a matter that threatens National Security, and says that he will leave Madrid immediately and travel by helicopter to investigate the matter personally.

So now I need two people who I can actually trust to deliver *los dos paranoicos* representing the Columbian team to La Comisaría de Policía in Málaga, and I have to look no further than my future wife and stepdaughter.

I then call the Málaga cop shop, and I'm put through to López's sidekick and inform him of the situation. And while I have more than a smidgen of doubt as to whether I can trust him, knowing that the director of the CNI and his team of investigators are in the air right now is likely to sharpen up his act.

And even if the disks somehow disappear, I have made copies and there is the original hard drive to back this all up.

And the second thing you ask Natasha to do?

Keep your hair on; I'm coming to that.

The second thing I asked Natasha to do was to move the Bentley and to drive one of the Mercs into my garage, then to tie both Vlad and López's hands behind their backs and to place them in the boot, before driving them to Málaga.

I thought this was a particularly nice touch, and I tell them that this is for their own safety, as nothing would make Messrs Dempsey and Nikolaev happier than to put a bullet into them. But in reality, it's payback for the treatment I received from Vlad this morning.

The last thing I ask Vlad before slamming the lid is if he has any of that chloroform left.

Understandably, he didn't see the funny side of this.

And the third thing I ask Natasha to do is to ring the number I gave her, ask for Pablo González and tell him to get his ass, along with a camera crew, down to La Comisaría de Policía – and pronto.

'And be sure,' I add, 'to give him a broad outline of what's happened.'

SEVENTY-THREE

TODAY, 21.13

So, like I said a minute ago, I'm at the Costa del Sol Hospital for two reasons.

The first is to have Sofía and Daniela checked out.

They appear to be fine but, certainly, if this had happened in the UK they would be subjected to all kinds of trauma counselling. And who am I to say that's not a bad thing just because I managed to avoid it?

I could stretch the point by saying that waking up in a pool of blood next to a girl whose throat had been cut – by myself, it transpires – probably entitles me to a session or two of rehabilitative therapy, but I'll be happy to settle for a few beers, a decent steak, a damned good shag and an early night.

Ever the romantic, aren't you?

Correctomundo, amigo.

And the second reason, of course, is to find out what the fuck is going on with the woman who I used to regard as my best friend?

But as we're heading to reception to find out where she is, Doc Brown comes careering down the corridor like human tumbleweed.

'Ah, señor Malone,' he goes. 'You didn't call me for the result of your blood test.'

'I've been kind of busy, Doc,' I tell him.

'No matter, boy,' he goes. 'No matter. It conclusively evidences a significant infusion of scopolamine.'

'Eh … in English, please?'

'It confirms that you were drugged, señor.'

So that's good news, I tell him.

It is good news because it will clearly come out at some point that not only had I hacked open Olga Antonova's throat, but also that I had dumped her body on wasteland in San Pedro. And so to do a Ronnie Reagan and repeat 'I don't recall' without scientifically evidenced justification is only likely to result in me sharing a cell with *los dos paranoicos*.

Doc Brown tells me where to find Maria, and off we trot.

***

She's sitting up in bed watching telly.

And while the second joyous family reunion I have had the good fortune to witness today is taking place, I happen to clock that the news is about to start.

Pablo's there, standing beside a black Merc that's just pulled up, and the boot opens. The camera zooms in to show two men, bound, struggling and cursing, as uniformed officers arrive and draw their guns.

385

'We have just received information from an anonymous source that the two men in the boot of this car will shortly be charged with the murders of four men and a woman at a villa belonging to bestselling author Richie Malone this morning.'

Good girl, Natasha, I'm thinking … never miss an opportunity for a spot of free publicity.

'The man on the left – here the camera zooms in on López – is Mateo López, a senior police officer originally from Bogotá, whose remit was to investigate organised crime on the Costa del Sol. The other man – the camera zooms in on Vlad here – is believed to be Vladimir Popov, better known by his underworld name of Vlad the Bad. Both men are believed to head up a powerful Columbian cartel that has recently overtaken Russian and Irish gangs as the most prolific traffickers of drugs and prostitution throughout Andalucía.'

The cops have now hoicked López and Vlad out of the boot of the limo, with – I'd have to say – a gratifying degree of violence, and handcuffs replace the ropes before the pair are marched off to be formally charged. And by now, Sam and Natasha, who managed to keep out of camera shot, are back in the car, and off they drive.

'In addition to these charges, it is believed that the two men will be charged with the attempted murder of a second woman who was shot and seriously wounded in Marbella earlier this evening, and the kidnap of two females, one of whom is a minor. We understand from our anonymous source that the hostages have now been released.'

I zone out as he drones on about how Rodríguez and a team from the CNI are on their way to head up the investigation. I turn the telly off and that breaks up the reunion, as all eyes turn on me.

'Hey, Malone ... turn the f ... turn it back on again,' goes Maria.

This is the first actual thing she's said to me? No thanks for saving my daughter and granddaughter; no look, I'm really sorry for dropping you in the total shit ... I could go on, but I won't.

So I turn to Sofía, who's wiping tears from her face so hard she needs a pair of fucking windscreen wipers.

'Sofía, darling,' I go. 'Could you take Daniela to the café? Maybe buy her a nice wee ice cream? I'd just like to have five minutes with your mum. Oh ... and you should get yourselves checked over.'

'Of course,' she says, and smiles at me, 'but we're absolutely fine, so there's really no need,' she adds, and off they trot.

I'd have to say that Daniela is – by the way – an absolute stunner, and a dead ringer for Salma Hayek.

So, we're left alone now and there's this long silence. I'm wondering whether she's going to thank me or apologise first, but she does neither.

Instead she just bursts into tears, and then she's howling like a baby, and I'm there hugging her and patting her back and saying shit like, 'there … there.'

When she finally calms down, I ask her how she is.

'I'll live,' is all she says.

And then she adds, 'I just couldn't trust you, Malone. I couldn't trust you to get them out of there. I am sorry, I promise you. Sorry for what I put you through. But if I had to, I'd do the same again. They told me if I ever hid anything from them, they would kill them.'

I just shrug and hug her because deep down I know that if it comes to a choice between family and friends, blood always wins.

'So, what's going to happen now?' she asks.

'What happens now is that I'm going to arrange for my window to be repaired, then get cleaned up and hit The Orange Tree for a steak. And if I get my arse in gear, I might just make it before they close.'

'That's not what I fucking mean,' she says, and of course I know this. 'Will I go to prison?'

I sigh.

'Sam's not an expert in Spanish criminal law, but she reckons you'll avoid clink if you cooperate and testify against López and Vlad. You might even get off with community service … maybe around four hundred hours of lifting dogshit from the streets of Marbella? A dirty job, but someone's got to do it.'

And with that, the door opens and the good-looking nurse who tended my wound this morning bobs in and smiles at me.

'Señor Malone,' she says and winks, 'we just can't keep you away from here, can we?'

Then I'm told that I really have to leave now, as the patient needs to rest. I kiss her forehead, squeeze her hand and off I go to find Sofía and Daniela and take them home.

And so that, amigo, is pretty much all there is to tell.

SEVENTY-FOUR

TODAY, 22.11

I don't know about you, but I don't like epilogues, so I'm not going to write one.

But I want to round the story off by telling you how my day ends.

And no, I'm not going to go into details about what Sam and I got up to in the bedroom department, but I will say it was particularly spectacular and definitely the highlight of my day.

And doubtless you'll have a few questions for me, amigo, before you close the back cover and tell all your mates not to bother reading this.

I just have the one, actually.

Go on.

You turned the security cameras back on this morning after López had called, when you began to suspect that Maria might not be what she appears to be. Correct?

Correctomundo.

So … if she had turned them off last night, how come they filmed López and Vlad carrying you and Olga Antonova inside?

Ah … good point. I'll tell you why. The entrance lobby is the one place in the villa where the security camera cannot be turned off, at least not easily. This is because it operates as a failsafe system to record the activity of anyone turning off the security cameras. This camera can only be disabled by entering a code, which no one other than Sam and myself knows. And when this happens, it triggers an alarm at the Marbella cop shop and the duty plod has to ring me to see if it was disabled by a bona fide person. *Claro?*

Claro.

So, we're sitting in The Orange Tree.

And there's just Sam, Natasha and me, as everyone else went home ages ago.

Truth be told, it was a toss-up whether Aileen would turn us away, but – I'm assuming here – curiosity got the better of her; and the fact that I'm with not one but two women, one of whom I was here with last night, probably swung it for us. And not only this, but Francesco, who owns the place, is hanging about, and as I would class him as a mate, he probably gave her the nod.

There's a curious sort of atmosphere as it's been one hell of a day and none of us has had time to digest what's happened. But there's one, shall we say, elephant in the room, and now's the time to get it out.

I'm talking about *Seven Days*.

Aileen's just offered us a drink on the house and I opt for cognac again, and it's almost déjà vu, except that Sam's here.

This time last night I remember thinking that life couldn't get much better. And now I'm thinking that it really can't get any better, because in addition to a book deal that means I no longer have to write porn for a living, I am getting married to the most beautiful woman in the world, and I will also acquire a resourceful and charismatic stepdaughter.

And no ... I know what you're thinking ... there is definitely not a pornographic novel lurking in my mind waiting to be unlocked.

'Okay,' I go, and take a deep breath, 'I think we need to tell your mother about *Seven Days*, Natasha ... don't you?'

She just shrugs.

'Your funeral.'

Sam, of course, knows how I ply my trade.

'You know that your daughter has written a bestseller, don't you?' I ask this with a degree of uncertainty, as someone who didn't know that the *News of the World* was defunct quite possibly has never heard of *My Father and Other Animals* either.

'Of course,' she goes. 'I read it. It's hilarious.' She looks at Natasha. 'I have to confess that I've been semi-stalking you for ages. I'm sorry ... I couldn't help it. But I kept the promise I made to your father and never attempted to contact you.'

'Well ...' I say – if I'm honest – a bit tentatively? 'She's written another book, and it's brilliant ... but it's a bit pornographic? So, I've agreed to publish it under my pseudonym.'

Then there's this long silence.

'Why are you telling me this, Malone?'

'Because, Sam,' I reply, '... because I want us to be entirely honest with each other. I don't want to have any secrets or to hide anything from you, and I wouldn't want you to find out that I had conspired with Natasha to write this.'

She looks at me, and there's a hint of a tear in her eye. I reach across the table and take her hand, and I know this is the right thing to do. I can sense Aileen's eyes burning into the back of my head, but to hell with it; she'll just have to get used to it, because these are the only women who will be in my life from now on.

'Just how pornographic is it?' she asks.

I tell her.

'Fucking hell, Malone.'

Again, there's a bit of a silence.

'And there's going to be a movie?'

'Unquestionably,' I reply.

Pause.

Francesco's hovering in the background, and I know he's waiting to close up.

'Okay,' Sam says. 'As we're talking honesty, I've got some news for you too.'

'Shoot,' I go.

'Dempsey's offered me a job.'

I am literally not sure whether to laugh, to cry, or possibly even crap myself. I choose the former.

'What's so funny? It's only handling his legit stuff. I'm not getting involved in any drug money, prostitution or money laundering, you know. I've made that perfectly clear.'

I am literally pissing my pants with laughter.

'Good luck with that. Does he know we're getting married?'

'No … but he knows we're … what would you say … an item?'

'So, let's review this … situation? Here's a man who said that he would literally kill me if my shadow ever fell across his again, who's going to engage my wife in what is likely to be a full-time business capacity, and a dubious one at that, while my stepdaughter runs a highly illegal rival organisation, and is the daughter of the most powerful oligarch outside of Russia. Hello … Elvis has left the building,' I go. 'Now tell me who's losing the fucking plot?'

I pay and leave Aileen the obligatory fifty euro tip, which only slightly softens the cast-iron features of her face.

I can tell Francesco wants a word. Did I tell you, amigo, he's Italian, by the way? And almost as popular as I am-slash-was with the ladies.

So I pretend to go to the toilet, and he comes over and presses something into my hand.

I look at it. It's a small sachet containing some sort of liquid.

'What's this?' I ask.

He smiles at me.

'Looks like you're going to be a busy man tonight, señor Malone,' he goes, nodding at Sam and Natasha.

'It's not what you're thinking, Francesco. They're mother and daughter,' I tell him. 'And no … we are definitely not having a family threesome.'

He looks, like … disappointed, as if he would have expected better from me?

'Those days are all behind me,' I tell him. 'We're getting married … Sam and me. What is this stuff, anyway?'

'Kamagra jelly. Much better than Viagra. Try it … you'll not be disappointed. Neither will Sam.'

I look at the sachet. The girls are champing to go.

'Do I swallow it or rub it on my dick?' I ask him, and he slaps me on the back and laughs. It's actually a serious question because I haven't a baldy what to do with it.

'I should try swallowing it,' he goes. 'But, who knows, that may also work, but you'd have to avoid oral …'

'Yes, okay, Francesco, I get the drift,' and off I bob to join the girls.

'What was all that about?' asks Sam, and already I'm torn between the truth and fabrication. I choose the latter.

'Ah, he just asked how the rugby went yesterday. Marbella had their first league game.'

'It's going to be difficult, isn't it,' goes Sam, a tad – if I'm honest – reflectively? 'Not to have secrets around the family dinner table. But we must try, mustn't we?'

'I know.'

And this is precisely what I told you way back at the

beginning, amigo. No one is what they appear to be. If they tell you that they are, then they're lying.

'And Malone?' she goes. 'Don't lose the fucking plot again, or I'll kill you.'

THE END

The author begs your patience in waiting for the second in the **Richie Malone** series; in the meantime, he would like to introduce you to **Dave** …

Saving Dave

Dave hasn't made a will.

This is in part because he doesn't have a pot to piss in, and in part because Dave doesn't know what day of the week it is.

In fact, Dave doesn't know that weeks even exist because he's been a wheelchair-bound quadriplegic in a permanent vegetative state, locked in his own world for the past eighteen years.

But all this is about to change.

A week after Dave is awarded £10 million in medical negligence damages, he has an accident that leads to a miraculous recovery.

Trouble is, he doesn't know whether to tell anyone.

His father is trying to kill him.

His neurotic, bipolar mother existed only to meet his needs before becoming entangled in an affair with her therapist – and now she lives for the moment she can be free to run off with him.

His pernicious siblings want a home in the mansion the compensation will provide for him. And everything else they can get their hands on.

What should Dave do?

Although Dave has never heard an explanation of the word psychopath, he knows he is one.

He will kill them all.

Because ... after all, he has the perfect alibi.

ONE

THE "ACCIDENT"

Perhaps it was no great surprise that the first word Dave said was "fuck".

And the fact that this utterance occurred some eighteen years, two months, three days and seven hours after he was born caused considerable consternation; not least of all to Dave.

In fact, it caused so much consternation that the four other people who heard it actually imagined that they had heard it, or that there must be some other logical explanation for the fact that they all thought they had heard it.

And this was because there was as little likelihood of Dave saying anything – let alone "fuck" – as there was of the tennis ball that had just slammed into his temple reciting the entire works of William Shakespeare.

AUTHOR'S NOTE

A few thank yous and a couple of disclaimers.

Thank yous first ...

I suppose I should thank my parents, without whom neither Richie Malone nor I would exist. Having chosen my parents wisely (who had the good sense to refrain from further production of children after I was born) I have been fortunate enough to dodge what could be referred to as 'a proper job' for the past twenty years and to devote a disproportionate amount of time to honing my skills as a writer.

Dear reader, I would be the first to admit that there is still a considerable distance to travel on this journey, but at least I have produced a work of fiction that – for some reason – I feel proud of. *Losing The Plot* is the best book it can be, and I can only hope that you have enjoyed reading it nearly as much as I enjoyed writing it.

I would like to thank my editor, Nicky Taylor, whose enduring, highly professional work and encouragement I have greatly valued. If there are any mistakes within these covers, the fault is mine.

Special thanks must go to Monika, whose unswerving support and tolerance of my prolonged solitary writing spells in Spain – most of which were actually spent writing – have been hugely appreciated. Monika, you are my cornerstone.

Thanks also to 'Maria', a dear friend whose enthusiasm, support and advice on all things Spanish has been exceptional.

Thank you to my Irish amigos, David Stewart and Cec Lowry: the former, for his assistance with my research into the machinations of the Provisional IRA, and the latter – a fellow writer – for his support, enthusiasm and encouragement for the project ... even though, as he keeps reminding me, *Losing The Plot* isn't his sort of thing.

And thanks to the host of friends and beta readers who read my MS as it progressed and gave me invaluable feedback.

On to disclaimers ... as I've already said, this is a work of fiction, therefore any similarities to persons alive or dead are purely coincidental. If, dear reader, having read this book, you genuinely believe that one of my characters is based on you ... I'm afraid you flatter yourself.

There are only three living souls who have morphed into my characters: Gora, the Somalian sunbed wizard; 'Maria', who is not called Maria and is not a traumatologist; and Mr P, who is called Mr P and actually is a racist, bisexual Chihuahua.

Finally, to my dear friends at the Moët – the service is not nearly as dreadful as it has been painted, particularly with the advent of Ruben, who has *una pinta* and a bowl of tooth-shattering *frutas secas* placed on my table almost before my arse touches the seat.

Gracias a ti, chicos!

About the author

Richard Grainger has worked as a teacher, personal trainer, restaurateur and journalist.

His first book, *The Last Latrine*, is an account of his experiences in Nepal running the world's highest marathon. *Losing The Plot* is his debut novel and he is working on a second, *Saving Dave*.

Richard divides his time between Marbella, where he writes, and Wroclaw, where he enjoys Polish beer and teaches English part-time.

Visit www.maverickwriter.co.uk for more information about Richard's writing and future projects.